Praise for *We've All Life Before Us*

A remarkable, movingly authentic love story, told in the form of literate and passionate letters from a gallant young airman to his wife. Incidentally a historically fascinating glimpse into everyday life in wartime Britain.

Richard Dawkins, evolutionary biologist and author

This remarkable selection of letters and diary entries reveals that a generation so often portrayed as emotionally repressed was anything but. The intensity of the love and affection expressed in the letters as the pair move towards their sad denouement makes compelling reading.

General Sir Jack Deverell KCB OBE DL,
Commander-in-Chief Allied Forces Northern Europe 2001–2004

As a member of the Silent Generation, born in 1944, I grew up feasting on war stories, be they in books or movies, from Rockfist Rogan through to *The Colditz Story* and on to Max Hastings and Ben Macintyre. But here is a very different take on wartime life, one of innocence, love, sacrifice and tragic loss. It is the story of Robert Keddie, a young RAF flying boat pilot and his 21-year-old wife Diana, pregnant with their first child, widowed when his Catalina simply and silently disappears when on patrol in the North Atlantic near the Arctic Circle.

Caroline Cecil Bose has produced an extraordinarily detailed picture of English domestic and military life in the quiet early days of the war, drawn from the cascade of letters exchanged between these two impossibly innocent young people, as they meet, explore and develop their friendship into a love affair and then marriage. The wonderful minutiae of daily life, at home and serving in the RAF, devoid of any trace of cynicism or anger, tells of a kinder, more civilised England. And then the horror of unexplained loss, and Diana is suddenly a 22-year-old mother and widow and yet Robert's letters from faraway Sullom Voe keep coming for a while and then there are no more. A beautifully told love story of a different age.

Nick Hewer, journalist and media presenter

The importance of Coastal Command during the war is often undersold particularly by the RAF who focused on the Bomber and Fighter Commands roles, but the defeat of the U-boat threat was crucial to our nation's survival and the winning of the war, and Coastal Command pivotal in that context. This delightful book highlights the part played by the people who conducted the campaign over the cruel North Atlantic and the touching love story of a couple of the protagonists. The stoic bravery of those who spent often terrifying hours in what were relatively flimsy aircraft, well aware that falling into the sea meant almost certain death, should always be remembered. The interweaving with a love story reminds us that humanity transcends war.

Admiral the Rt Hon Lord West of Spithead GCB DSC PC,
First Sea Lord 2002–2006

This book is an outstanding and heart-warming collection of letters written by Flight Lieutenant W. A. Robert (Bob) Keddie, a Royal Air Force (Volunteer Reserve) pilot, to his wife Diana over a two-year period until his untimely death flying a Catalina flying boat during World War Two.

Bob was based at Sullom Voe, a remote flying base in the Shetland Islands from where he would captain his Catalina and crew searching relentlessly for German submarines. The importance of this task cannot be overstated as the sea lines of communication and resupply routes had to be maintained at all costs. Missions were long and tedious interspersed with periods of frantic activity when the presence of an enemy surface ship or submarine was encountered. Captaining the aircraft required unique skills of leadership, flying ability and patience. Maintaining morale and encouraging stoic vigilance among the crew during what could be a sortie length of up to 20 hours in cold, hazardous and uncomfortable conditions took special people. Bob Keddie was one of these special people. He died along with his crew of nine.

Coastal Command lost thousands of airmen but unlike many of those killed in Bomber and Fighter Command there were often no known graves. They simply did not return. This book is highly recommended and is a beautiful read.

Group Captain Bob Kemp CBE QVRM AE DL RAF (Ret'd),
Inspector Royal Auxiliary Air Force and ADC to HM The Queen 2000–2007

This is an extraordinary story of wartime romance and sacrifice. It captures the heartache of separation and the remarkable stoicism and dignity of a couple forced apart because of a nation at war. The letters are evocative and moving to read and a reminder of a past age when writing was an everyday reality. They paint a fascinating picture of wartime life on the home front. They also reveal something of the dangers and physically demanding nature of flying boat missions from Shetland to occupied Norway in often brutal weather conditions. It is a unique, tragic but heartwarming story.

Hugh Pym, BBC Health Editor

'I wish I could make you feel what it is like up there', Bob Keddie writes to his beloved Diana Ladner. But in these vivid, absorbing letters, skilfully edited by Caroline Cecil Bose, Keddie does exactly that. He gives a detailed account of his training and experience as an RAF Catalina flying boat pilot over the Arctic Ocean. They are all the more poignant because of the tragic outcome—his death in the spring of 1942.

Brian Holden Reid, King's College, London,
author of JFC Fuller: Military Thinker

WE'VE ALL LIFE BEFORE US

Bob Keddie and Diana Ladner—possibly their official pre-wedding photograph.
Diana is wearing a brooch in the style of RAF wings.

WE'VE ALL LIFE BEFORE US

A Love Story of the Second World War

Edited by
Caroline Cecil Bose

FONTHILL

First published in Great Britain in 2025 by
Fonthill
An imprint of
Pen & Sword Books Ltd
Yorkshire – Philadelphia
www.fonthill.media

ISBN 978-1-78155-960-4

A CIP catalogue record for this book
is available from the British Library.

Typeset in Sabon LT 10/13
Typeset by Fonthill
Printed and bound in the UK by CPI Group (UK) Ltd, Croydon, CR0 4YY

MIX
Paper | Supporting
responsible forestry
FSC   FSC® C013604
www.fsc.org

The Publisher's authorised representative in the EU for product
safety is Authorised Rep Compliance Ltd., Ground Floor,
71 Lower Baggot Street, Dublin D02 P593, Ireland.
www.arccompliance.com

For a complete list of Pen & Sword titles please contact
PEN & SWORD BOOKS LIMITED
47 Church Street, Barnsley, South Yorkshire, S70 2AS, England
E-mail: enquiries@pen-and-sword.co.uk
Website: www.pen-and-sword.co.uk

Or
PEN AND SWORD BOOKS
1950 Lawrence Rd, Havertown, PA 19083, USA
E-mail: Uspen-and-sword@casematepublishers.com
Website: www.penandswordbooks.com

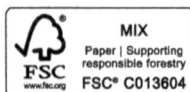

Acknowledgements

My former colleague Roy Hodson used to say that everybody has a book in them, but with most people it is best left in. Although my role in this publication has been that of editor rather than author, it took a great deal of pushing from my husband Mihir Bose to convince me that I could do the job, and without the help, guidance and encouragement of many other people, there would have been no book.

Penny Farquhar-Oliver was born five months after the death of her father, Bob Keddie. She generously agreed to her parents' letters and diaries being published. She has also provided fascinating information and stories, photographs and cheerful support, as well as a wonderful welcome over many years at her home in Herefordshire. Never having met her father or known how he thought, Penny described reading his letters so many decades after they were written as a surreal experience.

On one of my last visits to see Diana before she died, she and Tom, her son from her second marriage, gave me the correspondence and diaries. Diana had been keen to have the material published, and on that visit the challenge to achieve this was firmly passed on. I am most grateful for Tom's continuing support for this project, which has included supplying extracts from Diana's diary. Critically, Tom's daughter Zoe Pascucci saved the day by unearthing many more of Bob's letters before it was too late.

Richard Dawkins kindly offered information about his mother, Diana's sister, and his fascinating memoir *An Appetite for Wonder: The Making of a Scientist* (Bantam Press, 2013) has provided another family perspective.

Stuart Hadaway and Lynsey Shaw Cobden of the RAF Air Historical Branch put me on course to understand the military significance of aspects of RAF operations and life day to day. They also guided me towards the operations record book for Bob's squadron, the RAF Casualty Files at the National Archives and the map of the patrol areas of the Norwegian coast, parts of which are reproduced in this book under Crown Copyright.

To the Ends of the Earth: 210 Squadron's Catalina Years (Paterchurch Publications, 1999) captured the squadron's story before everyone passed away. Written by Bill Balderson, who flew on operations with Bob on a few occasions, and Mike Seymour, it was an invaluable source of information during my research. It was wonderful when I managed to make contact with the publisher John Evans, whose interest, support and photographs have been a boon. John also put me in touch with Bill's son Martin who kindly provided two photographs of Bob, which have been reproduced in the picture section. Soon after, Sandy Copland introduced me to Jeffrey Boyling, pilot and shareholder of the only Catalina still flying outside the Americas. It was a privilege to be invited by Jeff to IWM Duxford to be shown such a rare example of the aircraft Bob had flown, albeit a later model. David Legg of the Catalina Society also helped me with some vital details.

The account of the Catalina flight in the prologue draws on descriptions in *Arctic Airmen: The RAF in Spitsbergen and North Russia, 1942* by Ernest Schofield and Roy Conyers Nesbit (The History Press, 2014) and *Catalina over Arctic Oceans: Anti-Submarine and Rescue Flying in World War II* by John French OBE DFC AFC AE, edited by Anthony L. Dyer (Pen & Sword Aviation, 2013). Some members of 210 Squadron are mentioned in Bob's letters and, where possible, I have tried to clarify any names that were ambiguous. Their many achievements and great bravery have been beautifully described in these three books mentioned above.

I have tried without success to contact the next of kin to seek permission to publish Pilot Officer Bellerby's letter to Bob's mother, and that of Walter Hutton, Bob's commanding officer, to his father.

Stephen Bartley, the archivist for the St Moritz Tobogganing Club, gave me helpful insight into Bob's spectacular success on the Cresta Run.

Priscilla Osborne has provided incisive editorial input and, in the process, discovered that her father could well have known Diana and her second husband, Bill Dawkins, when they were in Sierra Leone after the Second World War.

Several people helped to transcribe the letters—no easy feat—and provided much enthusiasm for the project: Nicky Kruger, who also unearthed a mine of useful information, Shanna Martens, Eliza Halling, Rose Chisholm and Charlotte Melville have my considerable gratitude. Rose stayed the course for much of the project, providing assistance in too many ways to record, and Charlotte's active interest continues.

Peter McLelland made some helpful discoveries, as did Annabel Brown, and Glyn Russ applied his investigative powers to great effect. Martin Adeney gave valuable feedback on the manuscript and I appreciated Derek Wyatt's encouragement too. Steve Harris's guidance is always spot-on and his help with this project has been no exception.

My brother Richard Cecil's interest and observations helped and informed me. Julia Taylor, tower captain at St Margaret's, Downham, provided information about the bell installed in memory of the Keddie boys. Susan Hauser listened and encouraged.

My sister Jenny Mills and her daughter Eleanor gave me calm, expert advice, as did my colleague Patricia Knox, whose insight, skill and friendship have guided me during many years of collaboration. Susanna Majendie and Michael Croxford provided diversions when needed.

I am most grateful to Alan Sutton and his team at Fonthill Media for publishing the book. Jasper Hadman has steered me through each stage with skill, enthusiasm and patience, which I have greatly appreciated, and George Kalchev's design work has been wonderfully evocative.

Mihir, who changed my life when he married me, changed it again by inspiring me to complete this project, which I have found utterly fulfilling.

Caroline Cecil Bose
London
January 2025

Contents

Editor's Note

Diana had known my mother, Alison Foster, since they were small, and later introduced my father, Anthony Gascoyne-Cecil, to her. She was my younger sister's godmother but mistakenly had my initials engraved on her silver christening bowl. Therefore, when my parents died, she said it was only right that I should become an honorary goddaughter.

During one of my visits to her in Devon in her final years, I mentioned that I had come across the Second World War Experience Museum which had been established by a cousin of mine, Hugh Cecil, to capture the memories of those involved in the war. Little did I know that Diana had kept Bob's correspondence and the diaries they both had written sporadically, and that she had sought to have them published. I have tried to rise to the challenge she set me in giving me the letters and diaries, and to provide a fitting salute to her and her lost love.

Diana was a great correspondent, but few of the letters she wrote during the war have survived. Reading Bob's letters, however, which have survived so well, showed me how much that generation went through: so much more than most of us in the West have ever had to cope with. Yet their hopes and dreams were the same as those we today hold dear for ourselves, our children and our grandchildren.

By the time the letters reached me, they had been much copied and parts had become very faint and difficult to decipher. Pages and whole letters were missing, and much was out of order—some letters must have been lost, whether mislaid by the postal service or sunk by German torpedoes targeting ships carrying mail back from South Africa, where Bob had completed part of his training. Transcribing the letters and diaries prompted my extensive research into the context surrounding them and the references they contained, which were sometimes quite obscure.

My explanatory notes appear in square brackets or footnotes. The letters were written in the age before decimal currency when 12 pence made a shilling and 20 shillings a pound. For approximate 2025 values, multiply by fifty.

Once I had finished putting the book together, Diana's granddaughter from her second marriage, Zoe Pascucci, found all the original letters and diaries. It was wonderful to see them, many in their envelopes, written with a fountain pen and so much easier to read than the copies. There were about half as many again. Some had been written on scraps of paper—one was on a small, white paper bag—because paper was in short supply and expensive. I was suddenly able to unscramble some of the previously illegible parts of the letters. I went back to the drawing board ...

Prologue

In the very early hours of Saturday, 16 May 1942 at RAF Sullom Voe, a Royal Air Force station on the Shetland Islands, the take-off time for 210 Squadron's next patrol was announced for half an hour before sunrise.

It was less than a year since Hitler had invaded Russia, completely changing the course of the Second World War. Responding to Russia's desperate calls for help, the British and Americans were sending shipping convoys with weapons and vital supplies to the Russian port of Murmansk on the border with Finland. Fittingly, in local dialect Murmansk means the edge of the earth.

The Germans were aware of the convoy traffic and by the spring of 1942 had stepped up their efforts to stop the ships getting through. They increased Luftwaffe activity and sent warships along the convoy route past the Norwegian coast.

No. 210 Squadron's job was to provide the Admiralty with detailed reconnaissance reports of enemy movements. The best aircraft for the job was the Catalina, one of the most famous flying boats of the war. It could travel great distances but could only take off and land on water. It took three aircraft each day to keep a twenty-four-hour watch over each patrol route. A member of the squadron recorded that there was 'a shift in attitude—things were becoming dodgy' and everyone was kept very busy.

Early that morning of 16 May, the captain of Catalina AH535/J, Flight Lieutenant Robert Keddie, accompanied by his navigator and wireless officer, went to the operations room for a final briefing. Their patrol route was to the west of Trondheim Fjord. They were updated on the latest weather reports—a critical feature of flying so close to the Arctic Circle—and they were given feedback from the returning crews and those currently airborne. Two Catalinas had reported sighting German combat aircraft, and one had run into a hailstorm and been forced to return to base.

The second pilot and rest of the crew collected the rations for the flight. With gruelling non-stop missions lasting eighteen hours or more, the crew would heat up food and drinks to consume as they flew.

The crew was transferred by dinghy to their Catalina, which moved around constantly on the water. They had to negotiate the Browning machine gun as they climbed into one of the two transparent 'blister' gun positions behind each of the wings. The blisters, like enormous bugs' eyes, gave the gunners great visibility, but they also made the aircraft easily identifiable.

The engines were started, the final checks were carried out, the mooring was slipped and the Catalina was taxied towards the take-off spot on a runway formed of moored dinghies fitted with lights. With the engines powered up to full throttle, the Catalina threw up a waterfall of spray as it moved through the water onto its keel. Taking off required fine judgement and a lot could go wrong. If the flying boat started moving like a porpoise as it neared lift off, its nose would dive under the water creating a disaster for the aircraft and crew. But Flight Lieutenant Keddie had no difficulty in lifting the Catalina safely off the surface of the water and into the air.

Soon the Catalina was cruising at 100 knots. As the sun rose, the crew tried to get a clear view of the state of the sea. Visibility could be extremely murky. Everyone had to keep a lookout for enemy aircraft, shipping and submarines at all times, as well as fulfilling their respective duties as observer/navigator, wireless operator, flight engineer, rigger or pilot. All knew how to operate the guns in extremis.

There was rarely time to sleep and the on-board heating system was not able to cope with these long, cold reconnaissance sorties. It produced foul fumes and little heat and so was hardly ever used. Instead, the crew wore many layers, including a life jacket partially inflated for extra warmth, which made moving around the restricted space even more difficult.

Radio silence was enforced when the Catalina crew reached their patrol area off the coast of Trondheim, sufficiently far from the Norwegian shoreline to avoid detection. The aircraft started flying circuits of the patrol route, each of which could take more than two hours to complete. At 1739 hours, one of the crew requested a forecast for landing back at Sullom Voe. Whatever happened next was to have tragic consequences. Probably the Catalina had turned for home. At 1804 hours, RAF Sullom Voe called the Catalina with the forecast but received no reply. The aircraft was never found. All of the crew were reported missing in action.

No one knows what happened, but as with every death in war, the story did not end there. Diana, the love of Robert's life, who was carrying their child, kept all the letters, diaries, sketches and poems he had sent her over the previous two years. In that preserved correspondence is the deeply poignant yet still joyous tale of their love, a story that is both unique and, in its example of tremendous sacrifice and loss, characteristic of their noble generation.

Introduction

Wallace Arthur Robert Keddie loved writing, and his zest for life and wit shine through in his letters and diaries. Known to everyone as Bob, he was the first child of Annie and Frederick 'Wallace' Keddie, born on 14 January 1917.

He had two siblings. Dick was seventeen months younger and John arrived in 1921. The family lived in Westcliff, near Southend in Essex, and later moved a few miles away from the coast to Downham, near Billericay. Downham Grange was a large house with a wonderful garden, including a swimming pool and tennis court. The boys also enjoyed sailing on the Essex coast. It was an idyllic place to grow up.

At school, Bob was a talented sporting all-rounder. He won medals in swimming, two boxing championships and a place in the school rugby team. Later he became a keen motorist and the proud owner of a Frazer Nash sports car. In 1937 he passed his flying certificate at Southend Flying Club. This was probably when he was recruited into the Royal Air Force Volunteer Reserve, created the year before to provide airmen in the event of war.

After school, Bob trained as an accountant with the firm Josolyne, Miles, Page and Co. (now part of Ernst & Young) based in King Street, off Cheapside in London. The training was to equip him to go into the family business, the eponymous Keddie's department store in Southend, but he still found time to indulge in adventurous sporting pursuits.

In January 1939, Bob and Dick made their first attempts at the Cresta Run, the world-famous natural ice toboggan track at St Moritz in Switzerland. Bob's star shone spectacularly on the Cresta against illustrious competition. He 'took everybody by storm', winning all the key races, and his performance in the Curzon Cup received much media coverage. In a long article in *The Field*, another competitor, Colonel J. T. C. Moore-Brabazon MC MP, described Bob as a star performer, saying that he had only twice seen a novice become a first-class rider in his first season: '[Keddie] possessed courage and dash [and] has the satisfaction of having some very formidable scalps in his bag.'

Racing came with danger. Bob badly hurt his mouth because his face brushed the ice as he attempted to keep his head low in a more aerodynamic position. The injury, known as a 'Cresta kiss', was common before the introduction of full-face helmets forty years later. It was a badge of honour and showed you were really trying. (The resulting scar on Bob's upper lip was mentioned as a distinguishing mark on his RAF Record of Service.)

As a result of this success, Bob and Dick, who was in the navy and had to return early that season to his ship, hoped to compete in the 1940 Olympics, but war was to intervene. And not only that—Bob's life was to be overturned when he met Diana.

◇◆◇

Diana Constance Ladner was born on 23 October 1920 at a nursing home in Plymouth run by her aunts. The story goes that she was considered dead at birth and was cast aside while everyone fussed around her adored mother Connie. However, one of her aunts decided to fish her out of the coal scuttle and, to everyone's surprise, managed to revive her.

Connie had married an electrical engineer, Alan Wilfred 'Bill' Ladner, whose speciality was shortwave radio. Their first child Jean was born in Ceylon, modern-day Sri Lanka, where Bill had been sent by the Royal Navy to build a radio station. Bill's work took him to Marconi College of Wireless Communications in Chelmsford, Essex, the year before Diana arrived.

Diana went to St Anne's and then Chelmsford High School. Her great loves were dancing and spending time in Cornwall, from where both her parents hailed. She enjoyed playing tennis all summer long and bicycling for miles. After school, she set her sights on becoming an actress, and just before the war she trained at the Central School of Speech and Drama in London. But when the war came the theatres went dark, and the only paid work she did was four weeks at the Plymouth Repertory.

Diana's beauty, her vivacious but slightly shy nature, and the joyful way in which she told stories made an impression on those she met. There is no doubt that these qualities and her interest in literature, poetry and nature, which she shared with Bob, drew them together.

They knew each other for only two years, but with Bob's death, Diana's life was shattered. The war was also to claim the lives of Bob's two brothers; an entire generation of the Keddie family was lost. What consoled Diana through so much tragedy was reading Bob's diaries and letters.

1

A silver cascade of notes hovers on the night air

The British had gone to war to defend Poland but initially it hardly impinged on people's lives. As Antony Beevor wrote in The Second World War, *'Apart from the risk in the blackout of walking into a lamp-post, the greatest danger was being run down by a motorcar.'*

Bob Keddie was enlisted in the RAF Volunteer Reserve on 2 October 1939, and was recommended for training as an aircraftman/pilot at an aviation candidates' selection board at Uxbridge in Middlesex. He then waited to hear whether the Air Ministry would give him an exemption allowing him to complete his final accountancy exams before starting his RAF training. In the meantime, he carried on his daily commute by bicycle and train from his parents' house in Downham to the City of London.

In January 1940, Bob's twenty-third birthday came and went uneventfully, but a few weeks later he joined a party of friends to see the Beggar's Opera in London. It was an evening that was to change the course of his life.

◊♦◊

BOB'S DIARY:

March, 1940.

A girl called Diana was there. She has a fascinating face. I didn't get a chance to talk to her ... oh blast, you fool, you will only get burnt. Is there no such thing as a hardened heart? Let her pass while you can ... but a voice inside says she may and she might and if you don't ...

April, 1940.

Life's a game, but a serious one, there shall be but one wife for me. Pretty certain it's Diana. I wish ten thousand times I'd never met her; she's ruined my peace of mind for what seems like eternity.

To Bob's joy, the nineteen-year-old Diana lived with her parents in Little Baddow, outside Chelmsford in Essex, only about 10 miles from Downham Grange. Soon the pair were writing to each other. In response to a letter from Diana, Bob wrote the first of the letters that form this book.

◇◆◇

L<small>ETTER TO</small> D<small>IANA</small>:

Downham
23rd April, 1940

12am. Dear Diana,

Must write tonight, now, midnight.

It is quite still, no breath of wind, no rustle from the elms. Even the house has hushed its creaks and waits. I can feel the night—warm, soft—drawing me out: off with the lights and softly pull the curtain, lean out and I, too, wait. The musty-sweet smell of earth and new-mown grass comes up to greet me.

The moon, filmy shape behind her veil of clouds sheds a shimmer of light to see the larch and ash bowed—intently listening. The tension grows and yet we wait.

Jug-jug ... jug-jug-jug, a silver cascade of notes hovers on the night air, rises breaks and falls like a shower of sun-caught spray back into the sea. An answering song takes up the theme and the larches relax and sit up straight, the garden sighs its relief and gladness, the house resumes its creaks, and I wonder why it is those first notes of the nightingale that are so important. The rest of his song is lovely, but it's the first few notes that thrill the heart.

Must go to bed now, devilish late, but had to write that: gone in the morning. Goodnight.

24 April, 1940. Thanks for your letter—I loved it, I'm still reading it, in fact. I agree with you that love and marriage must represent the highest state to which poor mortals can aspire. I believe that the only truth in this world and the only things we can take out are beauty and love. Their attainment is the whole of life.

Over-anxiety to fall in love might ruin a whole life—two lives in fact: which is why I am always suspicious of war-time marriages. Love itself must be so tremendous that it really hurts—not mere vague aches. It is sure of itself—once known. We cannot create it.

25 April, 1940. I haven't mentioned 'them' [children]. Please don't think that out of sight is etc ... I have to find someone else first. The thought of them makes my blood race and frightens me too. Am I old enough to know how to bring them up? Don't I love them too much that they would be spoilt?

My 'Zouave Milliet' in his red skirt and hat* stares down and says it's time for bed. So must finish. He is my taskmaster. I work beneath his benevolent (?) eye and his word is law.

---

*   Presumably a copy of Vincent van Gogh's *The Seated Zouave*, a portrait of Milliet, 2nd lieutenant of the Zouaves, a French regiment whose uniform featured a distinctive red skirt and hat.

And once more thank you for your letter and putting up with this (if you've got so far). Trying to make my mind intelligible for others makes it clearer to me and sends strange relief to seething thoughts: directs the brain down new half-explored paths.

Can you and Jean make tea Friday? Come early: I'll ride and meet you.

Tout à l'heure, Bob

◊♦◊

At the end of April, Bob took some time off from commuting to the City to study at home for the next set of accountancy exams. He rang Diana and suggested sailing with his younger brother John.

◊♦◊

BOB'S DIARY:

April, 1940.

Glorious, glorious day, oh! for some more like that. We went up the river against the tide with the jib furled back to catch the sun. Diana leant against my knees. I would have given a lot to be able to stroke her hair or lay my hand on her shoulder, to talk through touch and feeling. Ran down to a beach and landed for lunch in the sun.

Diana so unaffected I can almost treat her as a brother, but not quite, something holds me back, I am frightened too. We had a close beat back: we sat together too near for necessity, perhaps, and jointly sailed her in a glorious breeze. Diana dear, you make me so happy my heart sung for joy today. Diana asked 'Are you religious?' Hell of a question to answer, is the heart not enough? Must she have my soul too?

◊♦◊

It took time to absorb the vast number of recruits into the armed forces' training systems, so it was eight months after war was declared that Bob received the letter he had been expecting—and dreading. He was mobilised to start his RAF training at Padgate, near Warrington, on 22 May. By now Hitler's blitzkrieg in the west had seen the Nazis invade Holland, Belgium and France.

◊♦◊

BOB'S DIARY:

May, 1940.

It quite panicked me, wandered round all the morning doing nothing for more than ten minutes then moving on to nothing else. Am I afraid? I think so a little, not of personal injury, of losing a leg or being hurt and in pain, perhaps not even death. I think too I am a little thrilled at going, proud of myself in spite of myself.

Asked myself to tea with Diana and spent a pleasant afternoon picking primroses. She attracts me more than I like to admit and can make my blood run hot and my heart jump right out leaving an empty longing behind.

Holland and Belgium invaded. Bombs on Brussels and aerodromes in France and Holland. What does it all mean? Where can it all end? Is that man never satisfied? He must go on expanding, gaining centrifugal force with each new invasion. My heart goes out to Holland. Oh God! The misery of war.

Golf with John and Diana ... By hand and eye and touch, by voice and gesture we said to each other what we know we each wanted to hear, at last we parted at her house [18th May]. I see her standing now, if eyes held messages, hers did then, my heart was full, not goodbye, please God, not goodbye, Diana in her green blouse and blue mauve skirt, large-eyed and appealing, soft and flowing hair, cheeks smooth to touch, her grey green eyes, her nose, her mouth, all these will I keep.

Phoned Diana tonight. I think neither of us dared more than hint at what was in our hearts or express it by allegories, but after it was over I felt immeasurably sad and had to bury my head in my pillows and later go for a walk and lie down in the grass to collect myself.

I don't want to leave you, Diana, 'to meet, to know, to love, to part'* not part please or not for ever.

God! How I love her.

Locked up my desk tonight, preparing for tomorrow.

Letter to Diana:

Downham
20th May, 1940

Diana dear,

This is the third or fourth attempt to write and it must be the last—I shall soon run out of paper. I should like to send you pages filled with the thoughts and hopes and ambitions of my heart, yet it is a part of me quite gone and I cannot find the accustomed spate of words. Because I cannot trust myself to words (even if I could find them) so must I leave unsaid what I would most wish to say.

Diana darling forgive this awful letter. I just can't keep my mind on one thought for two concentric seconds. I'll write again as soon as I can.

Look after yourself, don't give in to this world and write to me if you feel depressed—in writing you'll find comfort.

My love to you, you've made me very happy.

x x x x Bob

---

* The slightly misquoted first line of a couplet by Samuel Taylor Coleridge: 'To meet, to know, to love—and then to part, / Is the sad tale of many a human heart.'

Bob's orders were to travel to the No. 3 Recruits Centre at Padgate. Arriving by train in Warrington the evening before, he found that there was no accommodation in the town. Nevertheless, he made the time to write to Diana, a letter that he finished the following day.

◇◆◇

LETTER TO DIANA:

The Exchange Hotel, Liverpool
21st May, 1940

Diana darling,

I'm as near drunk tonight as I've ever been. Here is my record of the day. I'm going to be very rude and ask you if you will let me have it back or rather will you keep it for me in case I ever publish my diary, as I have not time to write to you and keep a diary! You see how conceited I get under the influence of drink to ask you this, and even think of publishing my diary. This is not all. I also keep a personal diary. Not for your sight I'm afraid—yet.

Now 1am. Drunkish. Arrived London. Nasty argument with a rat of a man at Shenfield station after he had been rude to Dick at Billericay. Join the Army, my God! As if he had not had enough excitement as it is.* Knocked his blasted bowler in, the unnecessary letter.†

Just time to have another haircut and shampoo at Douglas's. A real Bond Street finish—wonder when the next will be. There is a curious analogy between the Cresta Run and a shampoo. In both, one lives in a world of one's own for the few rushing seconds of speed or water. All is noise and it is with some surprise that one comes back to life, on the one hand to people, cheers (we hope!), and the tranquillity of immobility and, on the other, to the tranquillity of the barber's salon, mirrors and the soft glow of lights, a warm dry towel and a lovely renascent feeling. I love a shampoo.

Caught the 4.10 from Euston. Met Wilson and fiancée on the platform. Started reading Huxley's 'Antic Hay' on the way up. Bee [*sic*] funny satirically but must be taken in small, concentrated doses. He is a superb moralist without over-emphasising it.

Train journey: 'Antic Hay' interspersed with dreaming from the window.

And I look from the window, again and again—
Beats in my heart the careless refrain—
Is it this, is it this, is it you, is it you—
Diana, Diana, please say it is true—

---

*   Bob's brother Dick had already been in action with the enemy. He had joined the Royal Navy at seventeen as a cadet, becoming a lieutenant at the start of the war.

†   Perhaps Bob was aiming to impress Diana with his literary allusion. They had seen *King Lear* in London together a few days before. In the play, the Earl of Kent calls Oswald 'Thou whoreson zed, thou unnecessary letter!' The insult referred to the fact that, in the fourth century BC, the letter 'z' was dropped from the Latin alphabet.

and on and on goes the refrain and I wish and exclaim and wonder and watch the countryside slip past the—hell! Window pane doesn't scan.

Next moment two rows of cottages. Door to door, back to back—filthy narrow endless street. A glance from the opposite window confirms suspicions. Coal-black refuse dump. Industrial England.

Warrington. Endless streets. Dirty newspaper. Rubbish. Tattered children. Christ. The Patten Arms—musty-smelling beer and fish, lovely white Bentley outside. No accommodation in the town. Back to the Patten Arms in despair. None there. Nice American 'Can I give you a lift? Manchester or Liverpool?' Liverpool at 70–90 mph and radio in the car. With typical and true American hospitality, he gave us our last slap-up farewell to civilisation. Lobster—chicken—mushrooms. Sherry, Burgundy (two bottles between three of us) and Kirsch. What an extremely nice man. Swapped addresses. Wondered how I'd get up from the table. Quite surprised I could walk straight. So put up at the Exchange for the night and private bathroom—sic transit gloria mundi—the only Latin I know. Feel just grand. Wish Diana were here.

22 May, 1940. Every five minutes in the night some bee train seemed to be coming straight in our window then miraculously passed further down the street. The bath this morning made the room worthwhile. Gosh! When next do I get a bath like that?

Caught the 9.30am back to the never-ending streets of Warrington, and then a few miles further to Padgate.

Hell of a hole.

The inevitable interminable waiting. Now 2pm. So far have been issued with towel, mug, knife, fork and spoon only and been shown my bed and living quarters. Wooden hut with thirty of us in it. Bed with springs of sorts, biscuit mattress, two blankets, pillow-case and sheet. Blasted radio blasting forth blasted disruptive music. By the time I'm finished with this, I shall be immune from all outside noises.

Lunch: meat, beans (white, hard and tasteless) potatoes and apricots and prunes and custard. Now we wait again.

Warrington—straggly, dirty, ceaseless streets, rows of sooty, once red-brick cottages. Girls on street corners, paper everywhere. 'The light was on in the Institute, the gas was up in the gym.'*

Someone says we are only here for a month then South coast. Hope so.

I've just read through what I tried to write last night. Diana you won't think me quite mad or quite drunk will you? I'm not and I wasn't. I admit the writing is very nearly illegible but the brain was clear. As soon as I find the address of the place I'll post this off to you. If you can't read it all I'll decipher it for you sometime.

Meantime, sweet, my love and kisses, Bob

---

*   Misquoted from 'A Shropshire Lad', a poem by John Betjeman.

PS We may move from here in a few days, few weeks or something. Nobody seems to know anything. Until I can give you any address would you write Post Restante, Padgate Post Office, Near Warrington, Lancs? xxxx Bob

LETTER TO DIANA:

Padgate
23rd May, 1940

Diana dear,

I long for a letter from you but must myself administer the coup de grâce preventing it. I cannot have an address for another two or three days as we shall probably be moving somewhere else for three weeks of the barrack square. After that we go to an initial training wing for theoretical work and physical training. After that we ought to be pretty tough and our table manners will, I fear, be not quite what they were.

Today we continued our delightful pastime of doing nothing until after lunch. We were then issued with kit and uniform. The latter is definitely scratchy and the pants are a real delight to the eyes. We've also been given buttons, thimble, needles and cotton.

It never seems to cease raining here or rather it never ceases for very long but today, for a treat, we saw a little blue sky and sun between 2 and 3pm.

There is little peace here to read your book of poems* for which I thank and bless you but what I've read I love. Just finished 'Antic Hay' and think you might like it. Very funny, satirical and sometimes lascivious, but the theme is tragic, though the treatment witty. The scene in the corner house early on made me laugh aloud. It's quite light.

No quiet here: get up 6.30am. Breakfast 8.00am—radio full blast thereafter till lights out—lunch 12pm—tea 4pm—supper 6.30pm. Perhaps why I can't write as I would. Thoughtful all day and now a vacuum.

Oh, Diana, when shall I see you again? You don't know, I don't know, neither does Hitler. I may get a few days in three or four weeks' time: you won't be evacuated to Plymouth [to the nursing home run by Diana's aunts] will you? Please ...

Did Jean get off alright?† I hope you were not left too depressed. Remember me will you when you write to her and send my best wishes etc? Do you feel envious? I do. She's moving from a world full of doubt and hesitation to a comparative oasis of quiet certainty. Lucky Jean.

Nearly time for lights out. Nice corporal in charge of us, most helpful, just back from Singapore.

Gee these boots are heavy. Not that I've got them on now. Flat on my bed. Cigarette-smoky room, over hot: will open the window when lights out.

---

*   Diana had a notebook in which she copied her favourite poems, quotations and some of her own poetry.

†   Jean, Diana's sister, had married John Dawkins the previous September. She was travelling to Nyasaland (now Malawi) where Dawkins was working in the Colonial Service.

When we move, I'll try and telephone: at the moment we can't go out and no telephone here. Altogether uncivilised.

Lights just going out. I'll think of you and you, just you. Your eyes ... xxxx Bob

LETTER TO DIANA:

Padgate
25th May, 1940

Diana dear,

The handwriting will be worse than ever tonight. Vaccination and two inoculations yesterday. Very stiff last night and today. Thoughts like grasshoppers today. Sorry.

Trying to learn the Lancashire language, it's very hard. Somebody shouts at you and you say what, they repeat themselves and you're none the wiser. Embarrassing. One trouble is that every other word or so is interpolated (that's the right word, isn't it?) with either 'bloody' or something else I could not offend you with. It's dreadfully catching too—as is the dialect accent, so three of us have a system of fines whenever we use either of them. It's expensive but we spend it on ourselves, and it's curing us.

Table manners also are going to pot. As soon as you sit down, you grab for the bread and slice off as much butter as you can, then you set to work. Incidentally the bread and butter is very good and plentiful. It's my staple food. Average time for a meal is about eight and a half minutes. Main complaint: no fresh vegetables, salad etc or fruit. To compensate, I eat half a dozen oranges a day. Sorry to harp on about food but it's one of the main preoccupations and I like to dribble on.

Each to the Other* describes this place perfectly. Wait and wait. Waiting for orders. Just a belonging of the army like a gun or something ... ticketed and labelled. Forget exact words.

Today we did less than yesterday (because of our arms). All we had to do was carry our bags containing our last civilised belongings to be posted home. I quite like it: lie, dream, sleep and read all day! Now almost immunised against radio and people talking. Thirty of us in the hut, some very noisy.

Trying to live on my pay (two shillings per day). As we are not allowed out, I'm almost succeeding. When we go up to eight shillings guess it'll be quite easy. Trouble is a couple of days leave and bang goes a month or so's pay. But leave is somewhere in the hazy distance. Told yesterday that all weekend passes stopped until September. But anyhow this place is one big rumour. It is as for certain as can be that we quit here Wednesday for Hastings (Hush! Walls have Ears). Hope so: fed up with dirt, rain and atmosphere of this place. The sunny South for me.

Do you mind all these letters? Ignore them if you like. I like writing. Don't feel obligation to write ... just scribble when you feel like it. Tell me what you do and

---

*   Christopher La Farge's *Each to the Other: A Novel in Verse* has several parallels to Bob's life at Warrington such as joining the armed forces, deciding whether to marry, choosing a wife and making a life together.

how the country looks. It's a funny feeling writing a one-sided correspondence. Tentative, a little afraid. Of what? Don't know.

Am beginning to ache so goodnight—darling.

26 May, 1940. Today we find out that by turning up to meals a quarter of an hour late we don't have to queue and also get the bathroom free for a few moments. One lives and learns. Also keep yourself looking busy to avoid fatigue duties and never, never volunteer to do anything. Another day of sheer laziness.

Wish these people wouldn't smoke, especially pipes, just before I go to bed. Lots of love and xxxx Bob

LETTER TO DIANA:

Padgate
27th May, 1940

Diana dear,

So here we are still here, sitting on our backsides most of the day. On Friday (have I told you? I've written so many letters I don't know what I've said to whom: not certain haven't told you) we were vaccinated—the left arm and had two inoculations. A painful night followed and felt deflated in the morning. In fact quite miserable. However, aspirin and Enos put me right by the afternoon.

So Saturday and Sunday I lay on my back and slept and dreamt and read. At times I managed to go off into a lovely trance-like dreaming. I can do that sometimes. Can you? It's what I imagine dope to be like—quite happy just floating and dreaming, no cares, no worry. It's all too rare a feeling. Idleness being a necessary condition.

Today to the Parade ground at 8.45am for some elementary drill. A very sympathetic, humorous staff sergeant. Most of them are very nice here. Little of that old staff sergeant-major about them. Result—we work much better. After parade we are asked if we would like a bathe in the afternoon and as one man ... etc. We marched for half an hour and then arrived at a near deserted road-house. A lovely bathe (no bathers here!) in warm sun for once and joy of joys—bathing steps. Comparative freedom. The sergeant met some girlfriends there which explains the luck of the bathe. Incidentally the first women we had seen for a week. It did the heart good. (Did you know they put bromide in the tea here—and in the Army: it is an anti-aphrodisiac, or whatever the word is? I hope you are shocked. I was disgusted at first but, in the light of reason, approve.)

It is also pretty certain that we get to Hastings on Wednesday—may I phone that evening or the next if I can?

Sorry about the pencil: pen run dry.

If you write, tell me what you do and what the garden looks like and what you see in flowers if you look long enough. Can you too get dizzy lying in the sun?

I'm thinking of you a lot: do you ever know it? Remember what you said about wishing hard enough?

Love and xxx Bob

2

Diana, only you can cure the ache in my heart

On 29 May, Bob arrived in Hastings, East Sussex, for the next stage of his training with No. 5 Initial Training Wing. That day, Diana wrote to him saying that his brother John had phoned to tell her that his—Bob's—exemption had been granted by the Air Ministry. This allowed him to take a break in his training to complete his final accountancy exams. She said she was thrilled about it but was not sure whether he would be glad or sorry. Having started his training, might it be annoying to rush back again?

◊♦◊

BOB'S DIARY:

30th May, 1940.

Do I leave tomorrow? Don't want to: going to try not to, I think, God it's hard to choose. I'm settled now.

1st June, 1940.

You fool! You b----- little fool, why didn't you get out of it and go back to her? Diana I cry for you. Diana I'm in love with you. Diana ... do I love you? Yes, Diana I think I do. I love you inside ... I love to see you, to hear you, just to be with you and God how I love you when you're not there. You leave an ache in my heart. Only you can fill it.

LETTER TO DIANA:

No 904036, A/C WA Keddie!!
2 Flight No 2 Squadron
Alexandra Hotel St. Leonards, 1st June, 1940

6pm. Your two letters today. The first in the morning; the second just now. Oh Diana I'm sorry—I can't really explain why I had to stay, perhaps you can understand, think you do. It tore me in two and your letter ... if it had arrived this morning I think I should have come home. I can't say all I want to. I am with you in spirit if not in person ... you're not out of my thoughts for long. Hell! How can I offer comfort with worn out clichés ... but what else is there to say? I know how you feel and it hurts me to think of you while I live mainly from one moment to the next. Our days here are pretty full—but I'll write of that anon. Have promised to go out 6.30.

Tomorrow Sunday: supposed to be working seven days a week but hope for afternoon off and retire to the cliffs. If so will scribble in the grass.

A dreadful place this. Nothing else to do of an evening and 'our gang' always goes out together. Sorry I can't phone tonight—it's too expensive—perhaps one evening next week.

Here they are to go out. My heart aches. Diane ... God bless you and keep you ... don't lose hope or faith. Don't despair. Must go. They're cursing me.

Diana, Diana, Diana ... I can sometimes find you by just repeating your name again and again.

Xx Bob

◊♦◊

The main evacuation of the British Expeditionary Force and French troops from Dunkirk, one of the biggest sea evacuations in history, had started on the night of 26 May. It was not completed until the night of 3 June. In Britain it felt as though invasion was imminent.

◊♦◊

DIANA'S DIARY:

1st June, 1940.

I think I want to marry Bob. I know we are suited, I know I like him as a man. Am I in love? I think I am but I wish I could see him again to be certain ... The men are getting out from Dunkirk and Flanders. How many people's lives are being destroyed? Life is passing fast and here I am wasting my precious days wishing them to pass so, in my ambitious dreams, I may attain peace. Noticing the days hurrying by when you're in love, my how time flies.

Going to the Chase Club tonight. Think I'd rather go to bed but I am off to a dance.

Gardened today, dug under the apple trees, played with Sheila, one of our evacuees. My new job, a kindergarten teacher in Danbury School, is not till July. What ought I to do in the next month?

2nd June, 1940.

Reading the Observer and the Courier. Italy will come in [with Germany into the war] any day. Germany have nearly all Europe and a lot of the north of the

French coast, therefore command of English Channel and French ports and air bases. The evacuation of children starts again and today even Mummy packed our silver to go to Mullion.* Feel scared stiff. Only in moments of active exercise or thought does one forget. Like dancing the old fashioned waltz with Jeremy last night. Jeremy in uniform.

◊♦◊

Occasionally Bob started writing a new letter without addressing Diana, as if continuing a conversation. Often, he wrote at snatched intervals during a day or over several days, updating the time or date within the letter. This was because postage was expensive and paper in short supply—he did not want to leave any part of a page blank. At the end of the day, he wished Diana goodnight even if he then added to the same letter the following day.

◊♦◊

LETTER TO DIANA:

St. Leonards
2nd June, 1940

6pm. Just bathed: washed my hair, some handkerchiefs and a pair of socks. Feel as clean as a whistle—quite a luxury here. Also dressed comfortably—shorts, singlet and pullover. Another luxury. Reread your letters in the bath: just saved one from drowning—now drying. Sorry to so maltreat them.

Oh hell! Dick† and Tony just came for the evening pilgrimage to Leslie's.

We really meant to be back in time to write but it was a glorious evening and we, of all things, listened to a woman Communist on peace aims. Now a few minutes to lights out. After that we had to feed and we talked and talked of death. A subject I've not yet heard mentioned elsewhere: it doesn't lead very far—we three are all afraid I think. Stop: morbid.

... Hope no one comes in—your letters strewn over my bed. Perhaps I'd better turn in. Shouting down the passage 'turn out those lights': Goodnight Diana, wish I could write more: lovely night, warm and glowing. Just lie in bed count the stars and wish. Wish you were here to talk to and listen to and to be at peace with. Goodnight—God bless you.

Bob

3rd June, 1940. 5.30pm. No time to tell last night of the weekend's activities. Mainly wandering about on the beach. Saturday started with a visit to the CO

---

*   Presumably the plan was to remove the silver to the family holiday cottage at Mullion Cove, Cornwall, in anticipation of the invasion.

†   Dick was a fellow trainee in the RAF, not Bob's brother.

[commanding officer] where I signed a chit that I didn't want to take the [accountancy] exams—he wondered whether it meant I should be disinherited. A wise man.

The afternoon was ours except that we had to be in for tea at 4.00. We sat on the beach for a little then Dick and I left Tony waiting and went in search of crabs. Found an old bucket and a piece of wire and made ourselves weapons to poke about with. For the next two hours or so we poked and scratched and raised a catch of five crabs. Two or three quite large, four eels about four–five inches long and a few prawns. For the eels a small boy of ten or so helped with his net and we gave the eels to him. It was most amusing and reminded us both of childhood's happier days. Amused by small things. Later we went on things they call Whoopee floats built like this looking from the top. They're like small double canoes and you have one large double-ended paddle. Great fun standing up—it is so easy to come off.

We finished the day at 'chez Leslie' as usual. Have I described him to you? He's about thirty, six feet tall, fat all over, long wavy hair, small eyes, clean manicured hands, affected in manner, brilliant in wit and repartee and the voice of a woman. He fascinates us and so do the customers. Wish you could see him.

Yesterday church parade. Ghastly preacher, made me writhe. He said the fog over the channel and bad flying conditions outlined in the German communiqué were due to the day of prayer. Yes, I thought, so was Leopold's capitulation.* Also said God was like a bank cashing cheques of friendship ... a glorified YMCA. I suppose it's men like that that make one feel I never want to go into a church again. After lunch, we three walked as far as we could along the beach, to the old town of fishing nets and those tall sheds to drag them in, cottages, ropes, capstans, wire, wheels and the hundred little things left lying round that characterise the bygone days of fishing prosperity. Back again for another dose of crabbing (we'd had nothing more than a pair of shorts on the last two days) and then tea. A last bathe and we have arrived at the beginning of this letter.

Does our daily routine interest? Reveille 6.30am. Clean boots, buttons and selves. Make beds in the recognised fashion—blanket, sheets etc folded just so, 'There's only one correct way in the RAF'—and clean the room. 7.30am breakfast: meals of quite good standard, also nice servants and comparative peace and quiet, no rush or scramble, feel almost a gentleman again. 8.15am roll-call and parade: inspection. 8.30am–10.30am, 11am–1pm, 2pm–4.15pm classes, drill, PT, compulsory games etc. Break at 10.30am. There's quite a nice coffee shop just down the road. 4.30pm tea, then usually free till 10pm and lights out 10.15pm. Supper at 7.00pm if you want it.

Thanks for your letters (and bath powder): the last still hurts to read. Yet I would not have it otherwise: joy out of sorrow—gladness from pain. Don't stop please. I should be worse than mad if you did.

---

*   People turned out in strength to support the national day of prayer. Many claimed that the prayers led to the bad weather that hindered the Luftwaffe's ability to attack the troops waiting on the beaches at Dunkirk. On 28 May, King Leopold III of Belgium, commander-in-chief of the Belgian forces, had surrendered to Germany.

10pm. A little morose and depressed. Our usual routine—three half-pints with Leslie, a round of the dodgems and a little supper. Walk home along the front, glorious evening, it always is here. No thoughts of war, the RAF—the last place to be reminded of it. I miss you Diana. And yet you comfort me too. Strange, n'est-ce pas, that one can receive comfort and yet be thereby forced to require it only the more. Bad grammar: but does it convey what I want to say? The more one has the more one wants.

I wish—too. But too much wishing leads to eventual discontent with one's lot and thus unhappiness: and yet I go on wishing—and you as well.

Rumours here of evacuation to Torquay or Ilfracombe: hope not—I am just ensconced nicely now.

Just looked for seven stars*—still too light. I am going to do it this time or bust.

Funny, your book of poems—I seem to like quite a number of those unmarked and I presume not liked by you. We both like 'The blue flag in the bog' [by Edna St Vincent Millay]. Must finish tomorrow: will there be a letter from you?

Goodnight, Diana, Goodnight. Seven stars.

Tuesday, 1.30pm. Just had lunch and upstairs to find your letter. Enchanting: for a while I lived in a world far from uniform, discipline and the one-of-a-thousand feeling. Thoughts go back twelve years to Yorkshire: a pool in the bracken. I used to run away there and bathe with nothing on. Curious elation: feeling of freedom that is denied—almost the forbidden fruit—and how marvellous it is to feel the water on your skin then the bracken and sun on the back.

Your world and my world. Yet we're quite happy here. We live for the moment, little idleness, no time to be unhappy. And we really are treated nicely. It's surface joys. Yet it's a life I've never led before: good for me no doubt but I long for the return to your world. Flowers (thanks for the syringa: I've a cold, can't smell but it is in my Oxford Book of Verse waiting), little things, thoughts, dreams, absurd joys and disappointments. The spiritual, I suppose, as opposed to the physical.

Compulsory games in 10 minutes. I gave mine as swimming, hope to lie on the beach in the sun. Going to hide this in my pocket too.

OK, now on the beach, sheltering from the wind behind a breakwater. Very hot, very nice, and here we have to stay until 4pm. Just my idea of compulsory games. Trouble is I've forgotten all I was going to say—just gone with the wind.

Dick and I are waiting now for the tide to uncover our rocks and the place where we hid our crab instruments.

Must lie on my tummy for a bit, chest's getting too hot. Can't write like that, too many stones—using my knee now.

---

*   A reference to some version of the old wives' tale that should an unmarried person count
     seven stars for seven nights in a row, on the eighth day they will shake hands with the person
     they are to marry. Bob's interpretation seems to have been slightly different to this.

An hour later. Swam, done about a quarter of a mile or more out then along the beaches. Afraid to go out further—cramp. Felt it at last in my fingers and came in. Lovely feeling. It is good to feel really fit again. You've no idea how tough they're going to make us here. Then an ice cream and some chocolate. Oh! It's the life alright, if you like it: I should get bored if it went on too long. Now basking in the sun again. Dick and Tony bathing. Crabbing after that.

Can't forget you, that night at the Chase—your hair up. It seemed to do something to your eyes—or perhaps it was just me—or just you?

Are you in your garden now, I wonder?

Going in for tea now, will post this on my way.

So long Diana: forget the war for a while if you can. I think this recent holocaust has hurried up the end, anyway.

You're always with me, my dear.

All my love, Bob

BOB'S DIARY:

5th June, 1940.

Letter from Diana and phoned her tonight. My cup is full: I have not deserved so much—it can't last: yet it must: it will. Letter—more poetry straight from her heart I know: Diana you turn me inside out. I could, I do live my past again with you. Diana, and say it again, softly, Diana, Diana, la petite Diane, Diane, Diana, Diana, a world in a name.

Tonight on the phone—more than a day's pay: to hell with it!—how nice to hear her voice again. So much to say—no time to put in words, I would like to just sit one end and be quiet. Feel. But one must talk to get one's money's worth. Diana good night. Seven stars tonight. Fourth time—over halfway. Diana's done it: what did she wish, I wonder?

LETTER TO DIANA:

6th June 1940

8.30am. Just about to have a mathematics grading test. Hope to finish in time to get on with this letter if I'm not seen. Thank heaven that my maths is fairly strong—some fellows have got the wind up terribly about failing the passing-out exam in three weeks' time. If you fail you're pushed out, with no exceptions, and you have to get 70%—rather frightening if it is your weak subject.

9.30am. Just finished the paper. There is another hour yet, but I have not the energy to revise the test so have handed it in. The officer in charge is sitting about eight feet from me, I am hoping he won't mind me writing.

Diana, if you would grant any wish of mine please don't go into any WAAFs, Wrens, Wats* or whatnots. Please you won't, will you? I'd sooner banish you to Plymouth and I know how you feel about that. One has to assume a veneer of callousness and indifference to death and suffering when you belong to the services and veneer in the end looks like the real thing—you are not weak that you couldn't resist—but no one can be immune from the influences of hatred and lust to kill and revenge. It would not, it could not, destroy but it would spoil a part of you Diana—hurt and bruise a piece of you that I love. Must stop now. Got to learn about gases for exam tomorrow. Horrid subject. Look after yourself Diana dear, my love, Bob

7th June. 10am. Just done the gas exam. Crazy, crazy. They told us the questions yesterday and so we all had it mugged up. If you hadn't you could always crib. Just like the RAF.

Must get a new pen. Have lost mine and the family usually object to letters in pencil.

Seem to have been here for weeks and away from home months—it is just over a fortnight. Yet the days pass quickly enough: expect we shall be finished here before we realise it.

Will there be a letter from you today? Another two hours to wait. Lovely long break today, they seem to have forgotten we're not on parade.

2.30pm. Spoke too soon: got whisked on to parade and off for another injection—rapidly going sore and stiff: luckily had the sense to get my left arm done. But, joy of joys—'Callooh! Callay! O frabjous day! He chortled in his joy.'† We have the whole afternoon off—to do as we like. Needless to say I'm off to the beach. Will take this down but probably won't feel like writing.

Your letter got to me just before lunch—they are very far from being 'dull'. It's the 'little things' that really keep me in touch with you, and the life I've left behind. No time for more now. The beach calls and I'm lunch-lazy, no mood for writing.

7.30pm. Must go to the post now—last one 7.45. Letter from Mother says John expects to be here today. Well it is goodnight my love. I think and dream of you, Diane. Love Bob

---

*   'Wats' was Bob's joke—the women's branch of the army was the ATS (Auxiliary Territorial Service).
†   Misquoted from 'Jabberwocky', a poem by Lewis Carroll.

3

The whistle is almost due
to go now

Hastings: on the beach
8th June, 1940

Now nearly five—or as we say 1700 hours. Lying on my side on the beach, sun on my back, shade on the paper. It is not too easy writing and very slow.

Today we again had our photographs taken—this time individually for our records. The photographer was the quickest worker I've ever seen—he took fifty of us in about five minutes. Also had my photograph taken on the beach by a friend who joins our trio now and again. He is also Dick and is small, quick and a marvellous mimic and very witty. He can do Gillie Potter [an English comedian and popular broadcaster] perfectly. Our trio has been enlarged today by Tony's wife—Ruth—who is staying in an hotel about a hundred yards from ours. They've been on the beach with us all afternoon—we've been free since 12.00pm because of our inoculations—and we are all four going to have a slap-up dinner and then walk along for our beer 'chez Leslie'. If we get any more of this sun, I shall soon overtake your brown if I'm not as brown as you already but the trouble is that normally we shall only get out from 5.30pm onwards, unless we have 'compulsory games'.

Sun just gone behind a cloud.

Shall I post this tonight? No, not enough to have my money's worth. This 2½d post is a strain, don't you find?

Getting cold, going in. Pity, can't bath or bathe—bad arm.

11.15pm. Bought my pen tonight—doesn't seem to write very well—getting better! Just had to write to you but after lights out and all that so have to do it in the lavatory. Diana dear, I longed and longed for you tonight. You are most painful at times; I go crazy. Drink numbs the pain but only to redouble desire when the evening is over. Diana, Diana, Diana.

Had a bath when we came in from the beach and after that a clean shirt and collar—almost civilized. (Your clean silk frock brings visions of coolness and content midst summer's heat!) Had a good dinner—cold chicken and ham and salad with Tony, Ruth and Dick and then we started to walk along the Prom to 'chez Leslie'. On the way there met John, so took him along too. He is not going to say anything about his shoulder—heavens know what Mother will say if she finds out so keep it quiet. Personally I wouldn't do it, I think probably would have at his age though.

We then had a drink and then a round on the dodgems. Found Richard—he is the pert little fellow who sometimes joins us. I like him: he is great fun and a grand free entertainment. After the dodgems we went back for more drink and John to his hotel—he had to be in by 10.00pm (us 11.00pm)—and there we stayed till closing time—Richard telling me lovely stories.

Coming back along the promenade I counted my seventh lot of seven stars but saved my wish until I'm back to the peace of my bed. It is right by the sash windows and I can see a few trees, and the sky from where I lie. I sometimes drop asleep while looking out and dreaming—Downham, Essex, Little Baddow, Waterhall [Diana's home] and you. I save you up to last as when I was small.

I thought I had just pages and pages to say and now I find there's little else to say yet is all unsaid. It's hard to put feelings and desires into words. Must go to bed. Seven stars, seven nights. My wish. Diana darling, Goodnight. Take care of yourself. Goodnight.

My love, Bob

Sunday, 12.15pm. Church, some God-awful preacher, over by eleven o'clock. Straight to the beach. Hottest day we've had—no wind. Just swum so cool enough at the moment to write. Getting very brown, sure you can't be browner. Alone this morning, Dick has gone off with his family: Tony has disappeared somewhere with Ruth. Feeling drowsy—sun too hot—write later.

3pm. Had lunch and bathed. Met John on my way down here about two o'clock. He soon went back for his bathing costume but has not yet reappeared. Wonder whether he has picked up some female or got pinched for some duty or other. Never known anything quite so hot as this sun: almost painful. Marvellous.

A little while ago a group of about twenty-five boys and one girl, aged I suppose between six and eleven and mainly eight to ten, probably some school or other, all came down on the beach just beside me. They at once took off their shirts, shorts and shoes having little woollen trunks on and carefully folded the shirt and put it and the shoes on their equally carefully folded shorts. The whole is then wrapped in cylindrical form and then fastened by a blue and white belt with a snake (~) buckle like I used to have when I was small. You then place your gas mask against the sea wall and the little bundle on top.

Those that can swim then go in one after the other like a lot of little frogs or tadpoles from the breakwater. Those that can't have to wait for low tide and shallow water. (I know this because I've noticed them before.) Two of them—the little girl and a boy are busily engaged at the moment in burying someone—I think it is the son or a relation of the master and his wife (they also have a perambulator size kid), burying him under a pile of stones with which the beaches abound. Nothing like our Cornish sand here!*

They are fascinating to watch (and are useful to sit near too as they frighten other people off and never worry me). The only other way to secure peace is to sit down with a proprietorial air with some girl or other. I couldn't bear it. They can't talk, let alone think. I've never seen people so brown as some of these kids—quite a dark brown leathery colour.

Devil of a large bang just gone off. We've had guns rumbling most of the afternoon and continuously but this sounded nearer. Strange to think Hitler is nearer than London. If they try and land here or any of their funny stuff, we are reputed to be off to Torquay. Nice place, but I'm comfortable here at the moment.

Here comes the photographer: if only there were a devastatingly beautiful girl nearby (none in Hastings at all that I've noticed) anyhow, if there were, I'd have had myself taken with her and sent it on for comment.

Blast. Someone just dropped a pebble with some violence from the promenade above on to my posterior. Trouble is one can never catch them. No revenge.

Where the devil's John got to? Now nearly time to go in for tea. Curse is we have to put on uniform for all meals. For beach—singlet, shorts and gym shoes and tunic on top. All quite free and easy—think they might let us turn up for tea like that, such a curse changing.

Lying here on the beach, people all round but quite alone, don't feel lonely, don't want anyone to talk but miss you all the more. When there is someone else to talk to, occupy my attention, or dams to build, crabs to catch, the mind is occupied. High tide now, no sand to play with.

Try to imagine you here: sheer power of wish and thought. It works sometimes but never the same—more like a dream. You're here but you're only a ghost—it's your shadow, not you. No feeling of utter, complete content.

The rest of the world goes on instead of stopping, silent for us. Peace in tranquillity as opposed to peace in turmoil. A calm day instead of the still in the middle of a hurricane.

Must go in now—tea. Where's John?

4.30pm. Back on the beach. Sun not so strong—a little hazy. Wrong about the school kids—there are forty of them and two girls both with very fair hair, one pigtails rather like Mary Lucie Attwell's girls.† All in rows when I came down, eating sandwiches and drinking lemonade out of the bottle. Was it so long ago that I was doing that?

Sitting back to the breakwater now, facing the sun as far down as the receding tide waters will allow. Lovely noise of pebbles rolled round and round and up and down on each other. Starting with a little rattle and then rapid crescendo to

---

* Bob's family had a holiday home called Pentreath in Crantock, on the north coast of Cornwall.
† Mabel Lucie Attwell was a contemporary illustrator known for her drawings of adorable-looking children.

the gurgle-swoosh of the breaking wave (funny how they break in long curling lines down the length of the beach), next diminuendo rattling of the stones and we start again. Do you know 'Pebbly Ridge' (Stalky and Co) at Westward Ho!* Stayed there once: noise of the 'pebbles' some of them weighing many pounds is deafening close to on a rough day. Can hear it all night.

Poor Sheila, I hate the very smell of ether, thoughts of [someone] fiddling with my body. Ether makes me faint and even the waiting to be inoculated gives me a 'funny' feeling inside. I hate the sight of blood, mutilation, cuts even. Yet I'm not really afraid of being hurt myself, never have been—luckily—not even afraid of death itself, but I'm afraid of being dead—I so much want to live. So many hopes and ambitions to be tried, desires to be satisfied—or not—anyhow live to desire, the whole circle of emotions that is life itself.

There is a little boy now, almost silhouetted against the sun's reflection on the water (reflection artistically broken by breakwater's shadow pointing out to sea). He's sitting on a small stone which the bigger waves just submerge. As each wave comes in he throws stones to keep it back and, if unavailing, imperiously waves his royal trident of a spade—and gets his seat wet. Canute reincarnated.

The sun's not too hot—shall go in soon and take this to the post. Goodbye Diana my dear—you've been with me nearly the whole of today—I hope I'm not trespassing on your time—and thank you, it's been a lovely day. I feel all warm inside.

My love as always, Bob

LETTER TO DIANA:

10th June, 1940

1.45pm. Just a few minutes before we go on parade. The whistle is almost due to go now. Feeling most dejected—no right to be. 98% in maths exam. Two parcels from home and a letter from you. Perhaps your sadness is infectious. No: the real reason is—blast the whistle. You must wait. At least it is you that hasn't got to wait. It is I, until I get time again.

(This is a quarter of an hour later.) Just about to have a lecture on aircraft recognition—in fact it is now in progress. So must stop again—it is interesting— am I making you wait?

This man is not as interesting as I thought (ten minutes later), in fact he knows almost nix about his subject. He's quiet at the moment. Anyhow, as I was saying—the real reason is that we are very likely moving from here in about a week's time. (Careless talk! Keep it dark.) I think we go to Torquay, Babbacombe or Ilfracombe—anyway we go west. Torquay seems the most likely: so that rules out [meeting in] Bexhill I'm afraid.

---

* Pebble Ridge, the bank of cobbles at Westward Ho! in Devon, helps to prevent the sea eroding the sand dunes. It features in *Stalky and Co.*, Rudyard Kipling's novel about a British boys' school.

7.15pm. There's so little time to write: this must perforce be shorter than usual if I'm to post it tonight. Trouble is with you I find it most hard to write of 'debatable' subjects: each word is torn from its place to its context: each phrase, each sentence takes patience, time and labour. There is no flow: no continuity. I can usually write without ceasing, little effort, little thought and produce a fairly coherent whole. With you it is short, disjointed, rambling.

All I can tell of is 'news'—activities, people, the concrete. I feel so guilty: your long intensely interesting, delightful letters. I want to write. I can't. And so we have to fall back on the common round. Just going to supper, something inspiring I hope.

8.30pm. Dick came in just as I was leaving and told me Welsh Rarebit for tea. I hate it. So we went out to the bar underneath our hotel (not allowed for me of course*). Had some drinks so perhaps I shall now be more fluent. Here is a story anyhow.

Last night chez Leslie I spotted a girl in the next bar who seemed to have that poise and assurance that none of the Hastings girls have. Pointed her out to Dick and when she went upstairs Dick rushed to the telephone at the bottom of the stairs—along the passage. He had to wait ten minutes but nailed her on her way down and just after she'd passed fixed a date for tonight. He was fortifying himself just now. It is amazing what one can do in uniform though Dick has the nerve for anything. He's twenty and precocious, I suppose, as the youngest in a large family usually is. But it is the first female he has spoken to since our first night here.

We met John yesterday evening walking back along the promenade. He said he went out in a rowing boat. I wondered. He has just been in for a letter Mother wrote and sent to me. This life suits him down to the ground. I envy him in some ways but would not change places for a fortune—and more than that.

Damn! 9 o'clock. News roaring forth somewhere. So Musso has acted.† It tries one's faith in humanity. Soon, I know, I shall want to kill every German and Italian left alive.

To practical details—any letters you may post after Thursday evening will you send to Downham? I'll send you details if and when we move and where to as soon as I can but if you had sent a letter here it might never be posted [on to me]. I can't, won't risk that.

Brain won't work anymore. Must stop. No crabbing today. Parades all day.

Goodnight, Diana dear, keep me company and comfort. I know you will. You always do when I ask. Thank you. Take care of yourself.

All my love, Bob

---

*   The rank and file were not permitted in some bars.

†   On 10 June Benito Mussolini, the Italian Fascist leader, finally declared war on Britain and France.

LETTER TO DIANA:

St. Leonards
11th June, 1940

8am. Just time to say good morning, dear, before we start our labours at mathematics. Not such a good morning here but may clear—misty and overcast. Rather like the beginning of a really warm Cornish day. Have we seen the last of the sun? Consolation is [that] it may help the poor devils in France.

Hell here's teacher! (An hour later.) Done my sums just like school. Holding up one side of my exercise book so that he can't see what I'm writing. Felt last night like walking for miles and miles by the sea and hoping for a gentle rain, instead I had to go to bed.

Of all the crazy things! We've just been told to carry on in gas masks! Can you imagine us sitting round the tables here in a little room and all of us with gas masks? It's enough to raise a laugh from the dead.

Teacher's just gone out—to escape wearing his, I suppose. We take ours off a bit, for a rest. All pretty fed up with their maths. We are divided up into six classes. Ours is the top 90–100% in one exam. We could all pass easily now and here we are doing things and sums we can all do in our heads. Typical of the RAF.

8.30pm. How savage I sound and I'm still feeling savage. Why can't we know yet a day ahead?

> Wait. And wait. And wait some more
> For this is life, Privates, to wait and wait
> And not to know what you are waiting for
> Save further orders.*

Your letter came at tea-time: a ray of light through the darkness of uncertainty. Too eager to read I dropped the rose, unknown, through the springs of my bed. I've just recovered it and—titivated—sent it to rest.

I usually read your letters through and through, bit by bit and again and again. Often no words remain in my head—a phrase here and there or oddities in spelling ('nessesery')—and yet I know it all—feel it all going through me. Today three words remain. Stuck fast.

On second thoughts don't bother to stop sending letters here. I'll try and phone if we are told for certain that we move. Counter rumours going round today we are not to move after all. I think, am afraid we will. It may not be for a week or so, though.

'SWITCH OUT THOSE (expletive omitted) LIGHTS.'

Will resume tomorrow. Goodnight, my sweet and bless you.

My love, Bob

---

*   From Christopher La Farge's *Each to the Other.*

12th June, 1940. 1.30pm. Just had lunch after a most tiring morning. Our first hour was drill, and then we had half an hour from the Medical Officer—a very amusing man with an Irish accent tinged with American. Then we had a march in full kit—two haversacks, a 'satchel', water-bottle, gas mask and anti-gas cape. We perspired and ached. To finish off with they gave us a half hour of PT. I could sleep for hours—probably will do. It's maths for two hours.

Found out today you can write to me for 1½^d if you put 'serving with HM Forces' on the front but there is no such provision for us. Unfair, I think. Today too lazy to refill with ink.

Your letter yesterday got here most quickly. Apparently posted 4.30pm at Chelmsford and arrived here at 4.00pm the next day. Have you noticed how long mine take?

2.10pm. Now in the lecture room which is also the recreation room. It's law and administration—not maths—sitting on the floor, at the back, invisible at the front. Shall soon sleep ... drowsy now, the man reads on—'the legal status of an airman ... criminal law ... serving a summons ...' oh gee!

7pm. Post goes in three quarters of an hour. Day's work is done: tea is consumed. What's left of the day is ours—what is left of us. Just had my hair cut again. I hate it, but it is growing again on top.

It's a nice quiet evening here tonight. Why aren't you here to go for a walk with me?

Enclose my photo as on my identity card. They gave us one each for ourselves. I don't think it is very good—but there it is. What about a quid pro quo? Do you think I could have one of those stage photos of yours? They are not you as I know you but I should like to have a part of you to say goodnight to—as tangible evidence!—and a real picture is not for the world to see. I couldn't bear to have you exposed to all the inevitable questions; but a '<u>professional</u>' photograph arouses little comment. Anyway one of these days Dick should have some.

Tony interrupted: we're just off to the post and then for a drink below the hotel. I'll drink to you Diana.

I'll write to you again later, if time.

Take care of yourself—don't worry too much about the war, I think now it'll probably be over next autumn—if that is any consolation. That's a year earlier than I believed a month ago.

Dearest, my heart is with you in your garden, your room, your woods and your fields. Love Bob

LETTER TO DIANA:

St. Leonards
12th June, 1940

9.45pm. Posted your letter and went down to the bar underneath our hotel. Tony and Ruth there—as we expected—a double round of drinks to celebrate my win in the Derby sweep. Dick left us early. He made 'the incredible mistake' of not arranging another date with the girl he went out with the other night. So he now prowls around the pub we found her in. Apparently he arranged to meet her in a bar here which is out of bounds to ordinary airmen but allowed if you are with relations etc. He was waiting there when an officer asked him if he was waiting for someone. He said Yes, his aunt! And in she walked.

Have heard tonight that we may get a few days leave before we go to our EFTS [Elementary Flying Training School] in six or eight weeks' time. May ... may ... but it is a straw of hope to cling to.

Tomorrow I'm on guard, curse it. Means highly polished equipment and uniform. Parade immediately after tea and on duty all night: three of us in two hour spells. I'm on 8pm–10pm and 2am–4am. Trouble is one can't take one's (sorry about the one's) uniform off. However it will probably give me time to write. Trouble is with a noisy, smoky atmosphere shall not be able to write to you. All we get off for it is the early morning bathe, and I believe we are semi-officially entitled to raid the kitchen and fry ourselves some food. Reminds me of a 'dorm feast'.

Tomorrow evening one of the corporals is going to ask the CO if and when we move, so hope to include definite news in this letter tomorrow. Now don't read ahead! Please, please we shall not move.

With all this duty and being tired I have not had time to spend much—perhaps I'll have a priceless 2/6^d of telephone over the weekend. Perhaps you'll be at the Chase though on Saturday—so not that night.

Don't stop going out, will you? Meeting people, someone to talk to—especially new acquaintances—all take your mind off this war. I'd hate, too, to think of you staying in on any account for me. Not that I think you would—you've too much sense. Remember that, my mad Diana—I may never admit that again! Lights out, b---- it!

Goodnight, my dear, the stars are yours if they were mine.

Sleep well, love Bob

BOB'S DIARY:

13th June, 1940.

Letter from Diana: Jean's John called up in Kenya.* Poor Jean—poor Diana. When I finished reading, I could have written, phoned, telegraphed at once. But not yet. Why not? Why not? Uncertain? Not really, more like amazement. Unfair to Diana? 'Widow and kids'...? ... Afraid? ... Not afraid of marriage anyhow, my ultimate aim. 'Until death us do part?' As I should wish. Death doesn't part anyhow—can't—mustn't.

Diana you are all to me and all of me. I want you.

---

* Jean and John's son Richard Dawkins, the evolutionary biologist and author, later wrote that as soon as his mother arrived in Nyasaland, his father had to break it to her that he had been called up to join the King's African Rifles in Kenya. Jean managed to go with him to Kenya, disobeying army instructions.

4

One face, one image, one thought

LETTER TO DIANA:

St. Leonards
13th June, 1940

11.15am. Maths, as you may guess. Another hour and a half of it. There's only one thing to do and that is to find some controversial subject and make a good argument with the maths man. Yesterday I managed to make him waste nearly an hour by debating the relative merits of the metric system and ours. I quite surprised myself by the number of reasonable arguments I found.

I quite enjoy my morning bathe now: it is full tide of a morning early and we can just dive in, swim round and come out again. It is very enervating and gives us a good appetite. The trouble is that I feel so tired when we go for classes or lectures. And, if it is as boring as this maths, I should go to sleep if I had half a chance.

This afternoon is compulsory games but the tragedy (not tragidy, my dear, please!) there is no sun at the moment. It looks as if it might clear up though—it did yesterday. I could well do with some sleep on the beach as I shall miss a lot on guard duty tonight. Also a little more brown on my back would not come amiss. How I'd like to be a pagan and worship the sun—perhaps I am. How's your back turned out? Have you peeled all over, like a snake and left your old skin behind you? I'm now chocolate coloured all over.

This is written in many bits and pieces, as I have to stop whenever he thinks he'll have a look at my workings. Also I have to do a few sums now and again. Hope it makes sense: I'm always too lazy to read through what I've written. Do you?

Hell raining. Time to go too. No sunbathing today.

3.30pm. Raining like fun still. Therefore no compulsory games. Lying in my room—the other two have gone out to play tennis or something. Your letter arrived at lunch-time—the post gets quicker and quicker. I can't tell you how sorry I am about Jean and her John—and through them for you. Your letter moved me so much. I dare not read it again, it makes me want to do anything, everything. I feel so impotent: so impossible to comfort, give help.

When my love was away,
Full three days were not sped,
I caught my fancy astray
Thinking if she were dead,

And I alone, alone:
It seem'd in my misery
In all the world was none
Ever so lone as I.

I wept; but it did not shame
Nor comfort my heart: away
I rode as I might, and came
To my love at close of day.

The sight of her still'd my fears,
My fairest-hearted love:
And yet in her eyes were tears:
Which when I question'd of,

'O now thou art come,' she cried,
''Tis fled: but I thought to-day
I never could here abide,
If thou wert longer away.'*

I love your letters. Perhaps you write too much but in the end it is to ourselves that we must turn. It is only you (or I) who can get hurt. I think we know each other well enough to know the other's mind. I am content. Your parents—do they object? If you must restrain yourself—God forbid!—write, say, once a week but I shall consider myself also so bound.

Must start to polish now. If I can find out anything definite tonight about our moving will add it on the end.

Diana dear, don't let the world, life beat you. It's hard I know, but great are the victor's spoils. I hate myself offering these cold words. They are not meant for you. In two months' time I may be home ... I can hardly bear to think on it. The pain of disappointment would be too great.

Darling, my love, Bob

---

* 'Absence' by Robert Bridges.

6.15pm. Nobody knows anything about our evacuation. Now in the Guard room, I go on at ten o'clock till 12am and 2–4am.

Take care of yourself and God bless you,

xxxx Bob

LETTER TO DIANA:

RAF St. Leonards
14th June, 1940

Guard duty. Now 2.15am in the morning, I've just come on again for my spell. At 10.15pm the Orderly Officer came round to inspect us and see that everything was OK. At 11.00pm I was sent down to the kitchen—or rather I volunteered— to cook our supper. Huge piles of chips, an egg each and fried bread, cocoa. The kitchen was fun: there was also unlimited bread and half a pound of butter between the four of us. (Three on duty and the Guard Commander.)

At 12am, or soon after, we lay down to get what sleep we could. Must have your boots on and collar and tie, equipment—belt and shoulder straps—also supposed to have our respirators on but we don't. There are lots of dodges—undoing your boots and tying very loosely, unbuckling the belt, taking out your collar stud but keeping collar and tie on. Just as I was getting to sleep, the other man woke me up—it seemed the second after I had dropped off. So here I am, sitting at this wooden table with three bodies inert on the beds beside me and also the fire piquet [or guard] having a surreptitious nap while I write. Please excuse the butter marks.

Sit back and try to bring you before my eyes. See your face immobile for a change, hard to imagine. Asleep in peace, I hope. Hair everywhere—you don't do it up do you? (Why is it so nice to have your hair combed or hands run through, so nice to comb the hair of someone you're fond of? Animal instinct?) Face pale in your framework of hair, strands drifting across, veiling dark eyes ... must stop I shall soon be dreaming and asleep. Penalty two years' imprisonment or even death! Don't blonde your hair, Diana. I shan't know you—both senses.

One nasty blow tonight. The sergeant of the guard tells us that <u>all</u> leave in the RAF is cancelled till further notice. That's why we've had none here. So that is that until they amend the order. A bit tough—we're the only service with that regulation. Damn and blast it. I can almost imagine them doing it to me on purpose—curse them! Also told it is fairly sure that we shall move sometime in the near future. But there have been so many rumours. Today it was that we left for S Africa! Apparently we nearly went to Truro.

Your letter ... answers to queries (à la Dorothy Dix?*) Don't worry about John—they'll never let him fly with an arm like that—but he'll have a priority call on the doctor's services. The girls in Hastings? ... I had a good two hours watching

---

*   Dorothy Dix was an American journalist who gave marriage advice.

them this evening while on guard. They're all the same—and anyhow we have our bromide. It is not injurious at all—just sounds a bit shocking, that's all.

Remember well the Boyds. That night—a confession—I tried to interest Jean and so to interest you. I was crazy to get to know you and it seemed to me the subtlest and best way. Was my psychology of any use—or is that too much to ask? (Purely from a scientific point of view!) Do you remember the first time I danced with you? It was just (more or less) what I hoped people would think of me and yet you were so annoyed and hurt.

Remember ... remember ... remember ... that heaven, sailing, seems too close to be past. I'm still living it. Blessed last days of freedom.

Repeating words and words ... I can go on saying things which have no meaning or connection but they scan and sometimes rhyme or just words because they sound nice—Great and Little Sir Hughes [farms near Galleywood, Essex], St Just in Roseland, St Michael Penkivel [villages near Truro, Cornwall]—all these I love. And can you repeat a word so often it loses all sense and meaning?

Ten long minutes and not a word. Not an idea in my head. Just sit and read your letter through and through again.

● *- mop it up with bread* I've no blotting paper here. Another quarter of an hour. Two hours writing to you.

'One thing only will I remember ... '
One name only stands out.
One face, one image
One thought
Just you.
<u>You.</u>

Triangle of velocities ... last wanderings of a feeble mind ... must be nearly asleep. Not long now. Ten minutes. Some things to sign first, then loose my boots etc. Good morning to you, Diana darling. A gay and 'happy' day, I hope.

My love to speed you on your way. Bob

15th June, 1940. 10am. My dear, after we phoned last night, I felt tired no longer and passed the rest of the evening celebrating. Everybody was feeling cheery as it was payday and we had quite a merry evening. When I got back one of my room-mates presented me with your letter. I wanted so badly to write to you then and there but it was after lights out and they were getting nasty as quite a few people had come in a little drunk and were shouting and running all over the place.

I'm going to phone home again tonight to find out if they [Bob's parents] are coming tomorrow or a week later. If they don't come tomorrow shall phone you as well. I feel too full to write much. Ought to have written last night—in vino veritas and also lots of other things. I think I write better under the influence.

It is so hard to write: just sit and dream. If Diana comes down where shall we meet, what say and do? And none of these things shall we say. What would you like to do all day? Sunday—must find out the earliest we can get off. Might even get to the station before you. Doubt it. Where shall we meet? Station waiting rooms dull places.

I only know this town from our hotel to the pub (Leslie's) along the front. Could you face it? What would you like to make of our few precious hours? If it's hot ... the beach and a rowing-boat? Bring your costume—we'll see who is the browner. I hate our uniforms when it's warm. One perspires so.

10.45pm. Can I write straight? Phoned Mother up tonight, she said they would not be able to get down at all. I hate myself for being glad. Diana can you come? Will you come? Diana please, please, please. Perhaps I'm drunk, perhaps I'm very drunk. Perhaps I wouldn't dare write this if I were sober, so I must write it now. Diana darling ... next Sunday?

We finish Church parade at about 11.00–11.30. You go to Hastings station: it is only a quarter of an hour's journey from this hotel. If you ask for the front and when you get there turn right, our hotel is about ¼ mile from the Hastings pier. If you sit on a bench in a shelter somewhere near the Alexandra or in a deck chair on the beach, I'll find you. But have a paper or something to look at handy. There should not be many airmen about, but in case there are, I might get rough.

Oh my God! Diana I could never have dreamt of this. You are too good to me by far. I do not deserve so much. It is not right that I should have so much of life ... I feel as if I shall have to make good this good fortune with some future unhappiness. Diana, you are so kind, so cruel to my insides.

After phoning home I felt I could knock the world over. Take on all Germany single-handed. I am almost drunk. Perhaps drunk. I drank to you, and drank to you. I picked another flower for you. I dropped it. Someone trod on it. I searched but only a wreck was left. Third time lucky. Must write tomorrow: shall be caught with my light on if not. Diana. Next Sunday. Diana, oh Diana please ma petite Diane. Darling, all my love: God bless you. Bob

16th June, 1940. 2pm. Was I very incoherent last night? Won't re-read what I've written—might cross it all out, refuse to send it. I'd rather not. Raining here, or rather drizzling. Dick and I have had a good idea. Taken blankets down to the beach and pinched someone's tent. There's no one on the beach. It is just long enough to lie full length in and we reside in state admiring the sea. Very lazy, but peaceful and quiet.

Quite away from the RAF. He is sleeping now. Yesterday we had PT for an hour in the morning. Then had to go and change for 'room inspection' then change back for more PT, change for lunch, change for 'compulsory' beach in the afternoon, change for tea and change for more PT at 6pm. Sir Archie Sinclair [the secretary of state for air] had come down to have a look at us. I think I shall be a very good strip-tease artist by the time I've finished here.

Thank you for the flowers, dear: the syringa did not travel very well, but the cat-mint and thrift reside in splendour in my Oxford book. The smell also travels badly but the colour is all there. It's the only country I see. Also a part of you.

If you can come on the train, arriving 11.27am would be early enough don't you think? I could then just get to the station in time. Did I tell you to go to Hastings station? Not St Leonards. If I'm not there, but I told you? If you can face the front, it should not be too bad at that hour. It seems too good to be true. Daren't believe that you will really come. Will Patsy [Spencer-Phillips who introduced Bob and Diana] come too? What do your parents think! Hers? What will mine? I don't care: just cynically say 'I'm in the RAF now: most immoral of all the services.' Which would be quite true.

Sorry if I give you too much exercise—must be so infuriating if in vain. Good for your figure if only your figure needed improving.

Can't write more. Don't know why. Perhaps too excited. Perhaps later I shall start again. Anyhow will post this now.

I shall count each hour. But can't believe it will be true until I see you. Don't vanish then will you.

Goodbye, my darling, take care of yourself. My love as ever, xxxxxx Bob

LETTER TO DIANA:

St. Leonards
16th June, 1940

Sitting on the parapet of the lower promenade—bottle alley it is called—the walls are decorated with coloured pieces of bottles. Sometimes the effect is lovely. The tide is high just now—it is 7.30pm—later I think I shall bathe. Smooth water, soothing evening, a swim alone. Lost my wretched pen again: just had a look in our tent of the afternoon. Not there. Damn.

Once more into my arid days like dew,
Like wind from an oasis, or the sound
Of cold sweet water bubbling underground,
A treacherous messenger, the thought of you
Comes to destroy me; once more I renew
Firm faith in your abundance, whom I found
Long since to be but just one other mound
Of sand, whereon no green thing ever grew.
And once again, and wiser in no wise,
I chase your coloured phantom on the air,
And sob and curse and fall and weep and rise
And stumble pitifully on to where,
Miserable and lost, with stinging eyes,
Once more I clasp,—and there is nothing there.*

---

*   'Sonnet V' in *Second April*, a collection of poetry by Edna St Vincent Millay, first published in 1921.

I like it too. Rhythm, images and feeling. Beauty in despair. Hope despite failures. 'Fog in the throat'* yet faith in the heart.

Going now for my evening pint. Must get away early—to swim and write if I can. Got to rearrange one of Dick's dates, he's gone and made two for the same evening!

10pm. Dick had got my pen after all. Home too late to bathe. Leslie's bar is such entertainment we could not leave. You see all types there—especially the exotic.

Nearly time for lights out. Must clean my boots: saves time tomorrow. I'm getting really domesticated. Sewed two buttons on my trousers today and another three on my tunic. Got quite handy by the time I'd finished.

Diana dear, write soon and say you will come—I can't stand this doubt. I shall go crazy. We are almost certain to go to Torquay next week. Plymouth is only thirty miles away ...

Must go to sleep. Work tomorrow.

Good night my darling. God bless and keep you.

xxxxx Bob

17th June, 1940. 1.15pm. One long queue for lunch so just a few words while they get absorbed. I thought of something I wanted to say to you in maths this morning but it's gone. Oh damn! A letter from Mother this morning. She seems to be getting anxious [about the threat of invasion]—mysterious references to sending her few jewels and my gold cigarette box (have you ever seen it? I actually won it†) to 'a certain bank in Cornwall'. It's all so complicated. To add to her worries the family business is rapidly going downhill. I'm not afraid, myself, of going broke— I'm too conceited for that, but it would be very hard on one's parents.

Rumours flood around this place: today it is that France has capitulated. It sounds too bad but I would not put it past the new French government. They are a lot of fascist right-wingers. Still I hope it is not true.

The Germans in Paris. Germans in London? It is too awful to think of. Yet I suppose it is a possibility.

Let's not talk of it: you and I will out live wars even if we cannot alter the future course of mankind. If only you could have driven, you could bring my car down here, and I could take it to Torquay—they give us enough petrol for that. But you can't drive so what is the use of wishing. Still no-one knows the date of our departure, though we are sure to move. The whistle for parade. Adieu.

6.30pm. There are so many things to thank you for I must forget hundreds. Please be not offended, sweet, because, as you know, I have to write in bits and pieces and my brain is at the best a little erratic. Walking along today I suddenly thought I'd never thanked you for the painted flower. Diana, it is lovely—so light, ethereal it almost has a scent!

---

*   A reference to the first line of 'Prospice' by Robert Browning: 'Fear death?—to feel the fog in my throat'.

†   Bob won the cigarette box for the fastest time in the Cresta Run's Curzon Cup race of 1939.

10pm. In bed ... lovely moon but it is the other side of the house. Saw John on the front tonight and later in the pub. He seems to think Patsy's coming down too. Am I greedy Diana, I want you to myself—for a lot of the day anyhow. So much to say ... so little time. Picked you some flowers. Common brutes but the best the Corporation can provide, and I like the smell—intoxicating.

I'm hoping for a letter from you tomorrow—am I too optimistic? I get anxious now if I do not hear for a day or so from you. I've said so before, you spoil me. Yet don't stop, I beg you.

Scratchy beds tonight—the sheets have gone to the wash. I get used to everything, though.

Goodnight, Diana. We can't stop Time but I hate to think of you changing. Keep for me some of the Diana I know, some of the you's that I've known—some of the you's I may yet get to know—part of Diana as yet unknown.

Sleep now. Goodnight my darling. Sleep? How sleep with Diana's image dancing in front of my eyes? Diana, Diana -------- God bless you.

Come soon

xxxx Bob

18th June, 1940. By the time you get this I hope to have phoned and given you the heart-breaking news. We move early next Monday morning [24th June] and Sunday we shall be doing fatigues [cleaning or cooking duties] and packing most of the day. O darling, I feel as if I could weep. Savage and powerless. Blast and damn. Cursing is no good, but curses on the RAF. Just had lunch and go on parade in a few minutes. I feel too full to write any more. Will post this letter at once.

New address will be from next Monday or Tuesday—2 Flt, 2 Sqd^n— Windermere Hotel, Torquay.

Must read your letter before parade.

Diana dear, all my love

xxxxxxx Bob

LETTER TO DIANA:

St. Leonards
18th June, 1940

10pm. Diana darling, do you feel insulted or hurt when I write to you when nearly drunk. For that is what I am. I must confess it: it is better that you should know. I don't like doing it yet feel a savage delight in trying to find if it makes any difference.

Tonight I am as near drunk as I have ever been down here. Can just see what I am writing. I telephoned to you tonight and felt like an executioner. Could not lose the image my imagination had built of you in Hastings—arriving—you and I—you. There is some consolation in the bottle but tomorrow I shall regret it. I have a resolution that everything I write to you must be posted: shall hate myself tomorrow.

You are an ache and a gap—the end and the joy of my living and I get tight because of vain hopes frustrated. Weak, I always knew I was weak. Strong, perhaps, on the outside but rotten at the core. Diana, know me for what I am. I cannot see to write more. Despite it all Diana dear there is a cold, hard ache, sometimes an inward-ripping pain, sometimes an intense elation but most often half-hoping longing. All this is you. You, you, blast you, bless you. All this you do. Rend and recreate. Sear, burn, and torment—pacify, calm and soothe. I hate, I love ... Oh God! Diana. Damn lights out.

Goodnight, my sweet, how I hate you, bless you. Can I hope to see you soon? Goodnight dear.

xxxxx Bob

Diana's diary:

18th June, 1940.

11.30pm. Written during an air raid. The house shudders, there are explosions. My blackout board falls on top of me. Aeroplane drone. Air raid sirens wail. Don't feel afraid, horribly calm and interested. Seems very minor.

Bob phoned to say Sunday was off. They are being posted. Blankness.

France negotiating. Churchill's speech. Mummy and Daddy decide to evacuate me to Plymouth (Bob may go to Torquay).

Must sleep, air activity seems calmer. Now my blackout has knocked me on the head totally. More planes, one doing something to its engine, brrr brrr—brr brr—lots and lots more explosions. Shudder, shudder, shudder. I am afraid. It's like musical chairs as the bombers go over. Then pray the noise won't stop over your house or ... start. Trrrrp, trrrrp, trrrrp machine guns—it went down, a beautiful silver plane caught in the searchlights, twisting, writhing, beauty, horrid. It's fallen and now a blazing mass, a huge fire. The man, the plane, the beauty ...

It's horrid—the first time I've seen death and destruction. I'm shaking. Funny, these things should be ugly and it wasn't, it was beautiful. The silver plane, searchlights, starlight, garden flowers, darkness, now a burning mass that twisting plane, I can see it now.

◇◆◇

That evening, Prime Minister Winston Churchill had spoken to the nation on the radio saying: '... the Battle of France is over. I expect that the Battle of Britain is about to begin.'

5

Diana,
don't do anything 'dramatic'

LETTER TO DIANA:

RAF St. Leonards
19th June, 1940

7pm. Reclining on my bed, in my room.

Another letter from you today—it is bitter sweet reading of your—our—hopes and fears for Sunday. It would happen like that. Never mind—c'est la guerre. Is Torquay a possibility? I hate to press you to come, to feel I may be making you do something you may regret, might upset you with your family. Yet I ache to see you just once—and having seen, to ache again as you said.

I have been making one or two enquiries about Torquay—I'd rather live on hope for a while and be disappointed than have no hope—and there is apparently quite a good bus service. Rumour has it that we shall be allowed on the beach quite a bit of an afternoon and my evenings are nearly always free from 5.30. However ... nous verrons ... It is too just possible I might one evening be able to get into Plymouth on a late pass. There, dear are the possibilities ... I leave the rest, coward-like, to you. Please do not do anything to upset yourself, your parents. Plymouth will be thirty miles away.

Prayers ... religion ... God. I hardly know my own mind. Believe in him—yes. But once prayed for some weeks to Him and nothing happened. That upset me. I was then about seventeen and influenced by a sort of Oxford groupie.

What news of here? Yesterday after phoning you—feeling like an executioner—we sat and talked and drank: got very merry. At night the air-raid alarm 12.30am–1.30am. We emptied our hotel (two hundred and fifty of us) in seven and a half minutes with respirators and capes. We rushed onto the lower promenade and sat there. A lovely night: full moon over the water—thought of you, bombers over Essex, and fell asleep!

Damn here's the gong. Write later.

9.50pm. Dick has got the 'fire piquet' tonight and tomorrow, so Tony and I have just been round cancelling his dates or trying to. Whistling under balconies and peeping in all the pubs. Just finished with bacon and eggs on fried bread and coffee and home-made bread and butter. My favourite late evening meal.

But ... as I was saying ... our air raid. With that lovely moon and warm southerly breeze at any other time I should be glad to have got up to see it. Dream of one such night as this and you and I to enjoy it and ourselves together. Instead I fall asleep.

Today we had PT and drill all day: they say there is nowhere for us to drill at Torquay and we are getting it all over as much as possible. And PT will consist of going onto the beaches. How marvellous.

Do these air-raids frighten you? I wondered what you were doing, feeling. You must have had planes right over you. We saw and heard nothing.

Diana dear—an entreaty. Don't do anything 'dramatic': don't hurt your parents—not hurt, that's not the word; they are wiser than you or I, their advice would probably be sound. Do I dictate, sound paternal? I don't mean to be: if you were to go contrary to your parents' wishes for my sake I should not forget it, nor they. It could be a barrier forever. I long and ache for the day—our day but it would not be so fine if we had non-approval hanging over us.

Oh Lord, what am I saying? Raving mad? Trying to teach, dictate? But I know too well how you feel—must do something, anything, no matter the cost—I feel the same. Darling, write me please if your Mother and Father object.

Well, after sermon it's time for lights out. Goodnight my dear and I'll hope to see you in the not too distant future. I daren't say how much I want you. Diana ... Diane, goodnight ... Lights have just been turned out—10.25pm—writing in the last rays of light, can't see what I've written only a dark mark. Once more goodnight. Take care of yourself, of every one of the 'yous'.

My love, my love.

xxxxxxxx (enough?) Bob

20th June, 1940. On the beach. Nearly 4pm. Your letter at lunch-time—thank you, dear. I begrudged myself the few hours' sleep I lost but should have lost a lot more if I had known what you were going through. Diana I'm glad you are being evacuated out of it, more glad than I can say that I shall see you but a little nervous that you may hate me for dragging you from all you love. And last night—what happened then? We had a warning from 11.30pm till 4.30am: did you have it all again? Have seen no evening paper yet but they are too vague anyhow—just say 'East Anglia'. Wonder, too, what happened at home. Father up all night—[as] ARP [warden]—and Mother worrying for him. You won't be the only one needing comfort, reassurance.

We really are coming: Sunday night it is said. I'll try and ring Monday or Tuesday evening. Can't say which day yet will be best for you to come over but, if we get a whole afternoon off for 'compulsory games', that will be the day. That's what I've got now. But after today we start packing up—eating out of our mess tins—no plate —— no beds, no mattresses, sleep on the floor. Good practice, I suppose. Slept for three hours on the stone promenade last night, but they let us sleep till 8.30am this morning, thank heaven. We had no excitement at all except, twenty minutes after we had all gone in, one of our bombers, back from Germany, came down in the sea off the pier and got ashore in their rubber boat. We heard the explosion only.

Dartmoor, I'm afraid will be out of bounds: we have a five-mile limit here. It is rumoured twenty miles at Torquay but that's only a rumour. Torquay is nice and large though—large enough to lose ourselves. Expect it will have to be next Thursday or Saturday—compulsory games afternoon.

How can anything stop us now? I <u>must</u> see you.

Yet it is hard to believe: must not hope too much, yet hope I must, can't help it.

All my love Diana dear. Be patient.

xxxxxxxx Bob.

LETTER TO DIANA:

RAF St. Leonards
22th June, 1940

4.30pm. Just time for a short note, before I have to go out. Your letter just arrived and read. Had to write and tell you we leave Monday morning. So probably no time to phone you Monday but hope that we shall have Tuesday evening free, and will try and phone sometime after 7pm. Alright?

What are the shadows hanging over Plymouth and you? Before we try and chase them away, may I know what they are? I shan't really mind though if you don't tell me.

Dartmoor ... Dartmoor sounds marvellous. I know the feeling of complete freedom. Other places one can find it are mountains, sea, flying and sometimes, for me, in the Essex marshes, but that is more a depressing freedom not exhilarating. Both are nice. Perhaps—a very doubtful perhaps—I may squeeze one weekend leave: could we then go on the moors? It is too tempting to think of.

Today we loaded railway wagons with tables, chairs, beds, mattresses, lockers, clocks, benches and goodness knows what. Quite exciting in a way. Each thing loaded was one step nearer Torquay, nearer you.

Must finish now. Darling I'm coming. A week at the very most ... Do you know Torquay? Where to meet, where to go, what to do? Or do we explore together. Makes no difference. There's you and I anyhow. That's all that matters.

Coming dear, my love

xxxxx Bob

POEM POSTED TO DIANA:

RAF St. Leonards
23th June, 1940

Two or three nights ago I wrote to you
With a drunkard's pen, a pen that was
Bitter, bombastic yet full of desire.
I wished you could know me, my frailties and
Failings, I wished you could see me quite drunk.

I wanted to hurt, to wound and offend you
I knew you would hate it, hate me for showing
Myself in that light. Hate me for making
Myself such a fool. Hate me for writing
At all in that state. Was I just drunk?
Vulgarly drunk or wished I to show you
Myself as I am. Did I intend that you should believe it
That that was my end, my life, my ambition?
Or just want to hurt you. We sometimes do that
To those that we love. It was none of these.

I wanted to test you—yet that's not the word.
I knew the answers already, knew what you'd say.
Knew you'd feel sorry and comfort my mind.
I wanted to show that hurting your soul
Cutting and wounding your spirit
That in spite of all this, because of all this
You loved me and loved me the more.

LETTER TO DIANA:

RAF St. Leonards
23th June, 1940

This is Sunday—our Sunday that was to have been. If you were not in Plymouth now I should have gone quite mad: now 12.30pm and we have the rest of the day free—I could have got off at least an hour ago. But you, where you are, and I where I shall be hold out more hope, don't you think, than one day? And also (I had forgotten) you would not have been allowed here. No one is permitted in the town without good cause—in a military sense.

Last night I wanted to write to you, felt I could write all night but I was threatened with fatigues if I kept my lights on any longer. Had to undress and make my bed in the dark.

Everything gone now from our room: we pushed, pulled and sweated this morning—lockers (full of bedding) beds all slid and rattled downstairs. Rooms swept. All that is left is two blankets to sleep in tonight. It doesn't worry me though: I know tomorrow we leave for Torquay. I hate this place now—can't bear to stay here another moment.

Dick, Tony and I are perpetual shirkers, we do our utmost to avoid fatigues. Hate the dirt and getting hot and perspiring. Today, as they start at the top of the building and work down, we waited in my room at first until they'd cleared Dick and Tony's floor above, then we went up the back staircase and sat in Dick's room while they cleared below us. We were not caught, luckily, so all we had to do was to carry down our own lockers. We sat behind the door on our blankets on the floor with the door open which is very cunning if you think it out. It's quite an amusing and exciting a game because if you are caught you get let in for quite a lot extra.

5pm. On the beach. Swam out a long way today: have not had cramp at all this year and gain more and more courage. I love swimming right out alone—don't you. A lovely feeling of being remote, cut off from the world. Frightening, too sometimes: sudden feeling of panic—if I can't swim back … supposing I did get cramp? Could they get out in time? It gives an added zest to it.

Not that I ever run any risk of it—I'm much too frightened. I hardly ever used to swim out of my depth unless someone else was there but I really think the cramp has gone. I swim further and harder each day.

Apparently Hastings is gradually being evacuated. Folkestone, I'm told, is now an empty town—or empty of civilians anyhow.

8.45pm. We leave tomorrow … It's been a lovely day here—a day that I like: lie on the beach, burnt and dreaming, sound of the surf in your ears. A warmth glows inside, it's good to be alive. Only wish you were with me. Only twelve hours now, and we're ready to go—the train is in motion, we are waving goodbye. Silly! There is no one, no one to wave to. Time has been altered, did I tell you before? Reveille 5.30am and breakfast at 6.00am. Parade I suppose at 8.00am or 7.30am.

> Parade in full kit—heavy on shoulders
> Parade on the Prom. Last of the prom.
> Scene of our drill, our PTs and inspections.
> Dirty to lie on—handstands and press-ups
> Dirt in your nails, dirt on your tummy.
> Scene of the pick-ups, the airmen's flirtations
> Air-raids and kisses, mad combinations
> Bathes on the beach—the rocks at low tide.
> Bathes in the morning, no warmth in the sun.
> Bathes at midday, hot from our …

Hell! It won't scan. Needs concentration. Searching for words that make sense and using their rhythms.

Tomorrow we go. Tomorrow in Torquay. And after tomorrow? The heart jumps a beat. Diana, Diana, Thursday ... Friday ... Saturday. Shall I try for weekend leave next Saturday? Can I try—would your aunt have me? A hundred to one I can't get it but nothing like trying. Our CO's a good fellow—he might just relax ...

Sleep on the floor tonight. Got more things to pack up so goodnight, dear. God bless you. See you soon—my love xxxxx Bob.

10.10pm. Just collected all newspapers I could find and squashed them up to sleep on! Goodnight darling xxx Bob

DIANA'S DIARY:

24th June, 1940. Plymouth.

8.30pm. Saw hundreds of French sailors yesterday and French boats whilst driving with my aunt.

Jean and John sent a cable to say they are going together to Nairobi. When John trains, at least they are together.

10.30. He has phoned. He is there in Torquay praise be. And I am going tomorrow, ten to two at Town Hall.

UNDATED NOTE TO DIANA, SCRIBBLED ON A SCRAP OF PAPER:

My dear, We've got to go on parade now—1.45pm. Don't think I can get off till 4.30 at the earliest. Anyway I'll be here as soon as possible. So sorry. Why the blazes does this have to happen.

Darling, see you later, xx Bob

DIANA'S DIARY:

25th June, 1940.
Torquay and Bob. It happened and we love each other.*

26th June, 1940.
Memories of yesterday. Dressing for Bob, washing for Bob, making up for Bob, catching the bus for Bob. The extraordinary feelings and anxiety of the long bus drive from Plymouth, change at Totnes. Arrived at Torquay. Time seemed to stand still.

---

*   Diana probably meant that she and Bob had met and become engaged rather than anything more. When she gave me her diaries, she said: 'With hindsight, we should have just got on with it and slept together.'

Hundreds of RAF. Fear of not recognising him arriving at cinema. Handed note to say he was parading till 4.30pm. Wandered round utterly desolate. Went to film—Bette Davis and a prison film. Then again time stood still. Looked at clock every few seconds.

Cried. Came out and walking up to me was Bob. Took his hand in silence, walked and walked in silence. Gradually spoke of this and that. Climbed down to a little beach. Stayed there till eight lying on the rocks. The blue sea, gulls, clouds, jagged grey cliffs, rocks and Bob and I and we loved each other. Please God let us have life together and know the fullness of a 'happy married life', please, soon. Climbed back, walked back, had supper, hundreds of RAF. Caught bus. Cold coming back, rain, horrid.

My prayers were heard, we met, loved and it was heaven. And now I am filled with even more longing, but am happy in the knowledge of his love.

6

Was it I, was it you, was it really true?

Letter to Diana:

Torquay
26th June, 1940

4.30pm. Maths. My dear, I started to write to you after lunch but a parade soon intervened and I forgot to bring the writing paper with me—so I'll start this and go back again.

Tonight I will apply to the CO for weekend leave—'Dear Sir, I have the honour to request ...!' I'm going to try and find out later when I can expect a reply. We work now until 5.45pm so may not be able to get off on Saturday until then: it also means that it will not be really worth your while to come here again on a weekday unless I can get off earlier.

The maths master kept wandering around and I had to give up writing. We were supposed to be doing a test exam.

Lying on my bed, I can see the lovely blue of this bay and the sky and the red and yellow and green of distant cliffs, fields—full of corn, I suppose, and the woods. In the bay are three or four little sailing boats. One white hull and sail down, another with deep brown sails and white hull too, both bright shining in the evening sun, and, further away, a third one with lighter coloured reddish sails also reflecting the evening sun. A lovely, lovely view. I'm happy here, Diana, very happy but it is a happiness greatly dependent on you—if you were not near, I don't think I'd like this place as much as Hastings. There is more parading here, less freedom.

Just found out that tomorrow morning is the time to present my letter asking for leave, but nobody seems to know when I should hear whether it's been granted or not. If you get this in time there's no chance tomorrow of getting off before 6pm. This seems to be a letter full of broken hopes. Sorry darling ...

Diana darling, till Saturday or Sunday. Sunday is ours, no matter what. Just a few more days, a few more hours.

My love as always, Bob x x x x x

Darling,
  See you Saturday evening sometime. No time for more. Parade.
  I love you.
  xxxx Bob

Diana's diary:

28th June, 1940.
  Lying in the field by Welltowry Cottage on Dartmoor, tomorrow [Saturday] I am seeing Bob. I am happy. For one day I have a future and am content to wait and dream of tomorrow. Maybe we'll dance.

1st July, 1940.
  Bob came on Saturday to tea. Back home to supper. Talk absurdly and cried. Pain in my throat and heart almost past bearing. Run to bus. Pain. Bob got on bus alone. Alone. Walked back to nearby place—saw bus coming, couldn't watch.

Letter to Diana:

Torquay
1st July, 1940

9.15pm. Diana dear, I've gone and lost or mislaid a letter to you. It may turn up—my things often do but it had some verse for you on it and I have no exact copy. I used to carry it about with me everywhere, especially to maths, and jot down ideas at odd moments and now it is gone. I've been writing a lot this evening to make up for lost time and, in my hurry, I've also posted a letter to a friend—one of three, all men—in an envelope with a piece of lavender—also meant for you. It makes me feel wild and furious with myself. And you—can you forgive me? I can't think where it can be: the trouble is I've got everything packed tight in my locker and it is a day's job to tidy it all up so it may be in my dirty linen or some other place—blast and damn!
  No use crying ... thank you for your letter: how funny it feels getting a letter written to me before Saturday. I like it.
  Where did you go after you left the bus stop? I caught sight of you on one corner: I was not looking at you but just at the corner—one street was called Alexandra. Just looking at the corner and we were nearly past and suddenly with a shock I realised it was you. Still have a picture of your very definite image, probably not true. You just 'flopping' (not quite, perhaps wandering aimlessly) up the street, pulling a leaf out of a privet hedge through some railings, probably

going to eat it. Was there a hedge? Oh darling I know the feeling: I wanted to jump out of the bus and run after you!

Do you remember ... here is what I felt afterwards ... so long ago ... can't remember all of it ... some of it doesn't scan, doesn't rhyme. Some is forced—especially the rhymes.

> Today I can find little time to write
> And last night I could only sit and dream
> Dream of our day and of holding you tight
> To the sea's deep gurgle, the gull's high scream,
> Climbing the cliff, light hand touch on shoulder
> Jumping the rocks and rock back to boulder ...
> These were the thoughts as I sat on my bed.
> These were the dreams, dear that ran through my head
> This I remember and ponder anew,
> Was it I, was it you, was it really true? And whispers the echo back to my heart
> My darling, I love you, I love you, I love you.

More rumours today—probably some foundation in fact. We are supposed to leave here on the 10th or 12th: just possible forty-eight hours leave. And also, when we finish at the EFTS, we probably go to Canada for intermediate and advanced training. Darling, I don't want to leave you. I don't want to go.

Find it so hard to write these days—sometimes—and I want to write to you so much: perhaps it is using one's brain, concentrating all day uses it up. There's little chance of mid-week leisure I'm afraid. Thursday is the only chance but we are almost certain to work in the evening, dear. What a depressing letter this is.

Let's think of brighter things: I traced on the map today where we went yesterday—our railway line—its strawberries.

During navigation we had a large map of Cornwall and I looked at all the names I knew, you knew and what I thought we both knew. How exciting to re-explore Cornwall together—'Do you know this?'

It's getting too dark my sweet Diana Constance, so it's goodnight to you—sleep well—a kiss for each eye—x x. Keep well. Remember me to the aunts. I still love you darling, strange as it may sound. I love you very much, too much—my love. xxxxxx Bob

2nd July, 1940. 9.15am. Navigation class. Just finished my sums: a few minutes to write to you. A lovely day—very hot. I heard we shall be free at 4.30pm. Shall I ring you up? I hate to think of you coming all this way when there is still a possibility that we might get fatigues. I can't resist the temptation though. I shall have to do it—and I know you would want me to.

9.30pm. You've gone and a bit of me has gone too. Too much of me to be comfortable. A hungry feeling that's never satisfied for long: an ache and a pain, blast you—bless you. I swore I'd go through this war with no serious ties to my heart and that I'd enjoy myself (like Dick)—a short life and a sweet one. And here I am: enjoyment? What is it? I am happier than I ever dreamt I could be and at times more hurt and sad than I thought was possible. I still can 'enjoy' myself—I don't want to, because I know I would not. Beer sometimes helps for a bit but never heals, only numbs. Darling I love you, love you. Love you.

Nearly dark now: can just see by getting the light reflected off the paper. Diana asleep now? I like to think so. No air raids tonight for you I hope. Please not. Sleep well Diana: don't worry, keep well—for me.

Bay looks dark and forbidding now: sullen hills tonight, not soft as yesterday. Wish you could see my view. It is really lovely sometimes: early morning colours are superb. Can see no more now. Please excuse these scraps of paper. I fished them out looking for the last letter.

Darling Diana, it's only four days ... this afternoon has been very sweet. Goodnight dearest.

All my love, all me, all of this to thee—
xxxxx Bob

Letter to Diana:

Torquay
3rd July, 1940

8.30pm. My dear. We've just heard fifty of our squadron are going to Rhodesia at the end of the month—I'm not one of them. Am I glad or am I sad? Don't know: feel pulled and twisted first this way then back again. I don't know what it would mean to be going, what it means staying behind and where we shall be posted to. Wonder if John is going. Brain's a riot: one thing stands out—as yet I've still got you—we've got each other. I know you will be glad I'm not going and for that I'm happy—and I may not go to Canada at all. Nobody knows anything around here.

A bit later: somebody just rushed in and said the hot water was on so I've just had a bath. Feel marvellous. Darling, I want you, want you badly and I get furious with myself because I can't wait until Sunday—just four days and God knows, we may have to go four months without seeing each other before this war is over.

What shall I be like and you by then? If it goes on for years, how will we fare? Minds torn and cynical—mad and bewildered or saner, sadder but still confident in ourselves? Diana we must survive, shall survive to start and build our 'us'. You believe it don't you? And so do I. I have always had faith and belief in myself—that's why I'm thought conceited (not perhaps without reason)—and hope I shall always be so. Shall have to stop, people in this room are rioting and making a hell of a row (excuse the language). Goodnight darling Diana Constance. Take care of yourself.

My love, my love xxxx Bob

4th July, 1940. Nearly eight o'clock: in a few moments I shall have the room to myself—everyone out. I'll write Mother first then I can settle down to write to you ... Written to Mother and had a bath: for the moment peace. The lavender, luckily, I had sent to Mother: next time we march past that place I'll pluck a sprig for you.

Quite a lot of 'news' tonight. The first and worst, Dick fell about twelve feet this afternoon while climbing the cliff. He has had to go to the hospital to have his ankle x-rayed. Poor Dick! He was holding on to a piece of rock when it came away in his hand. We turned to see him falling backwards into about a foot or two of water with rocks underneath. I think he is lucky not to have done himself worse injury but a badly sprained or broken ankle is bad enough. To me it looked as if he had broken the bone of one of his toes on the top of the foot, but we shall see. It really is very bad luck.

Have no news yet of Sunday but we are almost certain to be off about eleven or twelve o'clock. If it rains I shall be furious, but we must leave it to our 'Gods': they have been very good so far.

Diana, I <u>would</u> like one of your stage—professional?—photos. They are all part of you—one of the yous—and, as I tried to say before, I can stick it up near my bed, whereas I cannot do so with a photo—it is too intimate—the you perhaps I don't want to share. And I do like—a piece of you to say goodnight to.

After my bath, my foot was clean enough to spot two troublesome thorns—they both are out now, thank heaven. And writing to Mother, I told of our scramble on Dartmoor, your aunt, and the strawberries.

Went and saw John tonight: he sends his love. He seems very happy and has a very comfortable hotel with very fine tennis courts close at hand. He has joined the Club—the best in Torquay—and gets mixed doubles any time.

I expect Saturday afternoon we shall be free at 4.30pm or earlier—I will phone on Friday evening if I know anything definite or put it in this letter tomorrow. Would you come two days running?

A letter from Mother said yesterday was the first night for ten days that they had had no [air raid] warning. Is your Mother coming down? Did you have more warnings?—air raids?

Can't write tonight, my dear, the 'mood' is not on: in fact, I found it easier by far to write to you 'of love and beauty' before I knew you loved me and I loved you. How funny. I wonder why? But I can always send my love—it is yours, darling, forever xxxx Bob.

5th July, 1940. Navigation class—tea soon. Just time to write a line or two. This letter seems so feeble—I hope to see you tomorrow—shall be phoning tonight—and you may not get it 'till it is all "past"'.

Hell. That is not true. It is now six o'clock and I've just had your letter. I was so full I dared not write but tried to pretend it had not yet come. But I could not write another word. Diana darling what have I done to deserve all this? And the tragedy is that I am sure they would never let you go even as my wife. Dearest I have always put you off before, held out a small ray of hope but I am afraid it would be impossible. If and when I get a commission, I would probably be able to get permission to 'live out'—on off-duty nights—and that is all I can hold out to you. My darling, I can say no more now. I dare not.

Diana, I love you.

You forever

xxxxxx Bob.

TELEGRAM TO DIANA:

LETTER TO DIANA:

[Address crossed out and replaced with a question mark]
10th July, 1940

9pm. In the train: we had no more time for writing or anything else. Got my telegram? Or won't it arrive 'till tomorrow? I gave it to a porter on Newton Abbot station.

Are you at Waterhall now? I was very surprised to get your letter—it arrived by the afternoon post just before we left. Thank you dear.

Travelling now up some Welsh valley. Past Newport about a quarter of an hour ago. Tony has smuggled Ruth into our coach and she and another RAF wife are in the compartment with us—eight altogether, all very nice. One Welshman who is just nuts with delight at being 'home' again. Going slowly now but getting faster—note better writing?

These valleys are very lovely: we've just passed the head of one, a view of trees and hills in a beautifully balanced pattern, down its wide V-shape. Ruth reading. Tony asleep. News from a portable wireless. Rushing down a more open valley now: writing needs too much concentration in keeping straight. Now stopped. Rhumba on the radio. Can I teach you to rhumba one day? It is such a lovely rhythm; I can't bear to be off the floor when a band is playing one.

Darling I want you, want you—shall I write home next time that we want to be engaged, ask the parental sanction and see what happens? Dare I ask your father? Pounds, shillings and pence do count after all and, at the moment, we don't know what will happen to us. We may be quite broke at the end of this war. It's silly for me to say I don't care, I've never known what it is to want. And may I tell Dick?

See Mother for me won't you? I'll tell her you will be coming: she will be pleased to see you, hear of me, I do not doubt.

It's rained all day today. We got quite wet marching to the station. Rain, rain and I was glad. Savagely glad. Why glad? Don't know ... the more miserable the weather the gladder I was. I wanted to be miserable. Did you feel like that? So, after all you got away first. Crewe in another two hours—midnight. Carlisle 04.05am. Prestwick 9.30am. We shall be bad-tempered in the morning. Hope we don't have to get out at Carlisle. Am going to sleep now dearest. You're mine, you're mine, the train is saying. You're mine ... you've given yourself to me and I to you. We'll keep each other for us until our day is come. I'm yours Diana, yours for ever with love xxx Bob.

P.S. Carlisle 4.45am. Posting this if time and I can find a stamp xxxx

Still love you.

DIANA'S DIARY:

11th July, 1940.

That day 6th July, Babbacome beach. Bathed, cold, cold water. After talked of Canada. Bob sweet ... We went to the country. Lay in field. Hitch-hiked back.

The next day, Sunday, met Bob, Tony and Ruth ... Bob and I climbed. Later Tony and Ruth came and John. We all went back to tea with aunts. Had supper in cinema. Caught bus back, slept all the way home.

Monday blank and unhappy. Bob phoned. Mummy ill. Daddy phoned.

Tuesday went to Bob's. He came at 4.30 then had to go again at 5.30. We went to the woods in the pouring rain and got soaked. We talked and loved and my tears flowed in the rain. I cried and cried and cried on the bus back to Plymouth.

The next day there was an air raid. I was sent up to London to accompany Mrs Browning [a family friend].

Home [ready to start her job as a teacher]. Bob—telegram—peace.

◊♦◊

*Bob's arrival in Scotland marked his start as an 'under training' pilot or 'leading
aircraftman' at the RAF Prestwick flying training school.*

◊♦◊

LETTER TO DIANA:

> WAR Keddie Esq RAFVR
> c/o Mrs Konnal
> Monktonhead, Monkton
> Ayrshire
> 11th July, 1940

Just arrived darling—into Paradise—almost except that you are not here.

My own room—clean sheets, towels, a trouser press and large chests-of-
drawers with lavender in them. An awfully sweet old lady of the house.

There's peace and quiet here to write and think and read.

As usual little time to write but will try tonight. Will ask tonight if it will be
alright for you or I to phone.

I love you dearest.

All yours xxxxx Bob

LETTER TO DIANA:

> c/o Mrs Connal etc –
> 11th July, 1940

8.30pm. I expect, Diana dear, that this will catch up the other note—probably
only one collection anyhow in this outlandish spot: I like it though. Do you
recognise the paper? You sent it blank once and disappointed me so you can
have it back again—

The house we are in: there are four of us—one of them a quiet, interesting
journalist (we get on well together) and the other two very good-natured if a
little ordinary. We all have our own rooms in this lovely house owned by [an]
ex-India Colonel*—a cock-sparrow kindly man, twinkling eyes, monocle and
his aristocratic tall greying very kind wife—a terrific gardener. She has a glorious
garden—I must get her to let me help her one Sunday (if she gardens on the
Sabbath—she might do: she smokes) and find out the names of all the flowers
and tell them to you. Besides those two I've seen so far: son-in-law, 45-ish or
more, and grandson aged two plus nurse, one housemaid and one parlour maid

---

*   Colonel Kenneth Hugh Munro Connal, OBE TD DL.

and two gardeners. When we arrived (dumped by a bus) at the lodge, we were pleased to think they were to be our billets, we never dreamt of this. Strawberries (unlimited) and cream for lunch. Fish, pork, cake, toast, home-made bread and scones for high tea.

You hang beside my bed, about four feet away, staring just behind my pillow. Mona Lisa smile. Rained hard all day. Wrote Mother tonight and said you might be over in a day or two. You will let me know about your mother won't you and your 'school'?

It is said we will be here six to seven weeks and it looks as if there will be no weekend leave—courage, mon enfant, courage—I hope to fly tomorrow and every day except alternate Saturdays and Sundays.

Going to bath.

10pm and time to go to sleep. Funny, you've turned round in your photo—looking straight at me. Trick of light? No! No! You've turned, I know, to say goodnight—so goodnight Diana—goodnight and be kissed, turn and sleep in peace. Shall I say it once more? I am yours—yours for ever: yours to command, yours to be trampled, yours to be raised to all eternity. Yours darling all yours Bob.

Sorry this is so short: I am so tired now can hardly keep my eyes open xxxxxxxxx.

7

We must have yet a little patience

LETTER TO DIANA:

Monktonhead
13th July, 1940

My dear, it will be hard to convey the feeling of peace and tranquillity—if not happiness—which is here. Probably the climate has a lot to do with it—warm and relaxing. Sitting in a chaise longue in a revolvable [*sic*] summer house I have nearly a semi-circle of garden in front of me. Trees are the background, mainly sycamores but some larches and silver beeches, a poplar, some mays and hawthorns: they form a triangle with the apex away from me. On the left, they make the edge of the garden and, on the right, they shield the lawn and garden from the drive.

There are flowering shrubs in front on the right but they are over now except for the last of a laburnum: and a few delphiniums lend colour. There is a path in front of the shrubs and the rest is lawn, mown right up to the trees on the left. In the apex, the path disappears into a clump of trees which fill up and round off the end of the triangle. They are about 50 yards away and, in front of them, is a pool with lilies and goldfish in a long, narrow pond.

Between me and the pool is grass, broken only by the old tennis court—no nets thank heaven. I have been here all afternoon except for a break to eat strawberries etc and could gaze for ever on the play of the colour pattern.

I feel so rested—it is our day off and have done nothing all day. Got up at 8.30 and wandered round with the Colonel after breakfast to the stables and farm and round the garden with Mrs C later. They are both very sweet. I admire him frightfully, keen horseman that he is—this is the first year he can remember being without hunters—he would not hunt last season because he thought it showed a bad example to the countryside, and was not quite right [during a war]. And after lunch—haggis or rabbit and strawberries and raspberries and cream—I've been out here all afternoon.

Now 4.30. The Colonel has visited me twice for a few minutes' chat and then trotted off with his two dalmatians. I felt quite worn out last night—the excitement of leaving, little sleep on the train, getting settled and so on and last but not least the saying goodbye and the feeling that for a least another six weeks ... But now I feel rested: not content, not really resigned but ready to live with an ache inside, prepared to go on and live in the knowledge that you love me, are mine and that we wait for each other.

14th July, 1940. 11pm. Hello darling, this must be the latest that I have written to you since the Exchange Hotel, Liverpool. Dearest, I wish you were here to share with me the atmosphere of peace and certainty which is in this house. Even the day-long roar of aeroplanes cannot dispel it. It's here, now, soothing and reassuring: I can almost imagine there was no war on and then I suddenly realise that, if there were no war, I should not be here with you three hundred miles away or more.

I am and shall be very grateful to these people: not only because they have removed the hardships and petty annoyances of serving in a modern war-machine but even more for this haven of refuge from an ever-moving, noisy, restless world. Am sure I shall do little homework here, the books, the garden, memories, dreams, all can now reassert their sway—and they are all here. But I cannot sit down now for long hours and peacefully drop off into a dreamland coma: before long, thoughts turn to Diana—given their head they find their own way back, even if by devious routes—and I wake up with a start: And turn and start and sway and gleam. O most individual and bewildering ghost.* Yet you are no ghost. No ghost could so upset the even tenor of my way.†

Anyhow it's time I went to sleep now. 11.45pm and up in seven hours' time. Mother says I need eight hours' sleep ... Hope I shall have a letter from you tomorrow ... please darling. I wonder how your mother is ... your father ... Jean. You. I feel as if I'd never heard of you, your family for weeks and am about to have an account of all your doings. Tomorrow Diana goes back to school. I hope you succeed, my dear. I believe you will—perhaps too well. You might unearth a few geniuses and give them modern 'freedom'—poor Mrs Holcroft [the headmistress?]!

Dearest, I really must sleep. I must hear from you tomorrow. I'm worried about your mother ... it sounded such a funny illness: hate things I can't understand.

I love you my darling Diana C. Love you always xxxx Bob.

15th July, 1940. 10.15pm. Tonight needs must be very short: tired and no mood for writing. Why write if the 'mood is not on'? There is only news to tell.

Today we flew: helmets came last night so from today we fly. Our brief holiday

---

* A slight misquote of a line from Rupert Brooke's 1909 sonnet, 'Oh! Death will find me, long before I tire'.

† A partial quote of a line from Thomas Gray's 'Elegy Written in a Country Churchyard': 'They kept the noiseless tenor of their way.'

by the seaside is over. Now it is business. But so far it could not be pleasanter. Fly for three-quarters of an hour and lie in the gear in the sun for one and a half hours then fly again. Home—you note 'home'?—for lunch, and back again for more flying. Home again for tea and a quiet stroll round the gardens: strawberry-beds.

If only you were here I would that this went on for ever. No mail today. I had hoped so much for a letter. It must come tomorrow and I'll send this. My darling, goodnight: flying is tiring business and I can hardly keep my eyes open. God bless you and keep you. I love you for ever xxx Bob.

16th July, 1940. Your letter arrived today just as I was leaving for the aerodrome. I read part of it as I walked down the road and finished it during Morse practice.

Dearest it was a bitter-sweet pleasure that yet left me happy—it is, after all, a part of you, a photograph or rather a film of your mind and thus I see yet one more facet and am still enchanted. I cannot help being sad for you, sorry to cause such pain, tiresome tears, yet sometimes glad I can do it. I don't think I should or could ever cry at having to part from even you but you make me do crazy things after you have gone and want to do still crazier: a good job I'm under RAF restraint.

Poor Diana, with the way of her kind, must cry. I wished you had cried properly whilst I was there, cried it out—you would have felt better. But let us not now live again those few precious hours, the sad pain of them is all too near to be thought of with equanimity.

Aeroplanes—I realised afterwards your plane must have been a Junkers 87B.* The other one might be any of these three [see below] (probably the middle one, the JU 88 dive bomber). Very like a Blenheim but the engines stick out a lot more. Don't you think my DO 17 [Dornier Do 17] looks like a dog's head (sitting up!)?

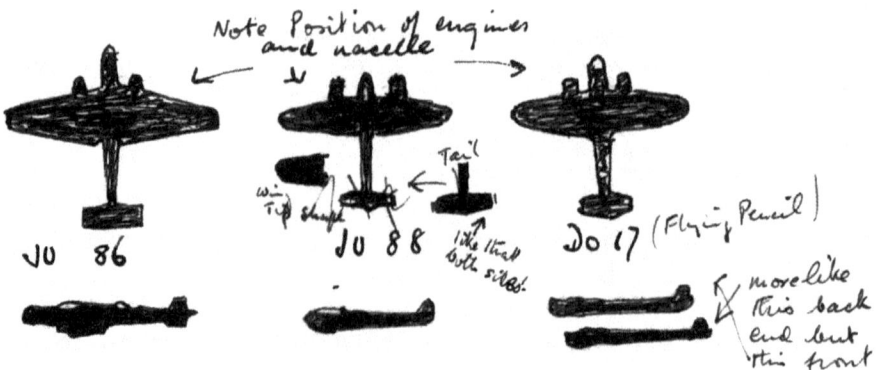

Note Position of engines and nacelle

JU 86   JU 88 *like that both sides!*   Do 17 (Flying Pencil)

Wing Tip Shape   Tail

more like this back end but this front

---

*   It was a nerve-wracking time. Later Diana described how she was bicycling the 3 miles home from school when a noisy dogfight took place just above her. She said she was so frightened that she threw her bicycle in the hedge and ran home. When she had to walk back to fetch it later, she felt ashamed.

Incidentally, your JU 87B has wings like this, nearly straight at the front but V shaped at the trailing edge.

That's the end of today's lesson children. I'm glad you got out of the way of that bomb, but I didn't quite get whether you were flattened by the bomb or voluntarily?

Mother tells me today the RA [Royal Artillery] may take over the house as GHQ. That will keep it going if nothing else. Trouble is Mother and Dad would then have nowhere to live. Perhaps they'll stay in two of the rooms. I can just imagine you (Oh hell! I've just realised that I am about to make a dubious double entendre, but let it be. You know my mind and what I mean). I can just imagine [you] sitting in your kitchen with nothing on, probably seated in an easy chair with feet up on the mantelpiece or something and in front of the fire, munching cake.

DHL [D. H. Lawrence] you'll find a personal biography—Father will lend it to you if you ask—in the billiard room. A 12/6 size book, brown with gold letters 'A Poet and Two Painters' [a memoir of D. H. Lawrence by] Knud Merrild. Very good on the man but not a literary criticism. In the billiard room, to the left of the fireplace somewhere about the middle of the right hand half—say five rows down. Lawrence understands the feminine mind, I think, as few other male writers have ever done. He had TB or cancer, almost certainly did not have drugs, was fanatical about sex, blood and earth, living naturally. Was probably a little mad; unbalanced anyhow. Very vain. Married to Freda, a German woman. Died of his 'disease' when about forty-five.

Wonder what you and Mother said and did? Where did you go? Take the dogs out? Up to my room? Throw Sieuwke [a former girlfriend] out of the window? I know you wouldn't want to do that. You have so much of me you could not begrudge her a little room. I wish she'd write anyhow. It worries me sometimes; perhaps she's thinking it might hurt me. The last I heard was that she was about to leave for Java to be married and she never sent her address and now Holland is invaded. Her mother and father were incredibly kind to me.

Polyfotos*—so far I have not yet been into Prestwick, have a guilty conscience—but it shall be done, Diana, I promise, probably tomorrow. I shall probably go in to see Tony and Ruth: they have managed to get half a house together and are feeling very bucked. I will go there to supper one evening and a flic afterwards.

Flying again this afternoon: I shall be off solo again in a day or two. It is nice to fly again, but there is now little time to look around and admire the view as of yore (I like that word, don't you?) because we have to concentrate on what the

---

* Polyfoto studios specialised in developing a proof sheet for each sitter of forty-eight head-and-shoulder poses. From this sheet the sitter could choose their best pose and order enlargements, or order booklets or cards of the smaller proof copy size. Polyfotos became very popular in wartime.

pilot is saying the whole time. How unimportant people, places look from the air. A large number of lovely homes round here with very large gardens, parks, pools and tennis courts. Nice rivers, trees and fields. Large fields on the hills, smaller in the valleys. The Isle of Arran, high cliffs sticking straight out of the sea, easily visible twenty-five miles away. It is good in the air.

I expect a parcel from Mother tomorrow, some more clothes. I shall try and pluck up courage then to break the news. It must be hard on one's parents to lose a part of their children, yet they, too, must take great pleasure in their new-found happiness. You, dear, and I as well I suppose, will be told 'no, much too young'— if not from our parents then from the Mrs Holcrofts. But we can just smile superciliously: the Mrs H's are ignorant. They have not got our knowledge. But supposing my parents (and more so yours!) say it and mean it? Or even think it. You are prepared for this? I know you are, but all will not be quite 'plain sailing' I know. And when the time comes to write to your father, I shall be in a blue funk. Suppose he should just write 'NO'? What would Dorothy Dix do next? Is he Dear Sir, Dear Mr Ladner, Dear Diana's Father? Gosh, and all this by letter. But all this is when we, when 'us' ... I dare not think so far.

Diana darling, how nice of you to have a name alliterative with dear and darling (a thoughtful father?), my dear it's time I went to sleep. I have to fly tomorrow morning and I can't fly well unless I sleep well so goodnight my dear—my fiancée, how odd it sounds!—please let me know how your mother is. God bless you. My love as always for ever, yours

xxxxxx Bob.

P.S. My 'billets' are nicer every day. I 'garden' with 'her': she's very sweet, not 'an old lady', spends all her time in the garden. He sends us into fits of laughter (suppressed) sometimes with his language!

LETTER TO DIANA:

Monktonhead
17th July, 1940

Two of my co-billetees elected to spend the evening in my room and it is now 11pm. I wanted to turn them out to write to you but they would stay and talk shop. Curse them. I wanted to thank you for your letter and now I am so drowsy that if I stop to think of a phrase, I daydream and then doze. Anyhow, Diana dear, I thank you for your letter and will reply properly tomorrow. In the meantime must go to bed. Darling I love you more and more—each day, each second. Sweetheart goodnight xxxxx Bob

18th July. Good evening, darling, how are you? Finished with school, finished preparing tomorrow's lessons and preparing for your bath? Now 9.20. Sun still a golden light on the fields and menacing blue-black mountains in the distance: it is light here till late—black-out 10.20. Lying on my bed now—hope my writing is not too illegible these days but I always write here as I've nowhere else in peace and solitude.

As usual, was yesterday so glad to get your letter, but this one moved me even more than usual, dearest. Your visit to Downham, sweet memories, confessions, and above all your verses left me feeling myself miles away in another world and then the longing to see, to feel, hear you. Fierce joyful pain of loving and being loved. It's funny how I, like you, wake and feel I love you more and so loving more and more can love no further. Yet the next morning it still goes on.

Poor Diana: surrounded by a horde of shrieking children: you are not fierce enough to be a school mistress. You ought to go into class cracking a large whip, then they'd all keep quiet. Tell me how you get on and what you teach, it intrigues me greatly. My memories of learning to spell are the ABC, the little picture cards like this ...   ... and so on. How else does one start? How explain to a blind man what colour is?

Prestwick is a small place and I could find no Polyfoto this evening. Perhaps there will be one in Ayr: if it is open when Tony, Ruth and I go in on Saturday (to see a flic), after I've had a meal with them I will have mine done for you. You will send yours 'if I want them' will you? Must I go on my hands and knees, dear, or is it being held as a quid pro quo?

Hope you do not regret your visit to Downham. Apprehensive—of what? You'll find it hard to know what Mother thinks of anyone, but she will tell me—I had hoped to hear from her today but nothing doing. I'll tell you what she says when I do and I must write back and tell them about us. Will let you know when I do.

We cannot, anyhow, get married until my commission because we should not have enough to live on. I really don't know what it costs, do you? But going on Pat's £400 minimum I should think we could exist then. A pilot officer gets, I think, between £350 and £400 year—anyway I'll find out.

We get no leave here and will get none I'm afraid for probably another three months. I have next Sunday off—entirely—and every alternate Saturday and Sunday i.e. Sunday one week and Saturday the next. On the other Saturday and Sunday we have to work till 5pm but that might be altered in a month's time. Nous verrons ... it seems a long way to come though—350 miles.

It's taken me an hour to write this. I keep on stopping to remember and thus dream or doze off! Must have a bath and go to sleep. Diana, my darling. I love you and love you and I'm yours forever and you're mine. Goodnight xxx Bob

19th July. 7.30am. Just off to fly, darling, it's a grand sunny morning, the best we've had—in fact too good to last. Have No Fear of this flying business, dear, we always wear parachutes anyhow! Nobody has been killed here for a very long time—it has the reputation of being one of the safest training schools and the best. Must go, all my love xxxx

8.30pm. After such a lovely morning it gradually clouded over and has rained off and on all afternoon. Went solo today for my first time since I've been here—a year's absence has not improved my flying! It's a grand thrill alone and in sole control—feeling of freedom and away from everyone—littleness of the world—no sign, no wash [as there would be on a boat] even to show from whence you've come. You must fly with me one day. I rigidly banish you from my mind when in the air (remember 'Each to the Other'?). Flying round an aerodrome with sometimes twenty or thirty other machines in the air demands all one's concentration and alertness. That's why it's so tiring when flying dual—that and the wind. Usually fly without goggles—like to feel the wind in my face.

I'm afraid I was a little too optimistic about a P/O's pay yesterday. I was talking to a corporal today who seemed to know all about it and he said the best paid man in the Air Force was the sergeant pilot—10/6—2/6 a day and flying pay—works out at about £275–£300 a year. But then he has no living or mess expenses, no uniform, and if living out also gets an allowance for that. Anyway I'll see what further information I can obtain.

Wrote to Dick yesterday to tell him of us. Wonder what he will say? You need not worry, I know he likes you.

Must have my bath—yes, as many as we like and it is the biggest bath I've seen, also nice comfy beds—and do some work. The mechanism of the Browning .303 Mark II* gun. Fires 1,150 rounds a minute at 2,500 miles per hour. Every Spitfire has eight of them—that's 150 shots every second. As our instructor says 'If you have a double-engined German in front of you and gave him two or three bursts you would cut him in half and the two halves would fly off.' like this:

The maid has just come in to pull my black-out curtains and wants to know why I'm always writing letters and not working!

Reading now and again George Moore's 'Aphrodite in Aulis'—find it very soothing. Started it last year ago and never had time to finish it.

Must really love you and leave you as my grandmother used to say.

My love, my love, all my love for you my love, for love is all and you're my all, my love. You are mine and I am thine—you and I and us. God bless you. Goodnight xxxxx Bob

20th July. This is now 4.30. Finished flying for today and just waiting for the word to go home. Four and a quarter hours in the air today. It was absolutely marvellous. I can't describe the view. About 5,000 feet up, people like pin-points, the Isle of Arran fifteen miles away and below us—mountain 2,000 feet high—and beyond Arran the coastline of rocky headlands, long peninsulas of land jutting into the sea for about seventy-five miles. Nearer to and to the right the Firth of Clyde merging with a bluish haze that is Glasgow. For twenty miles or so inland the fields, towns, woods, rivers and purple moors; but then a cloud bank merging horizon with sky—earth, sky and sea all one in the distance. Little cotton-wool clouds added the finishing touch.

Later—5.30pm. 'Home' now. Off in a quarter of an hour to have tea with Tony and Ruth and a flic after. Those two make me very envious and longing—why not us? Blast and blast. Your letter arrived at lunchtime, thank you darling.

Will answer it properly over the weekend. Your sample drawings incurred great disfavour at first: I thought that charcoal paper was a wrapping for your Polyfotos! When I've got over the shock, I can take a more unbiased view of their artistic merit or otherwise.

Oh darling, I want you, want you, want. But we must have yet a little patience. I will write and tell the family over the weekend. I could not get married without telling Mother because about three years ago a cousin of mine (Mother's eldest brother's son) got married secretly to a rather shady person and Mother said then that whoever I might marry, she'd rather be told first! Yet a little while ...

Oh God, you make me lose all self-control. I can't think, keep calm, my mind's a riot of desires and wants which all mean you. And I must think clearly now, it's not you and I just now, it is you and I and us. Dearest, what is best, what would be best for us now and forever? Because the future is dark and unknown it does not mean we can ignore it. Have I no power to make up my mind—a Hamlet procrastinating? Hamlet lost all: God forbid that I should do the same. I know what I want but I'm not quite sure how best to keep it—for you, for me, for us.

Must go and wash now. Then walk down the drive and hitchhike into Prestwick, post your letter and so to tea. Continual reminder of what we might be will not make it easy.

Diana darling you know I love you for always and someday soon our day will come. Dearest I am all yours forever xxxxxx Bob

8

Diana loves me
but will her father?

Monktonhead
20th July, 1940

A quarter of an hour to midnight, got back from the flics at 11.30, feeling miserable. It is a nice refinement of torture to have Tony answer the bell and show me to his—their—dining room and a few minutes later Ruth appears. We feed and then clear away the table. In every little thing I saw you and I: they are so happy. Their life is full for the moment. This must be torment for you too, let's stop.

But must just tell you: they live in half a house. Share it with another man and his wife (very nice). They have a bedroom and living-room and use of the bathroom and kitchen. It suits them very well and they are lucky because rooms here are almost impossible to get. All Glasgow seems to be holidaying here.

How nice to be able to be in bed now and think that I need not hurry off to sleep as tomorrow I'm off—breakfast nineish. How nice to write you before I go to sleep: but how much nicer ... stop. These thoughts will drive me crazy.

The picture was 'Another Thin Man': good but I was thinking 'we've never yet seen a film together just you and I'. Buses full on the way back, had to wait for one or two, but got one in the end. Short glimpse of an old stone bridge in Ayr with the full moon reflected off the river from between its arches.

You and I on the bridge watching the river flow by ...

You and I, you and I, us. In every little thing I do or see or hear—I think of it or rather I do not have to think—comes the refrain you and I and us.

Just after midnight: my eyes droop: I shall soon fall asleep writing. Hurricanes buzzing round above, practising night landings: it must be nice up there now. Full moon on the water, wonder if they can see Arran?

My Diana dear, just let me hold you tight just once, kiss and say goodnight and I will be patient—for about five minutes. Goodnight darling Diana

Constance, all of me is yours. God bless you my love. xxxx Bob

21st July, 1940. 5.45pm. Just going to get ready for tea: have just written Mother and Dad all about us. And now to wait in trepidation for the next few days. But just now tea. And to write and tell you as soon as the deed was done, although you will not know till after they do. Darling, darling, I love you, love you, love you—but just now tea.

9.30pm. In bed at last. Laundry packed, work done, buttons and boots polished, bathed and in bed. Feeling clean and 'nice' to write to you.

10pm. 'Bert' came in, blast him, for a chat. A nice old stick but I wanted to write to you. Now only ¼ hour left before I must turn my light out because of black out. 'Bert' wants me to go down to the cafe on the front with him one evening. He says he's never had so many girls make eyes at him before and 'some of them not half bad ... girls you wouldn't mind being seen out with, see?' A little unpolished our Bert, leaves his spoon in his teacup always, but a good lad. He said the sunset over Arran tonight was 'bloody marvellous'. If we get another fine evening, I'll walk up the knoll behind the house to have a look at it. It ought to be wonderful.

Today has been good. Slept in until eight o'clock then had a nice long hot bath. Breakfast then sit for ¾ hour on the veranda in the sun and chat to the son-in-law. After that upstairs and do a little gentle work till lunch time, making notes and writing up my flying log-book. After lunch the Colonel and I had arranged to go for a walk. I asked him after breakfast which was the nice direction and he said he'd 'take a turn with me'.

As we walked off with Barney and Liza, the two spots [dalmatians]—father and daughter—he explained how he had one gammy leg. The tendon broken on the Somme while he was trying to stop stampeding horses. It did not worry him much nowadays but the calf was much smaller than on the other leg. We walked for two and a half hours—about five or six miles and I think I was more tired than he at the end of it.

We went through a field or two, through a fence, a spinney—he called it a cover—by a field of corn then to some lovely beeches and all the time I thought, if Diana were only here, we could be walking this together instead of this nice old man. Then I'd realise he had spoken to me and I'd not replied. Did he think me mad or rude? And then through more beeches, lots of ferns, sun—pattern on the ground, the leaves above.

If Diana were here I could show this bough, that pattern, if she were here we could rest here a while, bury ourselves in those ferns—lost to the world. We came back by a lane, less exerting than the woods and the fields and my heart was more at ease. Roads and Diana: not quite.

When we got back, we repaired to the kitchen garden, he to the young peas, I to the strawberries. And then we arrived, or rather I did, at the beginning of today's letter and wrote to Mother. Now it is time my light was out. Is it too much to hope for another letter tomorrow? I love you dearest darling always and ever yours xxxx Bob.

22nd July, 1940. Hullo darling. Now just gone 9pm. Tonight is the best evening we've had yet but it is quite chilly. Always is of a night-time here.

Sitting on top of a 'knoll' as they call it, leaning against a baby haystack (I always forget what they call them) and hoping to see the sun set behind Arran. But I think I shall go back disappointed. The sun is already passed the peaks of Arran and will be at least another half hour before it sets. However, I have my sweater on and will wait until I get too cold. Wish there were no wind or it were blowing the other way. Could lie here for hours it is so peaceful.

Fantastic blue-grey-black of Arran in the shade, seventeen miles across the water and looking not more than ten. No light, no shade now and its two thousand feet peaks seem to rise straight and sheer from the sea. Resemblance to the Dents du Midi behind Lake Geneva. Countryside here is like Sussex near the downs, quite unlike Scotland. Some of the most fertile soil in Scotland, highly cultivated. Trees, waving corn, cattle and snug white farm houses all remind me of the south of England. Shadows, too, now lengthening across the fields. But, by the side of it all, this colossal mass of mountains. I must visit Arran one day.

No letter from you this morning. I thought it was hoping for too much. You shouldn't spoil me so because, when I don't get a letter nearly every day, I get bad tempered. No note or parcel yet from home either. I wonder what they will say and think when they get my letter. How is your mother now? I cannot, dare not, think what I shall or can say to your father when I write. Will he submit to losing his second daughter and only at the age of nineteen? (alright no rudeness meant!)

It must be very hard on one's parents—especially yours: mine have two other sons yet to keep them company.

Sun just going now below the level of the cloud bank. Sea has turned grey and cold. Arran blue—hard and icy too. No warmth from the sun. Half down. Hills all shadows too. Just the top of mine illuminated by the last rays. Now they are gone too.

I'm going in. Goodnight 'gaunt' Arran, made harder still by the pinkish sky behind your blue depths and heights. Only the topmost heights hazy in the clouds. Wrapped in mystery. Forbidding. Goodnight cold sea. Goodnight cold earth. All is cold. Me too.

10.15pm. In bed. Chores done bathed and refuelled—as you say it soothes a lot. But yet in soothing re-awakes my desire, aches and longing for you. Oh darling my whole being cries out for you. You, you, you ... Diana, Diana. It is good that you should be tied to Waterhall for a little while ... or else I know not what might happen.

You ought to have loved some stable, steady-going, pipe-smoking, feet apart, 12-stone, clean limbed young Englishman. Someone to laugh away your mad ideas instead of encouraging and rejoicing in them. Someone to point your way out to you and say there is your path and duty. Go to it or else I'll never marry you. And I, who should I have loved, my Diana? A vixen, hen-pecker or some plain bespectacled and skinny legged school mistress dressed in a modest blouse and romper suit? Some plain practical person.

Time now to close my eyes and dream of you. I have never done so yet. I dreamt the other night that the Germans captured our aerodrome and flew all our machines back to Germany, but of you I have never dreamt. Perhaps my subconscious changes you into something quite unrecognisable, knowing that otherwise I should wake up. Dearest darling, goodnight. God bless you. Do not despair, we've all life before us. I still love you, sweetheart. Yours faithfully Bob xxxxxx

DIANA'S DIARY:

22nd July, 1940.

Started my wartime work. A week of school. Take thirty-six boys and girls for everything—ages between five and seven. Sometimes I hate it, sometimes I love it. The children are rather sweet.

Love of Bob fills every minute of the day and floods and overwhelms me. Pray he'll phone tonight.

LETTER TO DIANA:

Monktonhead
24th July, 1940

Well darling, how are you? Not fed up with school, I hope. Are they any quieter or are you getting immune yet? Not 'wanting' too much? Your school sounds like hard work but very interesting and instructive if you've got the patience. I'm sure I could not stick it for two days. As you say individually you could cope very well and teach a lot but at that age in a group ...

I thank you for the drawings. I love them. Love the colour in one of the air battles. Children can convey movement and noise astonishingly well even if they do not do it intentionally.

Are teachers really supposed to live on £94 a year—36/6^d a week? A domestic, if well paid, would be better off. I suppose it is this modern world's value of intelligence. But you are not to work up here—I should be very cross. (Is this being tactful?) But neither of us could then work well and I might get the push if I did badly in the exams. And where would we be then? I would be spending all my time meeting you and, nice as that would be, I should have a guilty conscience that I should be working and then be annoyed with you for taking me from my 'duty'. I really do have to work in the evening—last night it was until 10.15 and I felt so tired I could not write.

A weekend would be just possible at the moment but later who can tell? And, in another month about, we shall be feverishly swotting for our passing-out exams. This training business is very hectic and I am afraid that until I'm finally posted to an operational squadron—i.e. when I'm fully fledged—that, until then, we shall be unable to see much of each other. It is bitter, I know too well; it is unjust too, unreasonable and heart-searing, but it is war. Regard it if you like as our testing time—not of our love, we know that already, but of strength of mind and character. It is harder on you than on me I know, but I shall love you all the more for it.

If you do ever come up here I shall have the following Sundays off as far as I can tell—August 4th, 18th, and 1st September if we are still here. I should be free on 5.30pm on the Saturday. It seems hardly worth your while travelling seven hundred miles in one weekend for an all too brief Sunday. You would make yourself ill my dear and I would rather face going without you than bear that. No, I'm afraid we shall have to wait and see where I get posted to next—it can hardly be further away. Well, my darling, you asked me to make you see it is impossible. Have I succeeded? They are the facts and facts are often harsh and unkind but it is usually best to know the worst. Sorry, my dear Diana Constance I can't tell you how sorry I am but, as I said before, c'est la guerre.

After that I feel too miserable to write any more so goodnight darling, will continue tomorrow when I hope I may hear from you and 'the family'. Sweetheart goodnight. My love to you as always and all me. xxxxx Bob.

25th July, 1940. Just in time for a few lines before I slip to try and catch the evening post: you may then get this before the weekend—enclosing the parents' replies. Don't you think they are sweet—and wise? Shall write to your father this weekend. I don't think it is fair to keep him 'in the dark' any longer and if your mother knows she must have enlightened him ...

Your letter has arrived today with the Polyfotos. Have not had time to examine them at my leisure yet.

The 'criticism' Mother refers to is that you were 'very quiet and shy, over-shadowed by Patsy'. It made me laugh. It's you darling and one of the yous I love a lot.

Your knowledge of figures astonishes me. So we could exist, then? I'll risk it on your assurance. Darling I love you and love you forever. We are now Each to the Other. Will write again over the weekend. All my love xxx Bob.

Letter to Diana:

Monktonhead
25th July, 1940

My darling, posted letters to you and Mother and Dad tonight: I feel so happy that they are quite content, or at any rate in no way opposed to us. It is much easier to have everything on our side. I have an idea to ease our paths with your father if it needs easing. I will tell him that we should like to get married when I've finished my training which will be in about four or five months' time. That should be enough 'testing-time' for anyone and, when I find that I shall probably be passed out in [just] three or four months, he may have got used to the idea.

What do you think or shall I ask straight out 'I want to marry Diana, please?' Perhaps it would be better vaguely—'in some months' time'. Must go to sleep now. Dreaming ... 'please sir, I want Diana' no, no, I don't 'want' I 'must have'. That's rude though. 'Please sir, Diana and I', 'I and Diana'? 'My betrothed and I' ... 'Dear Mr Ladner, may I have your younger daughter—Diana Constance's hand in marriage? My age is 23, I am 5 foot 8½ inches. I don't smoke, my tastes are varied, not always simple but can be if necessary, my income at the moment is 2/- per day plus flying pay 1/6^d per day, I have no prospects—not that anybody else has either unless they make guns—gosh where am I going. Goodnight Mr Ladner.' Goodnight my mad Diana: I am dear Madam your equally bats fiancé.

Yours faithfully

Wallace Arthur Robert

PS I love you—sorry I nearly forgot—I still do too xxxxxxxxxxxxxxxxx

PPS A bit later: I still love you darling more and more xx

28th July, 1940. Darling. Had to write three other letters tonight and as usual left yours to the last, and now it is after ten and leaves but little time to write, and I want to write to you tonight: feel I could go on for hours and hours. Last night and the night before I felt I could not write at all—didn't want to. At least I would like to have written a letter to you but didn't want to write—do you see the difference, or isn't there any? I don't know—it may be but don't think so. I didn't write because I don't want to send you letters which have been written when I don't want to write. Foolish? Vain? Probably. But I like to think it is overwork. Yes, really.

My brain has been working all day and must find relief. Letters do not often just 'flow'. They have to be thought out, and carefully constructed—or at any rate each sentence has to be. And at last it goes on strike. And so the night before the last, my dear, I read 'The House at Pooh Corner', and last night I was hauled off, not quite unreluctant, to Ayr to skate. And we skated from 8.00 until 10.00.

Our Bert picked up some piece in red who had a friend in blue. Bert wanted to date up red and I was to accompany blue for today. I didn't—because Tony and Ruth were coming to tea today. You need never fear, darling of my being 'ravished' by some blonde up here. Have, as yet, seen no piece 'I would be care to be seen out with' (Bert's dictum)—all are tough, fat legs, large mouths, half-ugly.

...Thank you for the photos, all my Diana, I send them back marked B, QB, F, QG, G, E, E* ... (Bad, Quite Bad, Fair, Quite Good, Good, Excellent, and the one-I-like-best). When I looked them all over again this evening, I thought that quite different ones were the best so it must all be a question of mood. When I made the choice I seem to have wanted you 'winsome'. First I chucked out the bad photography and those that looked bad. The rest I chose for you as I wanted you, you as I knew you, you that I haven't known, just you.

Have not written your father yet. Will wait, then, until he goes to Mullion. Will you let me have the address please: also where to write to you—Patsy's or the Foster's? (I suppose the address in Mullion doesn't matter: the PO [Post Office] will forward it.) Darling, what shall I tell him, how can I start? I'm scared, really frightened. Think if I wrote something he disliked it might just turn the scales the wrong way ...

It's time you learnt to spell <u>alphabet</u> 'my little school mistress'.

Today Ruth and Tony came to tea: 'civilized' tea to torment me, and yet to bring a joy of the yet-to-be and pride that soon we must have our turn ... I have been thinking, dreaming of you, of us. Silly little details. We must have patience sweetheart. I too feel cold and hard and lonely at times. Feel vindictive and mad at this foolish world: the only thing to do is to wait until the mood passes. Walk it off: burn it off, but don't sit still doing nothing. As you say 'school' occupies your time, less time to think. Mine is almost fully occupied. I'm lucky; at weekends the relief from work is so great that I'm usually too happy to get those moods. What can I say to help, Diana my darling? Only that I love and love and love you.

Morning noon and night. I live for you, now.

You will be miserable too at leaving Waterhall, poor you. I think they might have let you and Patsy stay on together. What a scandal for the neighbourhood. You might have taken in a lodger too.

My sweet, my love, my all goodnight. God bless and keep you.

Ever and always yours 'to have and to hold' xxxxxx Bob.

Letter to Diana:

Monktonhead
30th July, 1940

My darling—Mother is anxious that I should write to your father soon, so that she can write to you and your parents soon. So I hope to send a letter to him by Thursday morning's post. Have not heard yet what you think but hope to hear tomorrow.

Filthy day today for flying: clouds very low, only about 600 feet up, but it is seldom too bad for flying. We go up nearly all weathers.

I'd better go to bed—can't write two coherent sentences. You, my darling, are love. Sweetheart goodnight. Xxx Bob

31st July, 1940. 8pm. Your letter came today, dear. It made me feel very happy. Your questions—

Canada: I don't know but think we are very unlikely to go there.

The weekend 24th or 25th—we shall be here—but darling this place is 350 miles from London. The Colonel leaves tonight on the 9:30 train for London. Wish I were he. But 800 miles there and back for you—more than a fortnight's pay too in train fares alone.

Your father—I will write tonight or tomorrow and post it Friday: the hopes of two lives for one life all on a scrap of paper. Let's hope he'll say 'About time she got married and settled down instead of gadding about all the time with lots of different men'. Wish I knew him better: he me.

Writing in 'Bob' Lacey's room (he is the newspaper reporter) because he has a wireless and I wanted to hear the concert. Still here. Have sat through the news and couldn't tell you what it was but just then one of our Empire builders giving a talk said a few words we both heard 'young men with a light in their eyes and a song in their hearts'—and both rushed to turn him off. If he was talking about what I believe he was, he needs to be woken up. A few perhaps, in fighters, have the thrill before they take off—there is a thrill in shooting down aircraft, like shooting game as a reward for your skill—but mostly it is grim eyes and resolution with fear in their hearts. Gay eyes, singing hearts are for the skin deep. Now I'm getting emotional: I hate it.

Thank you for your sweet smelling flowers, your letter breathed catmint before I opened it. They are now in your book. Mrs C gave me a lovely jar of dark red and purple, with a few pale mauve, sweet peas for my room. She grows them all in the kitchen garden. They are too untidy, too much bother in her herbaceous border (she does it all herself) but I love to see rings of them in the garden. Do yours grow in rings or rows? Another thing she told me: a sprig of mint in the hat or hair or behind the ear keeps away the flies of which there are great numbers here.

We have mid term exams this weekend so the next day or so will mean scanty letters—especially tomorrow when I have to write to your father: it will take all the evening.

Flying today we did a practice forced landing in a field and the instructor got out and I taxied round the field after him while he picked mushrooms. They are a very human lot our instructors. Mine sometimes drives low over a little cottage to wave to his wife. Another often flies about 10 to 20 feet above the River Ayr looking for salmon to go and fish the next day. Or look for a pal fishing!

My sweet, it is goodnight now. Darling our sunshine will come, soon. All me to you xxx Bob

UNFINISHED DRAFT LETTER TO DIANA'S FATHER:*

Monktonhead
1st August, 1940

Dear Mr Ladner

I can find no better way to start this letter than to ask you outright if you will part with your other daughter, Diana, and give your consent to our engagement and marriage. It will be hard, I know, for you and Mrs Ladner to lose her, but is she not, in part, lost already?

When I pass out in a few months' time as a qualified pilot my pay will be sufficient for us to live on with a squeeze, but that squeeze should do us more good than harm.

---

*   There is no record of the original letter.

Monktonhead
1st August, 1940

11.30pm. It's done. It's written, stamped, and addressed. O God go with it. Too full for words. Goodnight my own. All my love for you for ever yours Bob.

2nd August, 1940. 11.30pm. Again. Darling I'm tired: today has been tremendously hot and this afternoon we were firing machine guns so, in the evening, we just had to bathe. The sea here is much warmer than Torquay but takes ages and ages before it gets deep. After the bathe (all four of us) we got some supper—tell you more about that over the weekend—and then we all went to the flics for a change. I was not too keen but perhaps that's why I didn't think a lot of the film—The Wizard of Oz.

Is there a Mrs Foster to be 'c/o of'? Suppose it would be improper for you to stay there if there wasn't ... Damn impropriety, it's only what people's nasty thoughts make it. And what does local gossip say about my angel now—and me? I suppose I am the big, bad wolf. Let them foul their own nests if they want to but don't let them hurt you dear. I love you so much that, if they did, I might go mad ... and give them something real to gossip about.

Oh Diana darling, I want you so much—one day I shall burst. You grow and grow in little jumps and each time bigger than the last. But you are mine, mine, mine. My heart sings to think of it and someday we shall be really us to share and share alike. When shall I hear from your father—Tuesday, Wednesday, Thursday? If he should say yes. I dare not think. Sweetheart goodnight. All my love, all me. Your Bob xxxxxxxxxxx

9

Can it really be true?

Monktonhead
3rd August, 1940

My darling, today has been full of many me's—damn! Just nicely bathed and clean and my pen then leaks over my finger, curse it. This morning early was a tired, little headache and cold in the head me. But breakfast and two aspirin put that right. Then before flying there was a quite peaceful me lying in the hot, really hot, sun waiting my turn to go up. Then me in the air learning how to do loops and slow rolls (from right way up onto your side then on your back, the other side and straight again). Very difficult to do well because an aeroplane's controls are such that they have a different effect when the plane is like this

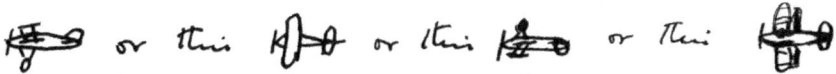

so you have a lot to remember. When doing rolls, you hang on your straps upside down while the machine is like that but in a loop centrifugal force keeps you in. When I got down to the ground again, I had got back my bee headache as well and also my tummy was not feeling too well. I was not feeling sick at all, it just wasn't used to working upside down and the result was lots of Turkish compliments. After lunch the tired me lay down on my bed and went to sleep until four with more aspirin and woke up very hot and sweaty. Changed and read 'Flowering Wilderness', one of the Forsyte tales, until tea. The after-dinner me was also engaged in reading and re-reading your letter, darling and ... but, no, this is about me—anyhow a kiss for you first—and then the after-dinner me finished the 'Flowering Wilderness'—as good as [all the other tales] are—while the others went out.

Having finished that, and feeling a lot better, a new me said get up and go out and, taking your book in hand, went out into the kitchen garden for some mint to keep the flies away and then wandered up to the knoll. No Arran tonight, too misty. But still very warm and leaning against my pile of hay.

> Today I dreamed of sand and sea
> Of climbing in and out the rocks
> Without a shirt, or shoes or socks
> Today I dreamed of you and me.
>
> Today we walked along the sand
> And paddled in the shallow pools,
> While sea-shells bright as any jewels
> Twinkled* to see us hand in hand
>
> No crowded beaches greeted us
> Swimming through the crystal water
> Father Neptune's son and daughter?†
> Naked as Our Father made us.
>
> And lying after in the sun
> And drying in the hot soft sand
> Soft touch of cheek and lip and hand
> And happiness of being one.
>
> Strolling home thus hand in hand‡
> Along our beach, beside our sea,
> A voice inside me said to me
> Keep this: it is your promised land.

And now the last me must go to sleep. Had to retire from the field about 8.30 because of the midges. Now nearly 11. All me goodnight my sweet my own xxx Bob.

4th August. In bed: bathed and hair washed.

10pm. Just written home and a note for John: he comes here tomorrow! Incredible isn't it?

Looked through yesterday's lines and added comments. It now needs the hard work of polishing: I always funk it—perhaps I don't really like—that's why I could never write good verse and add my difficulties for you to solve. Please teacher!

I didn't thank you enough for your letter: I never do. Can't tell you what joy they bring: I hope mine can do the same.

---

* A note in the margin reads '"twinkle" does not scan properly, what would you suggest?'

† Margin note: 'Hiawatha/touch? Just put into rhyme?'

‡ Margin note: 'too many "hands"?'

I'm glad other men have wanted to marry you and much more glad they didn't. I didn't know it—perhaps not unnatural. I don't think anyone has wanted to marry me except perhaps—your namesake. She would not have said yes if I'd asked but she might have wanted to. I don't know. I've treated her rather badly—met her three or four years ago in Switzerland (my 'happy' hunting ground?) and later in London. Then I never saw her for a year and hardly wrote. Saw her about once, vague promises and then a space. The night I saw her when you were tiddly at the Chase (hardly looked at me) was again first time for about 18 months. She was fond of me I know, but think she knew I didn't love her. It sometimes worries me—I should hate to hurt her: she's very sweet. Can you remember having any thoughts about her or were you too ... to notice much?

Keep happy darling, I like you best thus: or rather I'm happy too if you are happy and, if for only one of your reasons, keep happy for me and for us. I love you, sweet. You must be lonely, less happy in your strange home. Dearest cheer up: I'm thinking of you, loving you always loving you. Waiting, longing for you. In a few days now ...

Today we had to go into the aerodrome at 9am for a test. At 11 we were told it was put off till tomorrow. It made us just mutinous to think of our wasted hours that we might have been in bed. On the way back I hitch-hiked on a sand lorry but got out of it half-way when I saw the Colonel and the two spots on their way back from fetching the morning papers. I descended from the chariot and came back with him. I like him more and more: a kindly, enlightened, un-army man. He likes me, too, I think. It is amusing sometimes how he and Mrs C tell little jokes or fads against each other. She about 'her good man' how he will not have a tarred drive and when it gets bare always has just another load of stones on top. She hates walking up on these stones from the garage at the gate and he the thought (and expense?) of a proper road. So it has gone on since the beginning. He about the Cairn [terrier] always getting the tit-bits of food 'but better not say so to Kitty'. Attractive both.

After lunch we again went to the beach. A sort of inferior Cornwall. Nice sand but not so golden, and the soft unwashed sand not so clear. Glasgow in force leaves a lot of litter ... Still it was warm to lie in, to play and to swim.

And back to tea and, after some work, to Tchaikovsky Pathétique symphony. It made me sad alright. Sensual, tearful music. Not the hard dry-eyed feeling.

And so to bed and in touch with you. Goodnight my own, time we were both asleep: are you thinking of me, I wonder? I like to think so—to meet you in thinkingland. Silly.

God bless you Diana Constance, bless us. I love you love you love you, always and for ever yours. Bob

PS Will you be in Wednesday or Thursday if I hear from your father and phone about 7.15?

xxxxxxxxxx

Monktonhead
5th August, 1940

Five minutes ago I was lying on my bed reading your 'tear-stained' letter. Poor
darling, next time you shall cry in my arms and get it over or try to—that is if
there is to be a next time. It made me feel very sad and just then the maid
knocked on the door—'There's a young lady on the telephone for you.' I shot my
feet into my slippers and rushed downstairs.

'Hullo, hullo,' couldn't hear a thing, then very faint—'I am speaking for Diana
Ladner,' repeat please—yes right, yes, 'her father ... ', 'her father?' 'Yes, her father
rang up today and says yes.' Repeat all once more please—cannot afford to
make a mistake. It must be true: phone Diana. One hour delay—o curse, oh
curse.

What shall I say, what can I say. One look, one minute would say much more
than an hour on the phone and yet not say all. Who could have phoned? Whoever
it was must know. Was it Mrs Foster? Thank her for me if it was, kiss whoever it
was.

And now it's not if, now it is when. Whoever it was must have thought me very
rude: I said 'Oh yes, thank you very much, goodbye.'

Darling, darling, darling ... All I can think or say. I love, love you, love you, all
I can feel.

The phone again ... damn 'Ring you again in a minute.' ... and there it goes
again. 'Hullo' faint voice 'Hullo', 'Is that you Diana?' 'No! She's in bed with a
chill.' (Surely the same voice? Good lord of course) ... 'Will you ring tomorrow
night?' Never heard the tomorrow before. All is clear. A thousand curses, what a
disappointment. Blast, blast, blast.

And please Diana don't be ill: you cannot be very well if you can't even answer
the phone. Another thousand doubts. Darling, I won't let you be unwell.

Mind too jumbled now must go to sleep. It's only 8.45. Hell what does it
matter. The joy of your father's 'yes'—the pain of you in bed, they run round and
round and tear me in twain. But holding me together is our love. Nothing can
break it. My poor unwell Diana, goodnight, I love you.

xxxx Bob

Monktonhead
6th August, 1940

You poor darling, I hope your throat is not painful—laryngitis is a foul disease
and my heart bleeds for you. Please get better soon, I shall and am worrying for
you and will have no peace till you are better. After that I can recommend the sea

airs of Prestwick as excellent convalescence! What a time you choose to be in bed. I hope the Fosters are nice to you—let you alone when you want to be alone and amuse you when you feel like being amused. How many of them are there? It sounded like a girl's voice* last night but an older woman's (Mrs Foster's) voice tonight. Last night, though, was too faint to be distinguishable.

John arrived here yesterday and today a letter from him written a fortnight ago with a note from Father on the back 'Sorry, this has been in my pocket for ten days.' Inside were some photos of you and I and John. One dreadful one of me sailing with you and your red trousers—looked worse than bats. They were quite good photos though and will go into my 'gallery'. John is very pleased to be here and is now an LAC (leading aircraftman) while our poor course has not yet been 'promoted'. It is most aggravating as ours should have come through the day we arrived here. The whole point is that we lose £1.10s a week in wages by it!

Sweetheart I can yet scarcely realise that in three months' time ... can it really be true? Has your father really said yes? Perhaps I shall have a letter from him tomorrow to convince me. Vain unbeliever? And yet I know it is true: somewhere inside, a quiet peace reigns and there is almost a press of happiness. Oh darling ... Diana ...

The RA are taking over most of our house as HQ. I wonder what will happen to my books and things—if they have to store them, take out what you want darling—I shall hate parting with any of them: so will Mother, and I'm glad I haven't got to be there to see them go—I expect you will be over there when you are better. Tell me then what are they doing to my room. I never dare ask at home because I hate to appear sentimental. It is nice in a way, though, because it means the house will more or less keep itself for the duration. And I should hate to lose it.

I don't know, though, that I'd like to live there for always, with you. It seems so big—apt to get impersonal, one gets lost. What do you think, darling? Because I suppose that, following the good old English custom and assuming that after the war ... it will perhaps one day be my right to live there. Anyhow it doesn't matter: I wonder if all people of our age feel the same about large houses? Does one's sense of size diminish with age?

Must close now as it is 10.30pm and we fly tomorrow morning. Perhaps tomorrow there will be another letter from you or are you not allowed to write? If you want to phone before Sunday, I am in nearly every evening from six o'clock onwards.

One evening I must tell Tony and Ruth about us and go and celebrate—probably Thursday (after payday). I hope you don't mind me telling them—they are some of the few who know 'us'. In fact now, I suppose, we are semi-officially engaged. How detached I feel from that us and me.

---

* Mrs Foster's daughter Alison was eighteen.

My darling, goodnight and God bless and keep you. Get well soon and don't be unhappy.

Teach me half the gladness that thy brain must know,
Such harmonious madness from my lips would flow
The world should listen then, as I am listening now.*

Sweet for ever-mine, goodnight. My love, my mind, my body, my soul. xxxxx
Bob.

LETTER TO DIANA:

Monktonhead
7th August, 1940

9.45pm. In bed. It started to rain tonight and I wanted to be in the rain and I wanted some exercise badly so I put on my old grey slacks, an old shirt and sweater and ran for about twenty minutes round the wet fields in the rain. Mad ... quite mad, yet I enjoyed it a lot: afterwards a hot bath and so to bed. I feel so nice and clean: amiable too and very much wanting you. This crazy world that we must still remain apart. But we cannot grumble, our major battles are over and we shall soon enjoy the fruits of victory. Wonder what your father will say tomorrow, for the morrow must bring his letter. I think your parents are absolutely marvellous, they must know you better than you think and having only your happiness at heart could scarce forbear to say 'Yes'. It's nice, too, to think that we must have written very logical, compelling letters—

Diana-all-alone, Strange House, Toofaraway. What a marvellous rhythm it all has. But in bed with no beams to count,† none of your own books to read, not even able to talk, even to yourself—that must hit you hard, my poor darling. You know, you will never escape the accusation from me of being a chatterbox. All I first heard of you and the first words I heard from you were gossip, idle chatter. Not malicious I know—just prattling if you will—but chatter all the same. Now my Diana, live it down if you can or want to.

Letter from Mother today: the RA are to take over the house but leaving us the drawing-room (as dining and living room), the little pantry (as kitchen), Mother's, Dick's and John's rooms, and two bathrooms. An admirable arrangement it seems to me. Wish they would supply gardeners though!

Dick may be in an east coast port for his shore leave: Mother and Dad will probably go and see him—perhaps they've told you by the time you get this.

---

* From 'To a Skylark' by Percy Bysshe Shelley.

† Diana's home, Waterhall, was built in the sixteenth century, and she described her bedroom as 'all beams, slopes, plaster and nooks, with a lovely king post bang across the middle of the room'. Sometimes she would lie in bed and count the beams.

Exams tomorrow, must sleep and dream of us. Sweet dreams, I pray. Our life, new life together more perfect than the last, than ever before ... Darling, Diana darling, I want you now, want you here ... to comfort each other ... to have and to hold. How can this love bring so much pain as well as joy? And yet I love and love, and loving yet makes love grow stronger. Goodnight, my love, God bless and keep you, and us. All your Bob.

LETTER TO DIANA:

Monktonhead
8th August, 1940

12.15am. Bin' celebratin'. I love you more than ever. Want you more and more. You create and destroy. Bless you and blast you. I love you for ever and ever. All and always your Bob xxxx

LETTER TO DIANA'S FATHER:

Monktonhead
9th August, 1940

Thank you so much for your letter and good wishes. I cannot express how happy and grateful you and Mrs Ladner have made me feel by your consent to Diana and I becoming engaged.

While, perhaps naturally, we would both wish to be married in the near future, I quite understand that you would like to see something of me and my family first. I am sure we shall both be content to wait until you can see us be married with as much confidence in our future as we have. At the moment I am afraid my chances of any leave are negligible, but I hope that, when I start my next course in about a month's time, I may be able to get a few days off. Apart from that, proper leave is out of the question until I finally pass out in three or four months' time—

Diana seems to have chosen a most unfortunate and galling time to lose her voice. I understand she has got laryngitis—I hope it is not painful or enduring: she seems quite upset at missing 'school'.

I hope you find Cornwall just as enchanting as it always is for me, and that Mrs Ladner is now quite fit and well again.

With kind regards.

Yours sincerely,

Robert Keddie

Monktonhead
9th August, 1940

Hullo my darling, and how are you now? Can you yet speak in proper voice? Poor you, your lovely voice a mere croak: you must feel wild.

It is now 9.30pm—no nearly ten!—I've spent an hour writing to your father to thank him and your mother for saying 'Yes': I have not yet quite got over it.

He said '... my instinct cautions me to refuse ... if she now feels sure of herself as you say you are, then I feel it is a time when both your wishes should come first ... but as we do not know you or your people, we feel the question of an early marriage should be deferred until we have some further acquaintance and know what your people's views are in the matter.' I said, '... I am sure we shall both be content to wait until you can see us be married with as much confidence in our future as we have.' Perhaps not good grammar, perhaps an impossibility—in fact I know it is, but the sense is good.

I hope you are content to leave it at that for the present. I am, much as I should wish to be married tomorrow, today. We've asked a lot and we've been granted much. I should hate to seem impatient—not sure of waiting—not grateful for what we have received. Oh darling I love you and only you and ever you and wholly you. All of you with all of me.

Will stop this letter now and take it downstairs for the postman to collect in the morning—it is our day off tomorrow and I want you to get this on Monday, and I can tell you all about last night and today and tomorrow during the weekend.

Dick tried to phone tonight but somehow he never got through properly. I could hear him but he could not hear me: and then he had an argument with the operator who wanted to know where the call was from and Dick was not allowed to say!

Dearest Diana—tomorrow you phone—no! It is the day after, but I shall stay in tomorrow just in case. I love you so, I love you so ... 'in sickness and in health, for richer ...' When will this be said over us?

Always and ever all yours, darling Bob

xxxxxxxxxx

10

Alone, alone, when my love was away

Monktonhead
10th August, 1940

9pm. My own, you have just phoned: I knew you would somehow. Tony and Ruth wanted me to go with them to a little modern pub on the way to Glasgow but I told Tony that you had just written to say you might phone, a perfect lie, and yet you did! How marvellous to hear your voice, to feel you the other end. I know I asked the most ridiculous questions, said the most ridiculous things. Why can't we just hold the telephone tight and say nothing? Something, surely, flows along the line. Oh darling, darling.

Are you really coming in a fortnight's time? I believe it is supposed to be proper—I can never tell what is and what isn't: it all seems so futile to me. Founded on an out-worn code.

We must just hope for the best about my time off—they change everything about at such short notice here, and one cannot get personal interviews about leave etc., all has to be by letters which the sergeant probably opens and the CO never sees.

A place for you to stay may be hard to find in Prestwick. Would you like a farmhouse nearer me but further from the town? I might manage that more easily but some of these dour Scots frighten me. Perhaps the Colonel's name would help. Write soon and tell me what you would like. In a hotel we would probably have more privacy if it were wet and it often is here, but a farm I think is always nice.

10.15pm. Bathed and in bed now dear. Lovely clean white sheets, and they are sort of corrugated, herring-bone fashion and it feels just marvellous. Never seen any like this before, have you?

On Thursday Tony, Ruth and I had a little celebration. Tony and I decided to have some supper and drinks at a rather nice little pub here and then go on to the flics. But, before we started, I picked them up at their little home or rather their half a house and brought a bottle of rye with me. (Remember we had a rye highball at Torquay?) And we nearly finished the bottle before we left for supper—three quarters of an hour later. It was a wonderful evening.

We just got in to the flics and just in time for the film—'Road to Singapore'—and just got a bus back in time for the rest of the bottle. I left at 11.30 and got a WAT [Women's Air Transport] to give me a lift half the way—she sounded very nice and intelligent, even London-ish—and walked the rest. I was very tired but very happy when I crawled into bed. Nice Tony, nice Ruth, I thought, but Diana better than any of them: sorry about these muddled sheets [the pages are out of sequence] but the other is still wet and I can't wait for it to dry, and too lazy to get out of bed for the blotting paper.

Darling, then you phoned. I love you so and love you so that when you ask 'Do you want me' (to come up here) in that soft tone of voice, I nearly go mad. I dare not tell you how much I want to see you, be 'us' again: I dare not encourage you or tempt you to do what may be wrong or may be bad for you, your health (it is a dreadful journey) or against your parents' wishes. We might go mad when we must keep sane.

Must go to sleep now, my love, my fiancée, soon-to-be-wife, my darling, my betrothed, my beloved. I love them all.

I, too, can feel a calm triumphant content inside. It quietly goes on and yet grows surer every day. How nice it is to feel really engaged. Just one step more—

Goodnight my sweet, my all. All me. xx Bob.

11th August, 1940. 10pm. In bed. Well darling you are just now in bed in Mullion, I expect. Wish I were, too: instead of shut away in the remotest corner of England [actually Scotland]. And it has been cold here today. Fine, but cold as October. Hope I come South for the rest of my training—more than one reason. If and when you come up, please bring warm things, won't you dear? It's very chilly when out of the sun. Let me know soon if your parents think it proper and will let you come. Wish I could get weekend leave and we could go over to Arran. Anyhow during the day I shall have to work, if I do I can probably get off about 3–4. Today I left at 3. But one never knows: the RAF do things so suddenly.

Had a walk round this evening with a co-billetee: we got within about 12 feet of a rabbit. Then we ravaged the kitchen garden, scrounging bits from everywhere—this between season gives little fruit but we had a greengage, white raspberries, red currants, two plums, a carrot, peas, gooseberries, raspberries and a few strawberries and finally an apple. Sounds a lot but they all took a lot of finding. Later we went and ate a little wheat and the lovely golden field reminded me that I always thought it would make a lovely decoration in a modern flat—tall vase with corn and perhaps white or blue or deep red flowers—lilies, cornflowers or montbretia—is it out now in Cornwall?

What grows there now? Chrysanthemums I suppose but what is there Cornish? All my typical Cornwall flowers are over. The thrift, veronica, fuchsia and hedgerow flowers.

And how does the Island look?* Revisit it for me and the little pool the other side. Is it still capped with a forest of giant weeds? Last time I was there—about five or six years ago—it was covered with those huge hollow things all dry and crackly. Where is your house? What I can remember of the village is this.

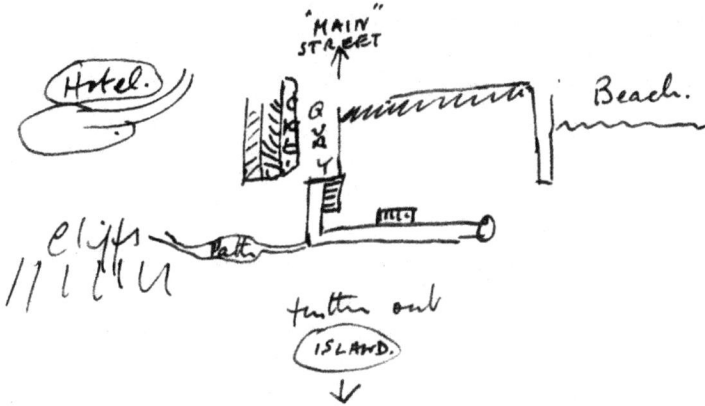

My memory is very clear on the details but no coherent whole stands out: I cannot see clearly the relationship of places to each other. I remember the little rocky path round the cliff from off the quayside. We once had lunch up there and fed thousands of gulls.

There is a funny smell in this room, I get it faintly nearly every evening and can't find where it comes from—sheets, pyjamas, pen, paper or what. The smell is of rubbed chests and warm camphor oil!

My book reading seems to have turned romantic. At the moment, I am immersed in George Moore's 'Héloïse et Abélard' and have just started too Stefan Zweig's 'Marie Antoinette'.

The parachute jump—I've just remembered. I never did it: was going to but it never came off. I would have told you all about it when it was all over ... women get such funny ideas in their heads.

Your last letter, how sweet your mother is about us: both our parents really only want our happiness. We forget that sometimes, I think. And your aunt too, I'd like to thank her for her kind words ... I've no doubt they helped.

And now for sleep. Flying all day makes me tired. Tomorrow a letter from you? Please darling. You, poor dear, will have to wait a day or so, then probably get two. I love you, still my angel. Get better quick. God bless you. Always and ever your Bob xxxxxxx

---

* The 'Island' was at Mullion Cove, where Diana and Jean spent many family holidays. The young girls boated, picnicked and swam. Diana was proud to have swum around the island.

LETTER TO DIANA:

Monktonhead
12th August, 1940

My dear, this is a bitter letter—sad news so be you brave. The 24th I am afraid will be impossible: we learnt today that we are going somewhere else that weekend—probably on the Saturday. And, please, that information must go no further than your parents. Oh darling, it is too bad, unkind, cruel. Yet do you remember that when you could not come to Hastings it was a fore-runner of better things? Let us hope that I come nearer. We do not know yet where and will probably not be told until the day we leave.

Diana dear, I was cold and furious inside when I heard the news but now only cold and sad. What is the good of even thinking of resisting the RAF? It means, too, more flying, more work. Today I had to fly again in the evening and it makes one very tired. Got back at 8pm weary and irritable and lay on my bed and snoozed. I wondered then what you would think when we are married and, having waited all day for me to come home, I just put my feet up and sleep. I'm not as bad as that, though; after half-an-hour life and movement return to the corpse.

But, darling, you have been warned, there are my dangerous moments when I'm really irritable and will you forgive anything I may say then? It won't be meant and I shall regret it.

LETTER TO DIANA:

Monktonhead
13th August, 1940

10.45pm. Writing relations ... 'thank you very much' ... flying until 7.30 ... very tired ... Goodnight my darling, my own ... I love you, love you, love you more and more each day.

All your Bob xxx

9.45pm. 14th August. Just in the middle of writing more thank yous. How kind people are to write but what a time it takes to reply. They are just playing Tchaikovsky's B minor piano concerto, one of my favourite pieces of music. It always takes me right out of myself—sensual, beautiful music. It makes me want you, too, and you are so far away. Oh darling, darling, Diana darling. Must write more relations now ... I tried and I can't: this music sends shivers through one. So many memories.

10.35pm. Now in bed. Written five letters. Not too bad but perhaps there will be some more to answer tomorrow. Darling, is there going to be an announcement in The Times—anything about us? I must buy a copy that day! Will post this tomorrow short as it is, then you will get it before the weekend.

We have had a most exciting day today. Some German parachutes were found at a lonely farm this morning and we have been flying low over the roads and moors all day looking for parachutists. If we saw anything suspicious, we flew until we found a nearby police car or soldiers and directed them to the spot by signs and diving. But they have found no-one yet even though at least seven parachutes have been recovered. Perhaps it has only been done to puzzle us. It's so odd that seven Germans should just vanish. The aerodrome is very strongly guarded tonight. The only excitement we've had up here!*

I hope you have recovered from the coughs and the train journey. You will find peace and happiness in Mullion, even though you may ache inside. Hastings did it for me. Stay down there until you are quite well—I hope you didn't tell your mother and father you wanted to come up here before I wrote that it would be impossible.

I'm glad I can't see you thinner because I like you as you are or were?—not fatter nor thinner.

Just heard tonight that cream is to be rationed or rather banned. How awful, Cornwall without cream—it will hardly be worth living there.

I like the Fosters more and more—are they relations of yours?—nice of her to defend you against the old lady Heigham. Do they really feel that Tom [Heigham, to whom Diana was close] has been unjustly done by?

It makes me so proud that you should light on me when these more accomplished 'worldly wise' gentlemen run after you. You ought to take me down a peg—I feel like saying 'I'm sorry this is my wife-to-be. You may admire but I warn you, she is mine, mine, mine and I am hers.'

Just after 11. Must go to sleep. Darling fiancée, Goodnight. Sleep well ... We see the same sea, more or less, even if we are seven hundred miles away. We shall see each other soon, I feel it. 'Faith, hope and love, and the greatest of these is love.' I love you dearest always and forever. And get well soon. Lots and lots of love and kisses. Your own Bob.

LETTER TO DIANA:

> No 2 Lecture Room
> Prestwick Aerodrome
> 14th August, 1940

Darling, I had about half a dozen letters today from relations and friends that Mother has told: shall have to answer them all tonight and will probably get little time to write to you. Your letter arrived this morning and made me very envious of you in the sun and peace of Mullion.

---

* The Glasgow newspapers reported that an enemy aircraft was heard over south-west Scotland during the night but no bombs were dropped. Twenty-nine parachutes with an eagle stamp were found although they were not the same as those used by Germans during the invasion of the Low Countries a few weeks earlier. No parachutists were found. It was concluded that the parachutes had been dropped to frighten the public. A farmer's wife said that, if that was their objective, 'they have completely failed'.

15th August, 1940. That was yesterday and I left this in my note-book. It is now really the 16th 0045 hours i.e. a quarter to one. We are doing a little night flying. Feel very sleepy. Went to bed for an hour or so with an alarm to wake me at 11.45pm. Dressed and walked down here to the aerodrome.

Never stop writing to me dearest—your letters only bring me sorrow that I cannot write as much to you. I love your letters, all of them ... you cannot write too much. They seem to bring us closer together for a while and I can more easily be with you. I read them again and again.

The letter post-marked Mullion 4.45pm Tuesday got here today (Thursday morning). If you are afraid of missing me with a letter, Mrs Connal will always forward it and I'll leave my address. Funny you should send me heather, I had just picked a tiny sprig of white heather for luck when we met the postman. Will see if I can get some more varieties. Must go and fly (literally) now. Goodbye darling. Goodnight or good morning my betrothed. I love you still, even now. I'm yours, all yours, to do with at your will. 'Knock and it shall be opened unto you.'

xxxx Bob

16th August. 11.30am. Hello darling, up and dressed again, but missed my breakfast: I shall be ravenous by lunch time—only an hour to wait. Last night was very interesting and good fun, but I expect the novelty soon wears off. The lights of the flare path to land and take off, the searchlight and the red, white and green lights of the aircraft made a lovely sight. To see a red and green light gradually growing larger and further apart, then suddenly an aeroplane appears lit in the beam of the landing searchlight.

You sit in your aeroplane by the side of the flare path with lights arranged like this . . . . ⋅ with a hundred yards between each. They are not flares but dim lights to show the line you must land on and take off. (The man in charge of them is known as 'Paraffin Pete'—a relic of an earlier age.) From where you are waiting you flash to the officer in charge (he is by the searchlight) your identification letter in morse •–•• [dot dash dot dot is the letter L in morse code]. If you get it returned in green you taxi to the starting point and take off. To land you again flash your letter and, when you get the green reply, you may come in. The tricky part comes next. You have to judge your approach so that you land just by the first lamp and, as soon as you get there, the searchlight is turned full on down the line of your landing. All the instruments are luminous and present a weird sight.

Your letter arrived this morning, again it seems to get here the morning but one after you post it in the afternoon. The silly maid came in at eight o'clock and woke me up and I cursed until I realised it was your letter. I read it and promptly fell asleep again.

This leave business is very vague but we have heard that we should get weekend leave at our next school. Proper leave will not be given until we leave there—in about two months' time now.

Lovely and exciting these thoughts of our new life of us-to-be. I, too, am not afraid but have the same sort of feeling as when one goes in for some test that you are sure of passing. We can and will succeed, but we shall have more worries and difficulties. But how nice to be the two of us to surmount them and how much better to feel that together we will have done it. I long to start but am content to wait until the day. Waiting gives time to think ahead, prepare oneself and the sweet delights of imagination.

We finish flying tomorrow. All next week we have to 'cram' and swot for our exams. I am fairly certain to get through but high marks mean better chances later, and I hate to be 'bottom boy'.

Oh dearest, I long to see you once again and pray that I may be sent south for my next course. If we were only within reach of London and can get weekend leave. Too good to think upon. Patience, patience is the only remedy. It's good for us, both of us, to have to wait, we are too impatient always. But I cannot. Must get ready for lunch now. Still loving you, my sweet. Always and forever yours, Bob xxx

LETTER TO DIANA:

Monktonhead
18th August, 1940

10.30pm. My dear, two days and I have not written one word to you. Two whole days and not a line. My reasons, darling (I know you won't want them, but here they are), my reasons are that on Friday I felt so full of headaches and funny inside that I just had a cup of tea and some aspirin when I got back (at 7pm) and went straight to bed and slept until nearly 7am the next morning. And yesterday I felt so well and rested: I flew in the morning and was allowed to just do what I liked as I had passed my tests and just had to do two hours flying.

I climbed up through a gap in the clouds and left the dismal grey of the wet day below for the white and mountainous country of the above-the-clouds. It was gorgeous and quite warm too as the sun was shining brilliantly there. I shouted and sang for pure joie de vivre and just threw the aeroplane in rolls and loops and spins and then flew about upside down for a change.

In the afternoon we had classes and I arranged for eight of us including Tony and Ruth to have a farewell evening in Ayr. We don't go till Friday but we have exams all this week so we shall be 'swotting' and not feeling like going out. We had some steaks and drinks, a flic and more drinks at Tony's place. We 'commandeered' cars in the car park to come home and eventually got back about 1pm [sic].

I was too tired and incoherent, no, not incoherent but my brain was a little muddled—to write to you then: and I remembered then that the last time—in Hastings—that I wrote to you while not quite my normal self I was so ashamed of the letter that it never got posted.

There, my sweetheart it has taken two pages to make my excuses, so I must have a bad conscience. Am I forgiven? I know I need not ask, but I feel so guilty receiving a letter from you every day nearly and then I go two whole days without writing you a line at all. Anyway here's this to welcome you back to Essex.

Now here is some confidential rumour for you. It is said that we shall be going to either somewhere near Moretonhampstead [in Devon] but, more likely, to somewhere near Bath. They are but rumours, so you must take this with a pinch of salt and please don't tell anyone—in case they were true: it's funny how these things can get about. I am liable for the maximum penalty—death, I found out—revealing any service information 'which may directly or indirectly assist the enemy'.

My poor darling, your letter made me very sad. I hate to think of you unhappy and not at peace with your parents. (Hell, just made a large blot of ink on the clean sheet. The maid will curse me to blazes tomorrow.) And I think you are not quite doing me justice 'your family mean more to you than mine'. You know all this me is mine no longer: I have given it to us and if need be would forsake all for our sake. But, so used to my own impetuosity, I cannot, dare not risk everything. No, not everything.

What am I trying to say?—To look further ahead—if we got married without our parents' consent, they would not completely ignore us but it would hurt them a lot and for ever there would be a small barrier between us. I could bear that for you and more but we might grow to hate ourselves for it, and, if I had to go abroad and you might in all probability have to stay behind, I should then hate to leave you anywhere but with your family or mine. But sweetheart, please think twice of the us-to-be: Joad (Professor) says that 'civilization is the ability to defer enjoyment', quite a profound remark.* Think of us in a year, five, ten years' time as well as in the next few months.

Now, thank heaven, that is over: hate me if you will for writing it, for being mother, father, teacher and moralist all in one. I know you are tempestuous and I love you for it, would not have you otherwise but I could not bear to see you ever reproach yourself for what you had done for me. My days are full, too, and longing for you cannot be intense all day long as it is for you: you suffer dear, and I suffer for you but can you bear with it a little longer?

I must get some leave from the next school—we have so much to talk about, there is so much I want to tell and hear and ask, and there is so much that we have got to see of each other's family that I am afraid that we shall be left such a little space together.

Just traced the 'camphorated oil' smell. It is the ink in my pen—'Quink'! How funny. I must be very unobservant.

---

* Professor Cyril E. M. Joad, head of the philosophy department at Birkbeck College, University of London.

Sir Walford Davies* on the wireless today quoted 'a high churchman is an altitudinarian, a broad-churchman is a latitudinarian and a low churchman is a platitudinarian'. I have been laughing at it all day, and so did the Colonel when I told him but I think it is a joke more appreciated by a man than a woman. Why I don't know—what do you think?

Must go to sleep now: it is 11.30 and we start revision tomorrow and exams at odd times on Tues, Wed, and Thurs. When I shall pack I don't know. Will let you know as soon as I know my new address, and will anyhow try and write again in a day or so.

Darling you really have all my love all me, my life that was. You are my present and future and you are me. I'll even be virtuous for you although you say you suppose husbands needn't be. Not that I think I am ever likely to be tempted—I would not have asked you to marry me if I did. Really, sleep, I must. I love you xxx Bob

LETTER TO DIANA:

Monktonhead
20th August, 1940

10.30pm. In bed. The wind is whistling round the house and edge of the windows, rumbling up the chimney and shaking the door. It is wild and blustery out, some driving rain now and again, streaks of scraggy clouds racing to their destinations. This is a cold country: I shall be glad to come south but hope it is far enough south. Around Liverpool again would be worse than this. It is at least clean here. We shall not know where we are going until Friday midday or soon after. And we may leave that evening or Saturday or Sunday. It is just possible that I may be able to get some hours in London or even get home but it's most unlikely. Still there is the faint hope and if I can I shall come.

Mother is at Immingham at the moment and I've just scribbled her a postcard telling her but said that if Dick is free [she should] stay there. When you get this it may be Saturday morning already and Mother may be already home if you want to ring up. But Miss Ladner, you are not to miss morning school on that faint excuse ... love, honour and ...?

John has been nice and singing your praises to Mother: she respects his opinion and above all common sense. Oh dearest must go to sleep now. Hope and pray for a move to the south but dare not hope very much because all the aerodromes down there are being bombed and that would interrupt our training. If we go to Canada which is unlikely I will let you know as soon as I can but I'm pretty sure wives are not allowed. You might not be able to get back too!

Darling, goodnight. I hope and pray for just a few minutes soon. God bless you, I love you so, all you's. I must see you soon. Your xxx Bob

---

*   Sir Henry Walford Davies KCVO OBE, Master of the King's Music.

10pm. 21st August. Dearest, tonight finished swotting in the evening for a little while. The day after tomorrow we have the last three exams. I'm glad of that: life is a little easier at our SFTS [Service Flight Training School] and after six weeks there we should be finished with exams. It is almost impossible to find out when we are likely to pass out but it seems that we shall be fully qualified service pilots in about three and a half months' time—depending, of course, on the progress and development of the war.

It seems probable that I may get a weekend or two off at the SFTS but whether it will be any good or not depends on where I go. Leave we'll probably get at the end of the three and a half months, but we might be speeded up to three months. I think we might ask to have our wedding (oh lovely words!) provisionally fixed for then. What do you think? And what do you think your parents will say?

Your last two letters have made me very happy. I was a little worried when you seemed so distressed. I expect my last letter annoyed or aggravated quite a bit. I'm sorry, darling, but still abide by what I said. We have too much at stake ... life is a gamble, I know, but I like the dice loaded in my favour, if possible.

I cannot advise you as to clothes. I know you always please me, whatever you wear even if it is done up with pins!* And I think you like my favourite colours for 'heavier' clothes—dark greens, browns and some reds—I like square-ish shoes, 'tough' looking ones, perhaps with crepe soles, suede. I like pleated skirts for afternoon and smart frocks, sometimes tailor-made's. I like jumpers and trousers too—you can wear them—for knocking about in. I don't think I'm fond of satin. I like black or dark skirts with bright tops. I like American clothes especially printed dresses and shoes. I like clothes from Dickens and Jones. Dolcis shoes. That is all I can think of offhand. Is it any guide? I shouldn't trouble about it anyway if I were you. I put full faith in your choice and eye for colours at all times.

The faint hope of seeing you within the next few days has been in my mind all the time I've been writing this and I've tried to shut it out, but it will have none of it. It is such a faint possibility yet I can't keep my heart from hoping ... I have nearly two more days of suspense—it is worse than the exam, hoping against hope. I shall probably be on my way to John O'Groats!

Poor Tony and Ruth: wives are not even 'encouraged' to live near the aerodrome at the SFTS. Tony said that the whole of the RAF administrative side ought to have been quite dead by now—after Ruth had had her say. So it is no good marrying me for at least two months!

Payday tomorrow: always a welcome occasion. Did you know you are marrying a husband who is still in debt to his tailor and, I believe, his garage? My family would be scandalised if they knew—but it feels almost a crime to pay one's tailor for at least six months and this time, when the time came, I had no money. However your husband will be solvent by the time he marries you. And

---

*   Diana created outfits by adding ribbons or fabric to the clothes in her wardrobe.

you had better from the start demand his pay and only give him his pocket money for money in his pocket—money to be spent and soon vanish. If you are like that too, heaven knows what we shall do!

Must go to sleep now—11 o'clock—only two or three more days up here. Perhaps ... perhaps ...

All my love, all me, sweetheart and I hope and pray for us. I still love you and love you more each day. Can there be no limit? It would seem not. Keep well, keep happy, three months is not so very long—I've been three months in the RAF now.

Darling yours faithfully (so far) your Bob xxxxx

◊♦◊

After such a comfortable billet in beautiful surroundings, on Friday 23 August Bob travelled south with little idea of what awaited him.

11

Last night your voice, tonight your letter—so near, yet so far

LETTER TO DIANA:

> LAC WARK* No 904036
> Room 4 Block 47
> 3SFTS, RAF South Cerney
> Cirencester Glos.
> 25th August, 1940

My darling, this place is hell after Prestwick and I'm so tired I can hardly write. But had to write to you if only to tell of our troubles and find comfort in the telling. We shall soon get used to it but after the 'holiday' we have been having this place is grim.

We travelled all Friday night and I could not sleep. We started at 9pm and changed at Kilmarnock, Carlisle, Crewe, Birmingham and Cheltenham. I'll tell you more about that another time, because there will be little news in this hole. We got here at about 2.30pm and were met at the station by a lorry with a flight sergeant (RAF equivalent of an army company sergeant major) who started cursing us before the lorry had stopped moving.

And now for the worst. No leave at all—not even evening passes. We work all day—start work at 7am, finish 4pm or 6pm alternate days and seven days a week with no half-days. We live in barracks twenty to a room and the food is poor. Discipline is strict—I could have sat down and wept. Tony has gone to Bedfordshire but this place is only about six miles from his home. That is about the only redeeming feature for me. I may be able to have a meal up there now and again. Ruth will probably be there as wives are not 'encouraged' to live near. Marriages are not allowed while here.

That seems to be the total of our miseries, but we ought to have expected this. Oh, I forgot, last night, our first night's rest for forty-eight hours, we had an air

---

* Leading Aircraftman W. A. R. Keddie.

raid warning from 10pm to 5am. Nothing happened, so I stole back to bed from the shelter at about 11.30. I hope there isn't one tonight.

Don't worry for me, once I get settled, routine effaces the little annoyances—and I hate change anyhow, the trouble was I had such high hopes for this place. The flying is quite good though—twin-engine aeroplanes, weighing about two to three tons. I shall finish on bombers, reconnaissance and flying boats from here. I sometimes wish I were going on fighters though—but it doesn't pay to have preferences. Now I want to get into flying boats (be stationed at Mount Batten?!)*

Dearest, must sleep now. Oh I love you so and because it is so impossible to be with you it only hurts the more. I shall be here three months. Oh God give me patience. One good thing, no time to think! Darling Diana xxx, don't stop loving me will you? Ever yours, Bob

PS Forgive this wailing and brief letter: too fed up to be interesting or readable. xxxxxxx

LETTER TO DIANA:

South Cerney
27th August, 1940

Last night your voice and tonight your letter—darling, they bring you so near—so tantalising and yet so far. I like to think of you at Downham, wandering around the places I know and love.

But—before I forget—the trains. They are not so good as I thought but they are not too bad, although you cannot just come down for a day as the last train leaves at 7.35 on Sunday.

I know no relations here unfortunately—the only people I know are Tony's: if I go up there this weekend or next week and Ruth is there, I'll mention that you are probably coming down—but then wouldn't that be more improper than ever?

It never dawns on me what is proper and what is not. What people do is no concern of mine and especially people who love one another should be guided by their consciences, their feelings for themselves, for each other and their own conception of God.

I know there must be some 'code' for a civilised society and that some things would certainly shock me, but, to me, whether or not people in love sleep together before they are married is purely between themselves. I may be blasphemous and I know many people would disapprove—Mother included—but it conforms to my idea of God and His wishes.

However, trains:

---

* RAF Mount Batten on Plymouth Sound, near the nursing home run by Diana's aunts.

<u>Leaving</u> Paddington 9.15, arriving Cirencester 12.03
                  Paddington 1.55, Cirencester 4.33
                  Paddington 6.30, Cirencester 9.03

I think all these trains run Friday too. The train leaving Cirencester 7.35pm arrives Pad'n 10.15. Monday morning 8.00am arrives Pad'n 10.55 and the 9.55 at 12.45. Well, dearest, there they all are. But if you come this weekend it will be a gamble because our lectures may be changed on Sunday. However, I shall be off at 4.00 on Saturday.

No time to write more, getting dark, and we've no black-out [curtain].

Dearest you know I love you forever. I think Patsy is right, you should go out—if only to see who else much worse you might have married! I feel much happier here after phoning you. I went 'solo' today, the first of our course. Love, love and love. All me in thee. xxx Bob

LETTER TO DIANA:

South Cerney
28th August, 1940

8.10pm. Not much light left now, but just enough to thank you for the letter that has come back from Prestwick. There is no news, dear, except one extraordinary coincidence. My instructor's name is Shaw, he is a flying officer and lives in Little Baddow, he has just got engaged and his sister went to school with you! Isn't that marvellous? It is a sort of bond between us and I get on very well with him. He is extraordinarily nice: very quiet and even-tempered. Dark, rather 'monkeyish' face and a charming smile. Do you know him at all? He can't recollect you. I felt quite annoyed with him that he didn't.

You make me long to meet your mother, I'm sure I should be charmed—but a lot of people have 'charmed' me and I only hope we are never at cross-purposes. I too can be very self-willed once my mind is made up. Can't see now, too dark. I love you darling. Goodnight my own. Your, Bob. xxx

29th August, 1940. Aerodrome 'somewhere in England'. 9.30am. Sitting on our aerodrome—it is away from the real aerodrome at So. Cerney and we all (instructors, pupils and timekeepers) fly here in the morning and do our flying from here because So. Cerney is too crowded.

It is a comic little place: there are three tin sheds, a few tents and half-a-dozen Spitfires for defence purposes. It is very new and very much more informal than the 'real' aerodrome. We sit about on the ground waiting to fly—there are only twenty-five of us altogether and there is a small canteen run for the Spitfire people where we can get tea, chocolate, fruit and cigarettes. Out here is the most pleasant part of our new station.

So here am I, 9.30 in the morning waiting for my aeroplane to come down in time for me to go up. My instructor is sitting on the top of a step-ladder two or three yards away reading a book. It is all very peaceful. I wish you were here to see us—in fact I wish you were here anyhow for no reason at all and for every reason. Oh, darling, when will we be able to look forward to each other at the end of the day?

Did I tell you that we might get some leave in about ten or eleven weeks from now? It is possible that we should get a week then, but one can never be sure—as we know already to our cost. Would you like to get married then or wait until I get leave again after that? The trouble is I shall not know if I am going to get leave until almost the day before it happens. Life is hard in the RAF—but this is war not peace.

Did I tell you too that I might get a commission when I leave here—some people do? Also I believe that, if I'm living out (as a pilot officer), I get £24 a month living expenses—with 12/6^d a day pay. That means nearly £500 a year but I then have some messing bills and have to buy my own clothes.

I lay in bed last night and thought of you receiving my telephone call—Patsy's excited shout and I imagined them all bundling out of the room and Mrs S-P probably wishing she could listen through the keyhole—not that she would, she is much too good a sport—and then Patsy's annoyance if she did. It kept me amused for some time.

30th August, 1940. Friday evening 6.45pm. Well darling, I wonder whether you will be coming tomorrow or not. I found out last night that, when and if I get into the officer's mess, I shall probably be able to stay out a bit later than 10pm. Not officially, but it is just one of those things that happens.

Another air-raid last night: I look forward to them now because I don't get up unless the flight sergeant calls me (and I return as soon as I can) and, in the morning, they usually put back reveille for an hour or more. Today we missed drill at 7am, which only happens once a week. We were very thankful.

Very warm flying today, I am trying to get a picture postcard of the machine I'm flying to send you. It's quite a large affair and has between thirty and forty instruments to look after. They are quite good fun.

I spoke to my instructor today about getting on to flying boats. He said that only a very few—the best of the pilots—get on to them, but I've not given up hope. I think my flying is as good as anybody's here. It would mean another ten weeks training, but as an officer. What will probably happen when I leave here is that I shall get posted somewhere else and they will probably give me one leave from there—so I should be able to find out beforehand whether we could live out or not because I think it would be wrong to get married on a week's leave and then have to live apart again for another two or three months, don't you?

There is just no news in this place. Must do a little work now before it gets dark. Darling, come and see me soon, if you can. I could fix a place for you in Cirencester but remember, in three weeks' time, I should be able to stay out later.

Diana dearest, I'm longing for you, for us to be us, and loving you more and more all your Bob.

P.S. I feel envious of 'the man' and sometimes a little jealous but I think he is good for you. The more men you see and prefer me to, the bigger my value, do you see? And it tickles my vanity!! xxxxxxxx

LETTER TO DIANA:

1st September, 1940

1.40pm. Sitting in the gun-turret of my aeroplane while we prepare to do a cross country trip—Henley on Thames, Bedford and back. Just going to pass over aerodrome at 200ft, 140 mph. Have got to mark our route on the map.

1.45pm. On our way.

2pm. Over Henley.

8.15pm. At three o'clock we were back home again. Was too busy marking our route to write anymore and, at half-way, I had to fly the rest. Tomorrow we go for a trip round most of Wales. Just think, in an hour I could be at Downham or Waterhall.

I shall be off next Saturday and Sunday at four o'clock. Oh damn! It's getting dark and I've got quite a lot to say. Some good news for you and some bad. It is rumoured and, my instructor says he thinks it is true, that sometime in the future we shall get a day, even two days, off, but what is bad is that he says that, if the war gets fiercer, he thinks we shall get no leave at all and we shall be lucky if we get two or three days when we leave here. Oh darling, can't see what I'm writing now.

Darling, I want you so and if I weren't so busy I think I should go crazy. My dear fiancée, I live for you and for us. Can you come and see me in three weeks' time?

Goodnight my dear, keep well and God bless you. My love as always, your Bob

LETTER TO DIANA:

2nd September, 1940

6pm. Darling, sitting now in my aeroplane waiting for it to be filled with petrol and oil before I put it away for the night, so I hope you don't mind this paper. On the other side you can see where we went: left at 13.54 and back again by 15.22. Most of the places are in Wales.

Here is the petrol wagon just arrived towed by the trailer. Wonder if there will be a letter from you when I get in. Hope so.

I am sorry my letters now all seem to be on odd scraps of paper and are disjointed, but we have such little time free, although we sometimes have some time on duty but doing nothing.

FROM	TO	True Air Speed	Mag Track	Dis-tance	Height	Mag Course	Ground Speed	Time	E.T.A.
BASE	SYMONDS YAT	130	300	32	800'	299	120	16	14.10
MONDS YAT	TREDEGAR	130	271	27	1600'	272°	121	14	14.24
TEDEGAR	HAY	130	023	26	2000'	019°	130	12	14.36
HAY	LUDLOW	130	051°	26	800'	046°	135	12	14.57
LUDLOW	WIRCESTER	130	131°	25	600'	132°	140	11	14.56
WORCESTER	BASE	130	170°	37	1000'	175°	135·1	17	15.22

Route and Orders :—

WIND 10/290

13.56

Route Forecast—see Form 2330.

Time	Position	Mag Course	Distance Run	Ground Speed	E.T.A.	Observation

Date............ Aeroplane............ Pilot............

Sent a letter to your aunt yesterday and as soon as I get time will write Jean. I don't quite know what to say. How does one address one's future sister-in-law?

3rd September, 1940. Again in the old gun-turret. Just done my cross-country test and the other lad is now doing his. Must post these odd scraps of paper tonight. Never got tea until 7.15 yesterday and it was dark by the time I was fed and washed. That's the curse of this place: rushed from one thing to another ... Must do my log now. Oh Diana darling, I love you so. Please God we shall soon be us. Keep well, and be good x x x all yours Bob

LETTER TO DIANA:

South Cerney
4th September, 1940

7.30am. Still feeling very sleepy: in the signals lecture room and the instructor hasn't turned up yet. Don't think I can really write a letter now but it seems too good an opportunity to waste. I got two letters from you yesterday—lovely surprise—one in the morning and the other in the afternoon. Went swimming yesterday evening so that they can choose a team to represent the station on Thursday against an Army team. I put my name down because I hoped to get off some work. After swimming we had a few drinks and then some eggs and bacon before we came back.

Dearest I agree with you—go in the shelter when the raids come. Fatalism is a nice comfortable philosophy but, if carried to its logical conclusion, means that all effort of resistance is futile. If there is a bomb or shell or bullet marked with Patsy's name or yours or mine, what need have we of any defence of our own. Cure her of the habit if you can—it's bad and defeatist. Not that, at times, it isn't safe to watch the raids—with a tin hat on—but is she in a place to judge? Tell her from me that I think she's either stupid or lazy—stupid if she knows what she is doing and is arguing for and lazy if she hasn't bothered to think it all out. I bet the latter. That ought to rouse her. I know that I don't go in the shelter here sometimes when we have a raid warning, but I should jolly soon go down if they came near us.

It is such a lovely day now: you must come here while the weather holds. I've been trying to look out good fields and woods and rivers to walk by—from the air. This is a lovely part of England. Oh come soon darling, can you, will you come this weekend? I wonder. Will you get my last letter in time to let me know? Let me know in time won't you otherwise I might have gone out for the evening. Tony is probably coming down this weekend and I shall probably see him in Cirencester on Saturday evening.

7.45pm. Now bathed—feel marvellously cool again. Will post this tomorrow morning as I shall have no time to write tomorrow.

Just starting to get dark now—it gets earlier each day. We never realise how the year goes by and how near now the fall is. (Don't you much prefer 'fall' to 'autumn': it's so expressive—a beautiful word.)

Found a lovely avenue of trees out of Cirencester today: it looks marvellous. We must walk up there when you get down here. It looked so cool, inviting and as if it had stood for years and years. Only trouble being that I expect half Cirencester will be there on a Saturday or Sunday.

Hell, people keep talking to me and it's getting darker and darker. Oh darling, I long for you so much: to soothe and caress me when I've finished work. To look forward to the evening with you. Home ... home ... our home. Dearest, I too want and want till it hurts. Too dark to write more. I love you still, my dear.

LETTER TO DIANA:

South Cerney
6th September, 1940

Darling, you would have laughed to have seen me last night. Got back from the swimming at 10:15 and found your letter on my bed. I took it into the bathroom and, with my feet in the basins and head jammed against the ceiling, I just managed to read it by the dark blue bulb! So pleased to get your letter and the lucky heather. This morning I put a piece of it in the wallet I won at swimming last night. I hope you're proud of your fiancé: he won the races! I got a cigarette lighter which I exchanged for the wallet, an address book (must now start with a clean slate, having written off all the old girlfriends!) and two chromium-backed hairbrushes in a leather case. Hope to give those away someday—I hate chromium.

When I said I could fix you with somewhere to stay I'm afraid I had rather skipped the propriety or not of it—I only meant rooms or an hotel. The only suggestion at the moment is with the wife of one of the fellows here. Would that be alright? Otherwise it will have to be the mayor! The best weekend for me would be the 21st.

Getting very dark now, that's a bit better—writing on the window sill. I hardly know how I should like you best—white or all modern; what do you think, dearest? Perhaps white is more traditional and significant. One thing I do know is that I should like it to be a very quiet wedding, wouldn't you? Who will officiate? I believe it is all the bride's responsibility (or rather her parents!) but if you want anybody I know Canon Morrow would do the job. He is an old friend of ours and married Mother and Father. However that side of it is none of my business!

Diana dear I hate to think of you in the midst of these air raids and wish I were there to comfort you and hold you tight. We get very few daylight raids but one or two solitary machines drone about at night. Too dark for more, dearest: Oh my love and all me, take care of yourself and God bless you. xxxxx your Bob

LETTER TO DIANA:

South Cerney
7th September, 1940

4.45pm. My dear, just going into the town for some food, a bathe and a haircut—weekend 'refresher'. Next weekend I don't think would be so bad after all, it seems quite probable that I could get off at 4 on the Sunday as well. If you are coming, let me know quickly and I'll phone next Friday night of what I can find for you to stay. I flew today to Peterboro' and Grantham and back.

There are people now throwing stones at my window to make me come out.

Darling goodbye for the present. I live and dream for the day when we will no longer have to say goodbye. My love to your parents and Patsy and for you, as always, all me dearest, my love, your Bob

◊♦◊

On 7 September the Germans launched the first mass bombing of London. The Blitz had started.

12

There's a glorious moon—oh, why aren't you here?

Letter to Diana:

South Cerney
8th September, 1940

6pm. Just been listening to the news—the first 'official' of yesterday's raids that I've heard. They really seem to be getting under way for the invasion now. Darling, I hope you didn't get any of the 'backwash' from the raids. I always feel that you are in a sort of secondary target area if they can't get to London. You will be careful, dear, won't you? We've had nothing here except solitary raiders at night. Occasionally they drop a bomb here or there but as often as not they don't even wake us up. So don't worry for me.

Last night I met Tony in Cirencester as he was having drinks with a fellow from the course in front of us and Tony asked me to dinner and to go into Cheltenham with them afterwards. When I told him I had to be back at 10 pm, the other fellow said that if I get in about 12 you could nearly always get away with it.

To cut a long story short I went and had an awfully nice dinner with his people and Ruth and afterwards we went into Cheltenham (Tony, Ruth and Tony's half sister) and met another couple in a pub. There had a few more drinks and finished at Cheltenham's makeshift nightclub. Got back to camp about twelve and unluckily for me got 'nabbed' and put in the guard room: but I got away with it by saying that we had been into Cheltenham and had been detained by the LDV [Local Defence Volunteers]! So, in future, when you come down I think it is worth trying again, don't you?

This new development and intensification of aerial war is going to spoil all leave I'm afraid darling. All leave was cancelled yesterday and I expect it will mean that our day off a week may be cancelled.

Another blow for you too: if I go into flying boats when I leave here, it will mean ten weeks' course at the air navigation school and I hear too that that is moving to Canada (keep this pretty quiet please!) However, it is quite possible that wives would be allowed too, although, of course, I expect they would have to make their own arrangements about getting across.

Well my Diana, I am afraid there are some bitter pills there for you and us. But, as usual, we must trust in our lucky star—it has been pretty good to us, so far. My poor instructor had got six days leave from next Sunday and was going to get married then and he is pretty fed up too. At the moment, too, we are not allowed out of camp: but I expect the scare will die down in a day or two.

Must stop now darling. To love you and leave you. How much longer must I leave you? Don't worry, I have patience although at times I get so furious with that man [Hitler] for stepping in and always spoiling what seemed like a good break for us. My darling, my own, goodnight and love to everybody. Always and every yours, Bob xxxx

10th September. 6.30pm. Sitting now in a little cafe in Cirencester and about to have some tea. Today was wet and cold this morning in contrast to the marvellous weather we've been having but the clouds lifted enough by ten o'clock for a little flying and we climbed up to about 5,000 feet right up into the sunshine with this floor of white mist below. It was exhilarating and grand. Like climbing a high mountain and suddenly looking around and seeing the glorious view on all sides.

It makes you want to do silly things in an aeroplane—to throw it about the sky round and round—sheer joy of living. It is in moments like these that I wish for you that you could be there to enjoy it all with me. And yesterday, too, when we flew over the Black Mountains in Wales. First crossing the Severn then over the Forest of Dean.

Two of us were with Shaw, being instructed in instrument flying. They put a hood over you and you have to fly on your instruments alone: it is not as easy as it sounds because sometimes you may feel that you are lying on one side and the instruments say you are on the other: then you must obey your instruments however strong the longing to do the opposite.

Anyhow the other fellow was under the hood on the way there and you can imagine his surprise to find himself cruising up a valley with mountains on either side. We went on then admiring the view with Shaw flying—sometimes just sliding a few feet (probably about 50) over some little ridge and all the time up and up to the tops of the peaks. (Please excuse the grease from my sandwiches—lettuce and cucumber.)

Once there, the view was marvellous all round and Shaw said he had often seen the Irish Sea from there. Then he cruised round the hills and up and down the ridges, from one valley to the next and I asked him if he had lost anything and he said he was looking for wild horses and courting couples—he had seen a lot of the latter a day or two before—'most interesting'. I laughed—a little self-consciously for I'd been thinking what a lovely spot for a honeymoon. We saw some horses—more like ponies—a bit later and then I went under the hood and we headed for home.

We are going to get our day a week off but when it will start we know not. Hope it will be Saturday week. Will you really come then? I had a brain-wave the other day: if your parents won't let you stay anywhere non-respectable, I'll ask the padre if he can't do something. Let me know what you think. I shan't be able to phone next Friday. Our phone is stopped for trunk [long distance] calls at night and I can't get out of camp that evening.

I think this shop is waiting to shut. Goodbye love, I hope to see you very soon now, and long for it each day. All my love and me. Your Bob xxx

LETTER TO DIANA:

South Cerney
15th September, 1940

6.45pm. Darling, just a line to let you know I'm quite alright. I go to the officers' mess tomorrow evening which should be very pleasant. I got back quite safely.* Tell you all about it another day. Must rush off now. Dearest my love as always. I felt so happy yesterday and a lot of it still remains.

All yours my Diana, forever, all my love xxx Bob

LETTER TO DIANA:

South Cerney
17th September, 1940

My darling, it seems ages since I last wrote to you and there is lots to tell so I'll start where we last left off being us …

The train was late at Shenfield and the connection didn't get there until nearly 5:30 but then the 'all clear' went and we whistled up to town. Just got up by 6:20 and I raced for a train but could not find one as the air raid warning had gone sometime before. In the end I didn't arrive at Paddington until nearly seven and the train, of course, had gone. The next one left at 8 so I went across the road to the forces canteen and had some supper. In the meantime the 'all clear' had gone. But a few minutes before the train pulled out we had another warning and so we rumbled on for miles at a snails pace. Eventually it arrived at Swindon at about 11:30 and I had to catch a taxi—catch is not the word, hunt is more like it!—and got back to camp just about 12.

I had lots of good stories ready to tell the guard but they only glanced at my pass and let me through. 'All's fine' I thought, but when I arrived upstairs to my room it was full of twenty-five new people and I wondered vaguely and vainly round looking for an empty bed. There wasn't one. I wandered downstairs to

---

*　　Bob got away to see Diana on 14 September or possibly the night of 13 September.

where the rest of the course were, but no beds there and futiley wandered back upstairs and wondered what to do and where to go. Just then one of the new occupants awoke and told me that I had been moved to a room opposite, where amidst fumbling in the moonlight I found my bed and laid me down to sleep.

Shaw was very anxious to hear how I'd got on and what Danbury looked like—I think he's marvellous don't you? Wish you could meet him, sure you would like him a lot. The next day though, Sunday, we were night-flying and luckily there was a moon which made it a lot easier and I managed to go solo my first evening. The day after that, yesterday, we had off and I slept soundly until midday. Then got up for food then a bath and later wandered into Cirencester for a little more congenial food and to collect our laundry which a lot of us had missed on Saturday. Then back here to move all our belongings from the horrid barrack room to this palace of luxury [the officers' mess].

Having moved, then a bath, read The Times (and seen our engagement!) in the lounge—a separate one for pupils and officers, I mean one each!—and then dinner. 'Potage bonne femme', sole something or other, Tartare sauce, Vienna steaks and spaghetti, choice of five vegetables and various fruits or blackberry and apple tart and cream, cheese and biscuits, coffee in the lounge. It's really too good to be true.

We live two in a room and a bathroom to every four rooms: woken in the morning and boots and buttons cleaned, beds made etc. There's a squash court here, radiogram, billiards and ping pong tables.

I saw our navigation officer today and I'm fairly certain he will recommend me for a navigation course when I leave here. That will mean six or ten weeks at St Athan in Wales and I shall have to try for flying boats from there. He says it is the only way to get into them. Rupert Cecil is there now and I hope to get some news from him of what the place is like.*

Must go to dinner now.

9.30pm. A good dinner and then a couple of games of shove ha'penny; life is a lot better now. Oh darling, in spite of this new luxury—perhaps because of it I long for you more and more ...

This morning we had to do instrument flying: we took off and, as it was bumpy, climbed through the clouds to about 8,000 feet.

I wish I could make you feel what it is like up there with these clouds below. Sometimes they are like a smooth sea or blanket but today they were marvellous— great towering lumps sticking up like so many grotesque mountain peaks. They look quite solid and yet soft if you know what I mean—like cotton wool. The sun was hot and the white clouds and intense blue sky were bright to the eyes. South of France ... snow in the mountains. We were Gods up there and looked down and laughed at the drab and dirty multitude below. I really felt as someone

---

*　Rupert Gascoyne-Cecil was brought up in Downham about half a mile from Bob. He went on to become a wing commander and was awarded a DFC and Bar.

aloof and above the world looking down. One day we'll fly together above the clouds and really 'superior'.

Well dearest I must go to bed now—my eight hours ... there's a glorious full moon outside: oh why aren't you here to share it with me? Will there be a full moon in a month's time? Will you be here? We have Saturdays off now for the next three weeks anyhow, and probably longer than that. When it does change I shall get Tuesdays off.

Really bed now: my room-mate is solemnly playing patience by himself! Diana my darling shall I say it once again? I love you till ... the end, if there be an end.

Goodnight, my own, your own all me—'with my body I thee worship, with my worldly goods I thee bestow' ...

Your Bob xxx

LETTER TO DIANA:

South Cerney
18th September, 1940

10pm. Oh dearest, I was so glad to get your letter: so much to say to you about it, but not now: feel so very tired and sleepy—just got into bed and my roommate is about to turn off the light and unfix the blackout and open wide the windows. Flew above the clouds again today, it is so nice and warm there (warm inside an aeroplane with hot sun streaming through the glass cabin) and it is so bright and clear, when down below it's dim with heavy clouds.

Letter from Mother—it is Father's birthday today, I forgot: I can never remember the date. He and I are alike like that: he starts wishing Mother many happy returns about a week before the day because he knows he will forget when it actually comes. Hope I do not do the same—yours is the 8th of next month isn't it darling?*

Really goodnight now my beloved, my wife-to-be. Take good care of yourself—don't watch these air-raids. So glad you still love me: and I do you, as always, for always. Forever and ever and ever with all me, heart, body, mind, soul and strength. All yours darling xxxx Bob

19th September, 1940. 9.30pm. My dear, perhaps again on Saturday I shall be able to come home! It is a faint chance, but if Shaw again lets me off at midday I shall try—if not perhaps next weekend. It was so wonderful to see you again and I can't resist trying again—not that I want to resist. However we shall see and if I come you will know before you receive this.

Today Shaw dealt rather a blow to my hopes of flying boats. I had never really expected to get onto them as it is the most select and difficult branch of the RAF to get into but apparently they want the best eight pilots of our course to be

---

*   It was 23 October.

instructors and I should be in that eight. Perhaps it is the next best thing to flying boats—we might go to Canada together pretty well for the duration—but I should like to do something a little more active and flying boats have always fascinated me. However, I'll tackle him again sometime and see what can be done.

I'm afraid I can offer you no other 'home' until this war is ended: and then ...? I cannot, dare not think—only hope and believe.

And children too sometimes worry me when I think of them. I, too, should love to have children of our own but where do we stand in this war-mad world. Would there be enough food and peace to have no effect on the child's future life? I believe that an incredibly large part of our minds are made and formed in early infancy (is it because I was born in a war that I love you in another?)

And if anything happened to me: I'm not worth much at present—after perhaps a year or two there might be something of a widow's pension. I hate and it hurts me to have to think of this but it must be done, dearest, and it will hurt you as much or more, I know. Apart from other reasons which I might distrust as selfish—I don't think they are really—I think we ought to wait perhaps a year to see how things are likely to turn out, if we can have time to fully consider everything. In the end, yours is the last say, my darling. My hardships could never be as much as yours.

Must go to bed now. Got drill at 6.45 tomorrow morning. I find it so hard to get out of this comfortable bed. Goodnight Diana, my darling. You are my life, my all: keep care of yourself, darling for us, and I will too. If not this weekend perhaps I'll see you the one after or the next when you may come. All love dearest and all me. Goodnight xxx your Bob.

22nd September, 1940. 10.15pm. Just to say I got back in good time last night, though feeling miserable and wanting you and loving you and cursing you for not being there and making me want you so. Must go to sleep now. Will write again in the morning if time as we have PT which I'm going to cut. But just now my roommate wants the light out. Goodnight my Diana, my treasure. Soon, soon, now. All love, all me, your Bob xxx

23rd September. 7.20am. Good morning dearest, a lovely day but very cold. Just off to get some breakfast and to post this before the post goes.

Still loving you, darling, even at this early hour and when it is as cold as it is. Diana dear, all yours forever and all my love and kisses, Bob

LETTER TO DIANA:

South Cerney
23rd September, 1940

Dearest, a letter from you today, written on 16th or 17th. Remember saying how hard you find it to write. I too cannot write anything logical or with any continuity. Pieces, odd scraps that go through my mind and interspersed with 'I love you's' for I do.

I got back quite without incident Saturday arriving here 9.30. Yesterday was the same as any other day—Shaw asked after you and he is now married:* I've not had time to ask where or when and today again there is no news to tell. I spent most of this afternoon above the clouds chasing in and out and down the valleys. A most exhilarating pastime: but I flew into one big black one and found a hailstorm inside, so quickly came out again!

Oh darling I'm waiting impatiently and expectantly for these next few weeks. Us married—one day a dream and the next as certain and as soon as tomorrow. Diana dear I know we will be so happy.

Keep well darling: I love you now and forever—yours faithfully, WAR Keddie

LETTER TO DIANA:

25th September, 1940

Dearest this is going to be a very short letter. Now 10:00 o'clock and I'm very tired as we were night-flying last night and only got this morning off. A few bits of important news now. We take our final exams here on the 28th October and I may get leave or get posted any time after that—they have cut two weeks off our course! Also I don't expect I shall be able to get home any more because in the new programme I have lectures Friday afternoons. Goodnight darling: your letter came today to cheer me. Oh dearest, I long and long for you each day, each hour, each second. Diana Constance all this Robert Keddie is yours forever, love and love, Bob

---

* Bob assumed that Shaw was married, but in fact he had not had time because his leave had been arranged at such short notice.

13

Soon we shall be us

Letter to Diana:

South Cerney
30th September, 1940

3.30pm. My dearest, I started to write last night, but some riotous people in the next room decided to wage war until about half past ten when I was too cross and tired to write. A pity, too, because last night I was feeling very happy again— the last week or so I've felt so depressed and miserable and I don't know why. Last Friday I went with the 'others' into Cirencester about five o'clock to do some shopping and get my boots repaired. I had felt miserable and rather liverish all day so decided to walk and get better that way.

When I got in, the shops were all shut and I felt just mad. We waited (I'd met the 'others'— you'd like them, 'the general', Johnnie and Tony) until the pubs opened in a little café sipping tea and where I left my boots. Then we drowned our sorrows—at least I did—until about seven. At seven o'clock I felt like dinner but the others wouldn't eat so I said I'd find someone else to eat with. They just laughed so I rang up Tony's sister (the 'Ruth' Tony) to see if she would have some food with me. She came down to the pub in about half an hour or so and we went on drinking until nine when we had dinner.

Dinner over at ten, I felt very muzzy and very tired—in fact quite considerably drunk—and so we sat in her car in the middle of Cirencester market square and talked and talked. And all the time I thought of you and cursed Tony's sister for being there instead of you and then I thought of Patsy, how she and I sometimes talked like this and thus again of you. It seems silly to say so but I loved you more then and wanted you more then than ever before. I was all turbulent inside and hated it and knew if you were there I should be at peace and so incredibly happy. Oh darling, you will be soon, won't you?

Well that's nearly all that 'confession' over. Apart from paying for my sins with self-hatred and annoyance with myself for getting drunk, I found when I got back that her father had rung up the camp to see if I was back because he expected her home at 10 and when she wasn't he'd begun to worry whether she'd driven off the road or something. Of course I wasn't in and the next day they asked why and gave me four days CB [confined to barracks]. It served me right but mattered not so much as loss of peace of mind. Darling, can you forgive your wayward fiancé and will you stop him going off, depressed, to get alcohol to revive his spirits? Will you still so bind him to you by an eye, an ear, or a look that he could not go even if he would?

7.15pm. Just played squash with 'the general': a little fellow with a glorious Guards moustache, a somewhat precise manner. He was about to take his barristers' finals when war broke out and very fond of his food, his wine and his women. Unfortunately, he beat me quite easily.

Diana dear, I wrote Mother yesterday and said our exams were on the 28th. Since then they are now definitely on the 14th October and I expect we shall leave here a week or two after that—probably the end of October. Also more news I've kept for you: I am afraid you will not be too pleased though—I probably shall not be an instructor after all because the navigation officer says I shall be 'wasted' spending the rest of the war instructing. Anyhow nothing is settled, nothing is certain. A piece of good news, though, to balance that: I may be able to get home this weekend (hope you get this in time)—but probably later in the evening so could you ask yourself over for that Friday night just in case?

Half past seven now. Must get some dinner before it is all eaten up. I love you dear, come soon.

10.15pm. In bed. Just written to Dick to ask him to be best man if he can get the leave. Oh Diana darling, all these little details and preparations bring you and us nearer. How nice for you to have so many little things each day to remind you and start the mind off on a new series of imaginations ...

Shaw came back from five or six days leave today—the first he's had since May. He had been back to Little Baddow and is most impressed with the 'war' there. I think the aerial torpedoes and mines quite surprised him.* He didn't get married though because the leave was sprung on him all of a sudden.

Dearest I feel so happy tonight: perhaps because I've told you of my sins, perhaps because in telling you how miserable I have been it just vanishes as if you were here: anyhow I am happy and loving and longing for you—to take you in my arms and hold you tight, never let you go, never, never, never. Oh darling, darling ...

I think it is a good idea of yours to wait until later before you get all your clothes. I'd marry you dearest even if you'd only one old set of things, or even without that! And afterwards, if I get a day or two's leave, we could go and shop together in London or if I were near Leeds or somewhere where there are good shops.

---

* The Germans used large blast bombs known as aerial mines, but aerial torpedoes were not normally used over land.

Must sleep now dear, and dream of you, I hope. Darling all my love and all me: even more yours when away from you and wanting you more when you are not there. Keep well, dear, and sleep well. Your ever-loving, if somewhat weak-minded fiancé, but still all yours if you'll have him. xxx Bob

◊♦◊

Bob managed to get back to Essex again at short notice for a fleeting visit.

◊♦◊

LETTER TO DIANA:

South Cerney
6th October, 1940

Hello darling—just a line to let you know I got back without getting into any trouble last night but that we passed through many tribulations before getting here. The car I got when I left you was a very lucky choice, it took me nearly to the other side of London and after he dropped me I soon got two more lifts to where I was meeting Tony. Actually I arrived there about a quarter of an hour late. I thought all was well but he soon disillusioned me. When he got there—about 10 to 6—he noticed a slight petrol leak and, as the pub didn't open up until 6, he thought he would be clever and repair it. Unfortunately he broke the pipe completely and when I arrived he was in the telephone box trying to find a garage. He tried garage after garage but all were shut and, in the meantime, I tried to fix the pipe with adhesive tape and rubber tubing etc. All to no avail and finally at 7:30 we abandoned the car and hitchhiked to Slough where we caught a very slow train to Reading.

At Reading we hoped to catch the train which should have left at 8:30. We got there just before 9 and it hadn't yet arrived because the air raids. So we went to the buffet and had some cold meat pies and beer and then suddenly I had a brainwave. We realised we were going to be hours late getting back and could think of no excuse which they would take. But I thought of the RTO (railway transport officer) so we rushed off to his office where a kindly private signed on the backs of our passes that we had arrived 7:30 and missed our connection because of the air raid. It was all too easy: we had expected to be asked which train we came by, how late it was and which one we hope to catch etc. But we just told him we missed the connection and he signed it!

As we arrived back on the platform the train was waiting and we piled in. It crawled and crawled and finally we got to Swindon about 12:30 whence we got a taxi with another chap to the camp. Luckily for us the RTO signature was a magic password and we sailed through but the other lad has been reported and will doubtless get CB. The only curse for me now is that I left my records in Tony's car and goodness knows when I shall see them again.

Today is miserable and raining all the time—a fine, misty drizzle, but I'm quite glad as it stops flying and I feel a little too tired to enjoy it. A rest is more welcome. God I felt tired this morning.

And you, dear, I hope you didn't worry whether I should get back in time or not: I didn't tell you but if I do get anymore CB, it might make a difference to my chances of a commission, so it's just as well I got back safely. I expect you stayed the night at Downham and go back today: I hope you don't get wet cycling home in this rain.

I thought coming back in the train that the most useful sort of wedding presents at the moment would be nice handy quick-packing things! Travelling suitcases and what not! Luckily I have got a superb travelling suitcase—a twenty-first present—and it's got lots of spare bottles and things for your concoctions!

Goodbye my darling for the moment. Will post this now even if I get time to write more tonight: I know you'll want to know if I got 'home' alright. Dearest it cannot be more than a few weeks now before we are well and truly Mr and Mrs K! I hope for leave even if my brain says it is most unlikely.

I love you darling more than anything else I have ever done or will do. Love you, love you, love you forever and ever. Be mine soon won't you?

My love to your parents and keep well my dearest. My love to you, and for you as always.

Your soon-to-be husband

xxxxxxx Bob

LETTER TO DIANA:

South Cerney
10th October, 1940

9pm. My dearest, yet another letter from you today—you are an angel writing so often and yet with so much to do. I'm glad you like the marriage service—I do too: suggest we have the 45th Psalm: read it through and you'll guess why. Anyway I like it for what it is.

I went and saw the MO [medical officer] today, he is an awfully nice man (plays rugby with me for the station) and asked him about not having children. Funny isn't it how easily men can talk to one another on things like that and not get embarrassed whereas if they talk about 'the Empire' you feel all hot and cold. Anyhow I asked him and he said he was not really the person to give advice as he had just managed to produce a baby more or less against his own inclinations! However he said he had found it almost invariably to be better if it was the woman who had to think about it and gave me the name of something which he said was not <u>absolutely</u> certain, but then darling, it's not as if we shan't be quite unable to afford a baby is it? He said it was so much more harmless than the other things that it was quite the best in his opinion. So shall I see about it? I hope you don't mind me speaking to the MO about us but he knows neither you nor me and is unlikely to see either of us again and it seems a good opportunity to ask one of those things which it is hard to ask one's own doctor.

Dick phoned up two nights ago: if you ring Mother up would you let her know that a call came from Devonshire—she'll know where he is. He hopes that he may get leave somewhere towards the end of this month and if so will be able to be my best man. The trouble is he may not be able to get leave so I'm going to ask John to be 'standby' and Tony Lane to be a final reserve. If none of them can come I don't know what I'll do. But anyhow I'd like to ask Tony and Ruth to the wedding wouldn't you? They've been so much a part of my service life and have known 'us' before anyone else: I feel they'd like to come very much too.

Our exams come at the end of next week—a week today: so I expect I'll be working quite a bit in the evening and have even less time to write to you darling. This weekend though, when I can't get home, I should be able to do some. But tomorrow morning I'm sleeping late I hope and in the afternoon playing rugger and later having dinner with the Lane's as Tony and Ruth are coming home. (I've got to be back by 9:45 though!)

Darling, darling I'm sure we're going to be so happy, I can hardly bear to think of it. It seems a dream yet too tangible for a dream. Here's the 'other Tony' coming to bed—can't write with him here. Goodnight my dearest—kiss your photo goodnight. God bless you. I love you now, tomorrow, tomorrow and always. Love you, love you with all me, all my heart, all my body, all my soul.

My sweet, my own so soon it must be, shall be—you and I, you and I—how wonderful.

More and more yours, my soon-to-be wife—all my love your soon-to-be husband, Bob

xxxxx

LETTER TO DIANA:

South Cerney
16th October, 1940

2.30pm. I suppose, dear, by the time you get this I shall have managed to phone up to say that our Saturday off has been cancelled. I tried to phone Mother last night but there was still six hours delay at ten o'clock. I'm going to try again tonight.

A piece of news I've saved for you darling—I thought you'd like to know first: I've been told unofficially that I shall get my commission alright when I leave here and have ordered a uniform on the strength of it. Would you tell Mother and Dad when you see them or phone as I know they'd like to know?

21st October, 1940. Darling I've just thought—if you haven't bought sheets and things and have the money instead we shall be able to get them wholesale at the family business. Why didn't I think of that before? But anyhow you would have to go to the London warehouses to find what you want.

Must go to bed now, darling, I'll write again soon.

I think Mother is suggesting to Dick and John that they give us a couple of entrée dishes. I hope nobody else has thought of that, have they?

Also Mother and Dad want to give us a cheque or war savings certificates but I said I thought it would probably be better to wait until the end of the war as the family is not too flush with ready money at the moment. Not that I expect they will have more by the end but we couldn't do much with it now anyhow.

Really bed now: I'll be in bed each night by 10.15 to beat you every night now! Darling it's only weeks, I hope, almost days now. Goodnight my angel, I love you now ever and always—more and more and more. Keep well, and don't worry we shall be us soon.

Lots and lots—in fact all my love,

Your Bob.

LETTER TO DIANA:

South Cerney
23rd October, 1940

7.10pm. My darling. Just a short line to say that I've passed my exam alright 8th out of about 45. I'm pleased enough as I did about a quarter of the work of most people. I am trying to phone you tonight to wish you many happy returns—hope they manage to get through alright.

Going in to dinner in a few minutes and have lots of letters to write. They've seemed to accumulate quite a bit.

Reading a good book—'Disenchantment' [by Charles Edward Montague]—an intensely interesting psychological survey of the Army in the last war. Very instructive and useful.

Finished my night-flying last night. Came back 11pm in the lorry. Lovely night: moon orange still, rising shrouded in mist vainly clinging and striving to keep it down. Tracery of the trees, many bare now, against the starry sky: the counterpoint rhythm of the searchlights, seeking—sinister coldly beautiful—the beauty of a marble Venus, a mummified Cleopatra. Sleek, shining, lovely but cold and hard. Swish in the trees as we went past, pulling back their silken petticoats to let a rude man have his way, leaning back when we'd gone to resume their intimate talk or renew their lonely sentinel vigil. Sitting quite still—all those stars, have they earths, are they peopled? God how small I am. Shivers in the cold. Think of Diana, dream of Diana—Diana and I—I and Diana. Where shall we be in a month, then a year? What shall we do? How is she now. What is she doing? Asleep? In bed anyhow—keeping her self-made vows. We are back at last ... sitting very still so as not to feel the cold, we never feel how stiff we've become ... stand up and stagger ... awake from a dream, blood starts to flow ... mind starts to work ... life goes on again.

Lying in bed, soon drift to sleep. Think of the night. God what a bad landing the first—the last two were nice though. Funny to think of us going round and round while the whole time, miles above, Germans were flying, eluding the lights, seeking their targets. Hopefully they can't see us. Dinner.

9.30pm. Written all my letters including John. Had a good dinner but no possibility of a call. Blast these telephone people ... anyhow many happy returns of what will be the day before the day before ...

We are told by Shaw that we leave here Friday week—i.e. about the 8th but we are behind with our flying and heaven knows what they will do. I don't expect any leave when we quit this place and the only chance is when we arrive at the next school.

Goodnight darling, all my love. Keep well won't you and don't worry about these air-raids and things. We'll soon be us ... Each day each hour it comes yet nearer—and the nearer it is the more I long for it.

Dearest I love, love, love you.

All me. xxxx Bob.

Love to your parents.

LETTER TO DIANA:

South Cerney
27th October, 1940

9.30. Darling, this must be very brief: from my letter to your mother you can see I got back quite safe and sound and in good time.

I can't think at all tonight, don't know why so can you be content with a small letter—will try again tomorrow.

That book I had was most extraordinary and diverting. 'Diversion' was what I needed to stop me thinking and remembering too much. There's nothing like a train and no book to read to jog the memory and refuse to allow it to be led away. Thank God for the book. But you had to cycle back with no distraction. Hope you lost no more gold chains. I must have a look one day.

God, don't know what I'm writing at all must go to sleep. I'm tired too. Goodnight, darling, I love you still and each day you come to be yet more me and I you. One. Us.

All my love. I'll try and write coherently tomorrow, will stop feeling as if someone's pulled the plug out of my brain and it all ran away. Only know blindly I love you more and more and more.

All you, Bob

South Cerney
28th October, 1940

10pm. Darling, just written some more letters.

I had my last—I hope—flying test to-day—I think I did alright but it might have been better. When we leave here, we get classed as 'exceptional', 'above average', 'average' or 'below average'. Shaw told me today that he had put me as 'exceptional' and said I was supposed to be the best pupil on the course which all goes to show darling ... but I expect you know the rest. I also got an official piece of paper today ... 'LAC WARK has been recommended for a commission and is hereby authorised to purchase a uniform' ...

Goodnight my love ... how much longer must we say goodnight a hundred miles apart? Please God not much longer: I shall burst. I hope to be home this weekend if I can. Will you be at Downham? Or are Mother and Dad still there?

Love, love, all my love all me is yours xxxxxx Bob

South Cerney
30th October, 1940

9.30pm. Your letter, dear, came at a welcome moment to comfort and cheer. I'm sick of this place, of the red tape and nonsense, sick of the pettiness and sick of waiting to marry you and wondering whether I shall ever get leave. And your letter comes like a breath of fresh air to a refuse dump: its gaiety and happiness are quite infectious and I suddenly felt glad to be alive again.

Rumours have been floating round all day—good and bad. That next Saturday off will be cancelled; that we leave next Tuesday, next Wednesday, next Thursday. I think Thursday is quite likely: we should leave then but we will have a job to get all our flying done by then unless the weather clears up a bit.

Written to Dick tonight with a marvellous code to tell him where I'm to be posted to and if I get leave. Will send a copy to you if I can't explain it to you this weekend, but I expect you'll want your father's help in deciphering.

Thank you for the piece of Jean's letter. She seems most depressed and unhappy. I do hope things will 'break' for her and John soon. If he could only break his leg painlessly and comfortably that they got some leave and time together. Perhaps he might swallow fruit stones and get an appendix or something.*

The rain is now hissing down, relentlessly beating against the windows with that unceasing remorselessness that only water can have. Someone in the room next

---

*   After the war Jean wrote that she had many happy memories of her time in Africa but also a
       lot of sorrow, fear and loneliness when John was away for long periods and there was no news.

door plays a 'blues'. My being, inside and out, is bored, tired and hating this place for keeping me; yet somewhere right inside is happiness locked up in a Pandora's box just waiting for the lock to be turned. I loathe this place yet I know it is not for long, doesn't matter. I'm miserable and depressed yet exultantly happy.

My turn one day will come to 'show you off' too ... My relations (Father's) are such funny people I don't know what they'll say or think of you. They always say the correct thing whatever they feel. Darling I know you will captivate them but I shall not be able to tell because they wouldn't gossip about it ... most peeving as I like gossip which is praise. It always seems more genuine! My Mother's brothers you will like, but they are apt to overwhelm ... they will be rude about me, tell you to keep me in order and, all the time, observe you carefully and, afterwards, tell their wives (my uncle Twig, the elder brother, glass eye, prisoner-of-war in the last [war] will do so anyway) and so it will come back to Mother. They'll shine if they are at the wedding: hope they are—they make any party go.

Must go to bed now. Can't think of anything to fill up the other side ...

though . Would you like a lot of kisses or do you get the same feeling from one like this ✗ and one like this ✗ or even this ✗ ? or what about

this ○ ◇ ◆ ○ ○ ? if you

... Mother or Father is looking at the back of this what must they think? Or what will my room-mate say if he comes in—he will do any minute? Bats quite bats. Perhaps we will grow up one day. How nice growing up together.

Grow old along with me!
The best is yet to be*

Good night my angel, sleep well and God bless you and us. 'We' can't be far off now. I love every bit, every one of the you's with all of me and me's. Yours ever and ever and after.

Your WA Robert K

---

* The opening lines of 'Rabbi Ben Ezra' by Robert Browning.

South Cerney
3rd November, 1940

7pm. Dearest,

Got back again quite alright on Saturday although I was a little late meeting my friend on the Gt. West Road. I tubed and bus'd to our rendezvous. It rained all the way, stopped yesterday morning but has rained ever since. The aerodrome is very wet and, if it rains much more, it will stop all flying.

We should leave here Thursday so I expect, if I get any leave, to be home Thursday afternoon or evening. I'll phone or wire as soon as we are told anything definite of our future destination.

Just written a letter to a friend who got engaged just before we did and now she's broken it off (and don't you dare do the same, will you?)

There's no more news darling, I'm afraid: the weather has been too poor for any nice autumnal shades or beauty—in fact it's been just one soggy mess. Mud everywhere. I expect the trees will have been stripped, too, of a lot of their gold and brown mantles. Dear, when we do manage to get a home, we must plant some beech trees (to console us in our old age? that life dies in one burst of golden splendour only to be reborn again). I've never realised what lovely trees they are at all times of the year. Their smooth straight trunks in winter and the most marvellous of all autumn shades in the fall.

Goodnight, my sweet, and don't stop loving me will you? I love you more and more and each parting gets harder and harder to bear. They must all end soon or we shall both just go up in puffs of flour and smoke. Goodnight, sleep well and sweet dreams. A kiss on either eye and one for luck. All my love and all me is yours.

Yours faithfully,
Wallace Arthur Robert Keddie

◊♦◊

Bob passed his exams with a mark of 80.9 per cent and was judged of very good character as an 'under training pilot'. He completed his training at South Cerney on Thursday 7 November. He was now authorised to wear his flying badge (or wings) and was awarded a commission as a pilot officer in the RAF Volunteer Reserve.

Two days later, on 9 November 1940, Bob and Diana were married at St Mary's church in Little Baddow, Essex, Diana's home village. Diana's great friend Patsy made her wedding dress and organised the wedding.

Right: Wallace Arthur Robert Keddie.

Below: Dick, John and Bob Keddie.

Above left: Bob's father Wallace Keddie in his First World War Royal Flying Corps uniform.

Above right: Curling in St Moritz: Annie Keddie, Bob's mother, also known as 'Cissie' because she had several brothers.

Below: Bob's parents at Downham Grange in Essex.

Above: Dick and Bob.

Right: Bob in 'civvies'.

Left: Bob and Dick at the Cresta Run. The message on the back reads: 'To Darling Bob—in the agony of thinking "what to say"—you're an angel ... With love and kisses Zolla'.

Below: The Cresta Curzon Cup riders, 1939. Bob is fourth from left in the front row. Standing on the extreme right is Joe Kennedy, the eldest son of the then US ambassador to Britain and brother of future US president John F. Kennedy. Joe was killed in action in 1944.

Above left: Bob at the start of the Cresta Run.

Above right: One of many messages of congratulations after Bob's Cresta Run wins.

Below: Bob, centre, with his Cresta injuries and all his trophies. His father is on the left, his mother on the extreme right, and a 'self-imposed' girlfriend, possibly called Mitzi, is second from right.

Above left: Bob relaxing at home at Downham Grange.

Above right: Sub-Lieutenant Richard Keddie (right) aboard ship in 1939.

Left: Dick was promoted to lieutenant in 1939.

Above: A young Diana Ladner at her parents' home, Waterhall, in Little Baddow, Essex.

Below left: Diana's 'stage photograph'.

Below right: The back of the stage photograph.

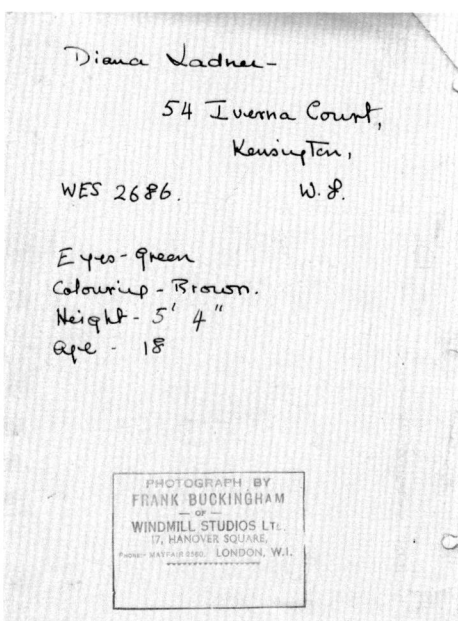

Diana Ladner —

54 Iverna Court,
Kensington,

WES 2686.   W. 8.

Eyes - green
Colouring - Brown.
Height - 5' 4"
Age - 18

PHOTOGRAPH BY
FRANK BUCKINGHAM
— OF —
WINDMILL STUDIOS LTD
17, HANOVER SQUARE,
PHONE: MAYFAIR 0160.   LONDON, W.1.

Left: Bob (with friend Tony in the background) somewhere between Torquay and Kingswear, July 1940. The photograph was taken by Bob's uncle Maitland.

Below: Diana with Dick Keddie.

John Keddie, Bob and
Dick's younger brother.

Bob with his wings.

Above: Diana arriving
at St Mary's church in
Little Baddow with her
father, A. W. (Bill) Ladner.

Left: Just married!

Leaving the wedding reception.

'Going away' after the reception. Bob is in the centre. Alison Foster is in the background behind Diana who is kissing her new brother-in-law, John. Bob's mother is in the foreground on the right in a dark coat.

Left: The happy couple at Downham Grange with Bob's parents' labrador. They both loved dogs and the sun.

Below: Bob and Diana with Bob's parents at Downham Grange.

Above left: Bob on leave in Scotland with Diana. Diana's daughter Penny said, 'Mum always liked this photo. My father was on leave from Stranraer when he and Diana spent time in what sounds to have been a hovel with no running water. I think he's washing in a bucket.'

Above right: Bob Keddie sailing on the Voe, 1942. (*Air Commodore Jack Holmes*)

Right: Diana scribbled a note: 'While we were stationed at Oban in the autumn of 1941 a squadron flew from Oban via Stranraer to Plymouth to be filled with small arms and from there to Tobruk in North Africa. Out of the blue Bob met his brother Dick in Gibraltar as he passed through.' This photograph must have been taken on that trip. Bob is pictured on the right.

Flying Officer Keddie's crew, plus extras, at RAF Sullom Voe, early April 1942. Back row, left to right: Ervine, Woodland, Short, Hall, Mitchell, Balderson. Middle row: Lonsdale, Woodward, Jenner, Harmer, Henderson. Front: Duffield, Keddie, Franklin. (*Bill Balderson*)

The site of the officers' mess at RAF Sullom Voe in 2024. The photograph was taken from a Catalina. (*Bob Kemp*)

A 210 Squadron Catalina taxiing to its mooring in Oban. (*John Evans*)

A Catalina completing a 'stall landing'. (*Eddy Edwards Collection / Pembroke Dock Heritage Trust*)

Diana and Penny at Downham Grange.

14

Little hope on the Cape of Good Hope

Bob had waited many weeks. He still did not know where he was to be posted for the next stage of his training but only that he would be going alone 'overseas'. By December, he thought that the direction of travel would be Africa.

◇♦◇

LETTER TO DIANA:

Royal Air Force
Turnhouse
Edinburgh 12
21st December, 1940

My darling

I don't suppose it matters you knowing where we are at the moment but we are only here to await our 'marching orders'. At any moment now, we should hear something (it is just after 11am) and we may have to go at a moment's notice or wait a day or two. I shall not be allowed to tell you where I go but I'll write every day. Thank you for your letter, dearest. I read it on the train yesterday. We didn't have too bad a journey; arrived just about seven o'clock and it's a very comfortable mess here, but very cold outside.

If we are still here, we expect to have a look at Edinburgh this afternoon: I feel I ought to, but inside I'd really like to go to sleep. Sleep and forget what I'm leaving behind. Forget ... forget. No not forget but just postpone for another day. A day that is now one day nearer coming.

8pm. Just going to Edinburgh.

Lots and lots of love—all of it xxxxx darling xx Bob.

Turnhouse
26th December, 1940

Still here darling, but not for long now, I think. On Tuesday we hired a car (Lindsey and two others from Prestwick) and went over to see Prestwick. It was very amusing there to see all the old people and instructors who also seemed very glad to see us. Then we went up to see the Connals (two of us were billeted there) and they too seemed very pleased to see us.

In the evening we went to the station dance which was one of the most drunken I have seen. There must have been at least a dozen girls carried out: my old instructor was as drunk as a Lord, and most amusing. And so we saw Christmas in. In the morning we had to return here and the officers go to the airmen's mess and serve the Christmas dinner to them. This lasts for a very long time as there are a lot of them—12.15 to 1.15. Then we go to the sergeants' mess for half an hour for drinks then the sergeants come to the officers' mess for half an hour and at 2.15 we had lunch—not so good as the airmen's.

After lunch, we all go back to the airmen's mess and dance with the WAAFs. At 4.30 some of us (and WAAFs) went into Edinburgh for tea and dumped the WAAFs back at 7.00 for their Christmas dinner. Lindsey and I went to a roadhouse till about ten—we went for one drink and stayed for several. Then I went back into Edinburgh for a little food. And so to bed at twelve o'clock. I hope to heaven I never have to spend another Christmas like it. At the roadhouse, too, there was a drunken officer who told us that we were not going anywhere near where we think which was most depressing but I don't put a lot of faith in him.

Today we got up about 10.30 and are just about to have our lunch. I'm going to try and play golf afterwards, even if by myself. Golf can be quite soothing and I feel like being soothed.

5pm. Managed to play golf—with a man of seventy-five and two others of over fifty I should say. Most enjoyable, though, and I feel much soothed. The post goes in half an hour so must finish this soon.

Tomorrow evening all of us go to the WAAF dance—I imagine it will be about a hundred WAAFs and two hundred and fifty airmen. If so I shall sneak away and have an early night for a change!

I'm keeping my Christmas cake for my birthday now—it seems silly just to sit down and eat it while we're still here. Hope it's still intact, I've not opened the tin at all.

It seems horrid that I shall not hear from you now for months, there is so much I want to hear. What you've done, are doing, will do and how sad you are without me! Incidentally I think that any letter for me had better be addressed to Uxbridge c/o PDC [Personnel Dispersal Centre], RAF Uxbridge, Middlesex. Nobody knows definitely where we're going or what we'll do so that should always get me in the end. Must finish now to catch the post.

Dearest Diana, do not worry yourself unduly will you: just remember that, everywhere, always you're mine and I'm yours, that I love you and you me. That one day soon we'll be together again—what is six months or a year—we have yet fifty years to be us.

Darling your husband's love, God bless you.

xxx Robert

PS Can't write with this news.* I'll write later.

10.30pm. In bed. Last night in England [actually Scotland!]? ... Playing part of Beethoven's Seventh Symphony after dinner made me very homesick. Why didn't I take my records? Dearest, darling, I don't want to go. But, hell, what's the use of moaning?

Did I tell you I've got seven hundred and fifty-two pages of a 'Musical Companion' for five shillings and sixpence to read on the voyage? It ought to keep me occupied. Hope there will be somewhere quiet to dream and read and write. I'll try and keep a diary for you. Remember ... you don't know when I sail ... or where: 'careless talk' might cost my life! Or others.

My wife, my wife, my wife—there is so much to say and I can say none of it. Perhaps, once on board, peace of mind and thought will ease the flow of words.

When and where we next shall meet ...
Will we be shy again.
Will hearts still faster beat
When eye meets eye again
Will age leave signs for each to see
When we gaze on each again
Will I speak first or will we be
Too full for speech again.

Will you laugh or smile or weep
Will you call out in your sleep
Will your hair be done the same
The day we meet again.
Will you keep your foolish dreams
Will you still foster madcap schemes
Will you please stay just the same
Until the day we meet again?
Dearest Diana, wife, mistress, friend
I have come to my very end.

A Happy New Year to all—
Sleep well ... I love you, love you, love you, don't forget it.
All of me, always and ever your husband and lover, WA Robert K

---

*   Bob was probably referring to the bombing in Britain or perhaps news of the war in North Africa.

LETTER TO DIANA:

Turnhouse
27th December, 1940

We had expected to leave tomorrow, my darling, but things have again been postponed for a day or two so here we are still—incidentally you must not mention anything about sailing dates even after I've gone.

Apart from that there is little news for you and it is so hard to write while we expect to go any moment.

This afternoon I played golf again: it was a gloriously warm and fairly sunny afternoon and was most enjoyable. Lindsey walked round with us—I played another of the officers on our course, a most likeable person.

Everyone here is wild because we could easily have spent Christmas at home—or you could have come up here even. I have wondered whether to phone or not but remembered that you said you'd rather not.

Have read a lot of light stuff since I've been here—two funny ones by Evelyn Waugh being the best. I never get up till about 10am and read in the bath too—it all helps to pass the day. That, squash and golf and billiards are the only recreations.

There's really no more news. Wish I could hear from you. Take care of yourself darling won't you? I love you too much ... Perhaps I'll phone just before we go: you'll know then what it means. Goodbye darling. I'll write tomorrow.

All my love honeybunch. Don't forget me xxxxx Robert

LETTER TO DIANA:

Turnhouse
Sunday 29th December, 1940

I am afraid it is goodbye, my darling, I funked the telephone in the end. I just somehow couldn't bear it. Last night all the officers attended the WAAFs' dance, quite a merry affair. Even the CO, the Duke of Hamilton, was there, and made quite a nice speech to the WAAFs.* This afternoon we've repacked for the umpteenth time and later Lindsey and I visited the ops room where all our fighters round here are controlled from. It is most interesting, especially when an enemy aircraft approaches the coast and our own people are sent up after it.

Everyone is very glad to leave here: there has been absolutely nothing to do and all are fed up and bored stiff. Yet still no-one really knows where we are going.

And still there is no news from you and can't be for a couple of months, I suppose. There is so much I want to hear and know. And I have no news for you.

---

*   Air Commodore Douglas Douglas-Hamilton, 14th Duke of Hamilton. In five months' time, on 10 May 1941, Deputy Führer Rudolf Hess was to land in Scotland asking to meet Hamilton, ostensibly to broker a peace deal with Britain.

The same dull life here. Get up about 11. Lunch 12.30, walk, golf or squash after lunch. Tea. Read, write or sleep or go into Edinburgh. Supper. Bed. It's so funny because it's not the same as just sitting at home with nothing to do. Here you can't concentrate on reading or writing and you can't day dream in peace.

'Taffy' Jones arrived here today: he had forty-seven confirmed victories to his credit in the last war. Did you ever meet Mrs Sells? He is her brother.

I got a Polish officer to swap a button the other day. It looks quite good. Wish I had got one of Dick's.

The b---- CO has just turned on the news, curse him; I'm trying not to listen.

I wonder whether you are in Cornwall now or did you manage to dissuade Pauline? Give her my love will you?

◊♦◊

On his passage aboard the Dutch ship MS Meliskirk, Bob wrote a diary.

◊♦◊

An African Journey

30th December, 1940.

Thirteen sergeants and nine officers were called this morning between seven and eight—quite a few hours earlier than they had been used to the last few days. They had been told to have their baggage ready at 08.15 and be themselves outside the officers' mess, Turnhouse, at 8.45. Somewhat sceptically they arrived between that time and 9.15 to be whisked off by bus for an unknown destination and unknown duties. For the last six weeks they had expected to sail for 'overseas' stations at any moment. It was, then, rather a jaded and faintly dissipated party that stepped into the bus. They were also poor after six weeks of farewell parties.

The day was raw and dour. An overcast sky and rain.

The driver said we should be an hour arriving at M—— [Musselburgh, Methil or Montrose?] our destination. He was wrong. Four hours later, after asking the way many times and turning back on our tracks more than once, we were handing our luggage gaily into the belly of a fat and dirty drifter called Lady ENA and proudly marked 'RN Control'.

Everybody tried to appear more unconcerned and casual than his neighbour but eager eyes were turned seaward and scanned each vessel in turn trying to find some sign to distinguish our own. The largest was picked out and 'it must be ours because it's the only one that looks like a passenger ship'. Someone turned and asked a red-faced, white-haired gentleman in blue suit and trilby hat whether he knew which ship it was we were heading for. He pointed out a ship somewhat deeper in the water than the rest and with her bridge and superstructure well forward. I asked if she carried grain and the reply was 'Anything from a needle to an elephant.'

We scrambled aboard one at a time up a large rope ladder lowered over the side. Our luggage was attached piece by piece to a rope and hauled over the side. The man in blue suit came too and quickly disappeared.

The ship can be described later when all its corners have been explored but the first impression is one of comfort and informality but there will be a rather cramped time, I feel, until the weather turns warmer and we can spread from our lounge and smoking room to the decks above. We are the only passengers and more than fill the ship: we are three in every double cabin.

At dinner the man in the blue suit turned up in clean white shirt and collar and the uniform of the captain. After dinner I retired to my 'bunk'—normally the daytime settee when there are two to a cabin. It is comfortable though and has a nice tray at one end 'useful for putting things in'. On it are my books, bottles, clock, photos and odds and ends. One thought must be uppermost in all minds tonight—when do we again see England, and at the back of our minds is still the question 'Whither bound?'—South Africa, Rhodesia, Egypt?

My darling, this diary is for you. I'm determined to write this only when I feel like it: if I write when I don't, the result should suffer. It is labelled proudly 'An African Journey', but so far it has all been rain and cold and no excitement or romance. I think I shall enjoy the journey; already I feel better, but I wish we could start soon. Good night my love, it brings you closer to say it thus even if you are miles away. 'Goodnight, my dearest wife. God bless you.'

31st December.

Spent on board: in the evening we celebrated New Year's Eve with simulated cheeriness—stories and lots of drink.

1st January 1941.

Two or three inches of snow all over the ship. Felt very ill and spent nearly all the day in bed. Sailed at 9.50 in the evening.

2nd January.

Felt better, still a little muzzy and slightly queasy, but quite fit and cheery by the evening. Passing up the snow-covered Scottish coast all day. Rather dull, but impressive at times. One lovely glimpse of pink-tinted mountains rising from behind the blue-grey rocks and land. Sailing about ten miles out, eight knots: one small single funnel destroyer and two armed trawlers as escort. Saw two or three Ansons.*

Goodnight angel: it's no good trying to forget you for an hour or so even by drinking. I miss you all the more when I'm feeling unwell. Wonder if you were unwell or not? A lovely night but very cold. Moon has just set. It's OK to send all letters Poste Restante GPO Cape Town. Goodnight my love, God bless you. I love you so. Darling, all my love, all me—

---

*   The RAF used Anson planes for coastal reconnaissance.

'Beauty will have passed away from me as the breath of a forgotten wind.'
From Aunt Ethel's book by Bradda Field.

3rd January.

Nineteen forty-one. What's in store for us this year, what will we be by the end of it?

Writing now in the sun-lounge. No sun though and a little draught. Got my flying eiderdown on and boots and a rug. The captain has just come out of his cabin to call his dog Nora because she keeps barking at us wanting to play games. 'Writing love letters?' he asks.

This morning after breakfast—from 8.30am until just after 10am, we watched the fantastically beautiful sunrise. Lights were flashing from either side of us and we could just see black shapes in which we imagined islands vaguely forming in the half light. As the sky behind us lightened, we began to distinguish the ships of the convoy strung out in line behind us: each a black shape against the lighter sky diminishing in size and evaporating in the distance.

On either side now the black shapes were just apparent as cliffs surmounted by snow-covered hills. The line [cliffs] was clear-cut and awe-inspiring by its very size and grandiose contours. Overhead now were flaming red clouds and a group of a dozen or so of us, wrapped up in all our clothes, waited for the sun.

At first, a few clouds low on the horizon turned pink, then blazed up in flaming gold: then a corner of the sun showed behind the hills and, being reflected off the water, seemed to suspend the hills between two seas of fire. Soon the whole sun appeared—large and very red. The hills turned pink then yellow, the clouds turned white, the sea from black to a dark green and it was day.

The convoy slowly reassembled into two lines as it was now through the narrow eight-mile wide straits.* We admired again and again the lovely line of Hoy and North Walls. Sheer hundreds of feet going straight down to the sea. And, on the other side, Scotland's lower cliffs but behind them the lovely snow-covered countryside and distant hills.

At eleven o'clock our cocoa or beef-tea.

Life is very pleasant and promises to get better every day. The ship is very steady and comfortable. She is Dutch: of 8,500 tons, maximum speed twelve knots. The convoy sails at eight knots. There is no vibration. She has about eight or ten double cabins and a sun-lounge, glass fronted but open at the back, all the glass is removable. A dining-room and tiny smoking room.

The captain and officers are charming and we have a delightful West Indian cabin-steward. Lindsey and myself share a cabin with a man called Batley—a Yorkshireman who luckily is not self-assertive and we get on quite happily. I have a bath at five to eight and breakfast immediately after. Elevenses. Lunch at one. Tea and biscuits 4pm. Dinner 7pm. Tea 9.30pm–10pm. We wear what we like but put on uniform at dinner. I don't shave. Bed about 10pm.

---

*   Between John O'Groats and the Orkneys.

We expect to put into port today or tomorrow and that's why I'm trying to get this finished. If this letter doesn't bear the Censor's stamp, you must not say anything about our route or sailing, and after this, I'm afraid you cannot expect to hear until we arrive. I believe we go a long way round and no intermediate stop so it will be sometime. I am strictly not allowed to tell you the name of the ship.

Just been up to the chart room to see where we are—just approaching Cape Wrath. A Hudson [an American bomber] flew over and round the convoy signalling to our escort.

Undated journal entry:

No more dates: it'll be nice to feel that time for once has not quite stopped—but ceased to count, ceased to matter. There is a daily news sheet on board but I need not read it. I can live on my self-appointed pedestal, unaware of time and the world, more or less independent in the sense that I need no longer take any thought for the morrow and need only associate with my fellow-beings for meals, live in my thoughts and myself.

Thus no more dates—time shall flow forgotten and unheeded. So, too, is this no longer addressed to my wife: I hope she will not mind. I find it hard to explain my reasons. The whole is still hers and written mainly for her because I know she is interested in what I write; but I do not want to include any feelings or messages which only the two of us can understand. This is my diary and my journal. I hope it will contain thoughts, happenings, verse and some more formal writing but I feel there is no place here for a recital of feelings and emotions which are there every day and all day and vary only in slight or sudden increases of longing. Thus, my darling wife, goodbye—but you shall have a 'personal' letter to take the place of omitted avowals!*

This now is Oban. As it began to lighten this morning, I went on deck to see whether there was anything worth watching. At first only a dark silhouette of a sky appeared on our right and was lost in a bank of cloud so that it was difficult to tell where skyline began or ended. But it was enough to show a succession of large islands rising to great heights and vanishing in the clouds.

Then suddenly, on our left, the hazy shape of the 'mainland'—actually the island of Mull—began to show. A high and lovely line of hills or cliffs—still only a black mass descending mist-shrouded to merge with the sea. Very soon the sky above could be seen as dark blue and turned gently to a soft purple where the hard blue-grey of the hills cut it short. These in turn imperceptibly changed to a misty mauve where land and sea should meet. But the sea too was lost in the mist and came back to us—through shades of foam-flecked green. The whole was

---

*   In fact, as the passage progressed, Bob lapsed back into addressing Diana directly and dating each journal entry.

now constantly changing colour. The sky got lighter, the hills grew softer in outline, and revealed shadow, the mist changed to a mauve and pink, the sea took more colour. First purple, then mauve, now pink dominated the scene. But, through the pink haze, a faint line of breakers could be seen, the cliffs took shape, the hills had golden-brown sides and the distant peaks were veiled in cloud. Then a white farm in a valley near the water's edge. It was daylight.

I felt privileged and dazed, humble, and turned to the other side. Quite close was a vicious looking ridge of black rocks at one end of which a light winked wickedly—who controlled it? Surely no-one lived on that minute outcrop? And yet it could not be mechanical because it was only turned on for the convoy. Behind these rocks were 'The Small Islands'.* High abrupt islands rising evenly, continuously from the sea to hundreds of feet. I looked from one side to the other and wondered whoever could have thought of it all. Such infinite variety, such perfect harmony.

At Oban. Got the letters off with our retiring gun crew. Everyone hangs over the stern looking at the land less than two hundred yards away and yet as far as ever—is it the last we shall see of this good earth for some weeks?

We sail tomorrow morning early. For America? For the Azores? For the Canaries? Or just into the blue? ...

Now we have been at sea for a few days. Everyone—including myself—is beginning to settle down although a few sharp words have been spoken: due I suppose to the lack of occupation and enforced contiguity. I sometimes feel very annoyed with myself that such small things should annoy me. As yet, too, I feel little like writing.

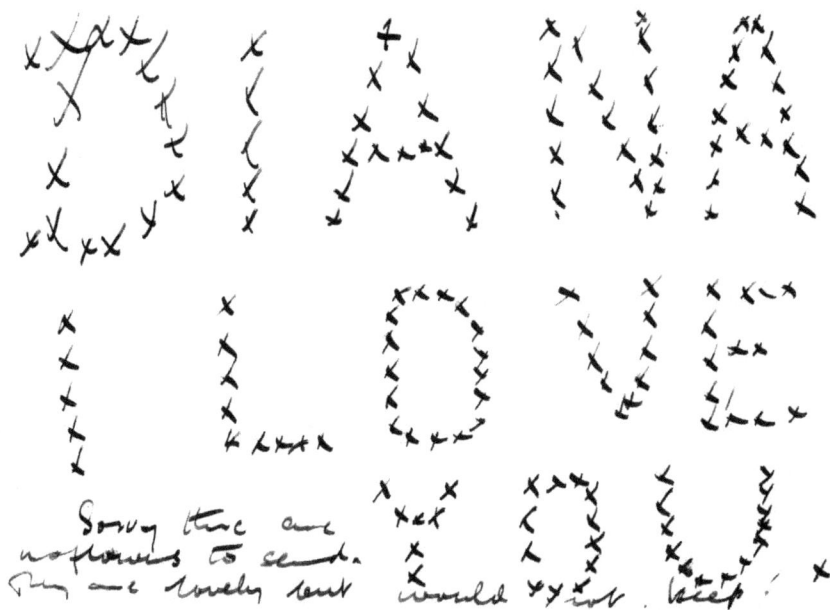

---

* The Small Isles—Rum, Eigg, Canna and Muck—to the south of Skye.

◇♦◇

At Oban, Bob hurriedly scribbled a letter to Diana for the gun crew to take ashore with the first pages of his journal.

◇♦◇

5th January 1941

My darling, We're just getting ready to drop anchor and I've only time for a short note ... Dearest Diana, remember I love you always and ever and nothing shall stop us or hinder us. God bless you darling and keep well and try not to worry. I shall undoubtably be better off than you. My Diana, always your loving husband Robert xxxxxxxxxxxxx

15

I shall be back soon

BOB'S DIARY, 'AN AFRICAN JOURNEY', CONTINUED:

10.30pm. In my bunk, MS Meliskerk—Atlantic.

Diana dearest—the dates as I say in my diary I'm trying to forget and it has been quite easy.

We arrived at Oban about midday the day before yesterday and sailed yesterday at about 6am. We were tantalisingly near to an island—within two stones throws—and there was a telephone kiosk in sight. However the captain was too frightened of having a passenger missing and we had to stay put. The next morning we loitered about a bit and then made touch with the main body of our convoy—another ten ships and six escort ships—three destroyers and three smaller ones. Since then we have steamed approximately west straight out into the Atlantic. Nothing at all has happened yet. This last night we saw the last of Ireland and today has been all sea. One ship in the convoy broke down as it was getting light this morning and was left behind. Today and for the next two days (while we are in the danger area) we man the two anti-aircraft machine guns.

Our defences have caused some amusement. First there was the kite—or rather kites. One morning, while sailing around Scotland, we came on deck to find the first mate and some men with an enormous kite on the deck. This kite was about six feet long and eight feet wide and made of bamboo and silk. It was attached to some wire which runs through a pulley at the mast-head to a drum on the winch at the foot. A rope on a loop ran free on the wire so that the kite could be launched by it. They got the kite up and let out the winch so fast that it dropped and slowly flopped into the sea. The wire broke and that was that. Two days later, or it may have been the next day, the spare one was got going properly but at night, when they wanted to pull it down (by the launching rope) the rope had blown out in the strong wind and, as no-one could reach it, the kite was left flying. A gale blew in the night and in the morning the kite had gone.

Winch — Pulley   KITE
Main Wire   Launching Rope.

Second come our machine guns. This morning one of the crew, explaining how it worked, got the ammunition belt jammed and, trying to free it, accidentally fired one round, narrowly missing one of the officers on the bridge.

Thirdly, we have our rockets. These are rocket things in fixed metal stands and are fired by pulling a string from about eight feet away. Now before we go further, another diagram is neccessary [*sic*—Bob was teasing Diana by using her misspelling].

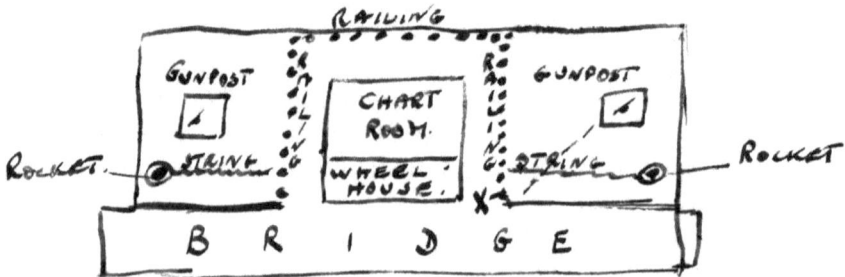

RAILING
GUNPOST   CHART ROOM   GUNPOST
ROCKET.   STRING   WHEEL HOUSE   STRING   ROCKET
B R I D G E

The above is the bridge. Wood all around except opposite the wheelhouse, then railings on the side. The two gun-posts are on open-roofing with no railing. Just by them are the rocket things. These are rockets which go up about five hundred feet then a parachute opens and trails a lot of wire cable to catch aeroplanes. They are fired by the pieces of string—one end is tied to the firing mechanism, the other to the railings: one just pulls and off they go.

I was on duty at 4.15 when the steward came for the tea tray which was in the gun-post. I was on the bridge talking to the officer, so I climbed over the railings (see x on diagram) and into the gun-post and brought back the tray. Meantime the captain's dog, with whom I am on very good terms, had followed to see what was up. As I climbed back over the railings, I saw the dog tied up in the string. Up went the rocket. Everyone on the bridge ducked. Connecting the mast and funnel is a stay which keeps them upright and holds them together.

There was a strongish wind blowing and so the rocket hit the stay with a loud twang and headed off sideways out to sea. The parachute soon opened about eighty feet up and sank into the sea. In the meantime the mast and funnel still stood although the stay (half inch wire) had been snapped, but the falling stay caught first on a wireless lead which snapped, and then on the string which works the hooter. This protested vigorously for a few seconds until this too snapped. Peace reigned again. The little dog laughed to see such fun.

I'm getting writer's cramp and it's now about 11.30pm so I think I'll close down for tonight. Just kiss you goodnight—I use that picture frame to write on—and then open the door and off with the lights.

Darling, you don't know how I miss you and miss not being able to hear from you— what you are doing, the local scandal, how you are and that you still love me. I know that but like to hear it all the same. Hope you don't mind my diary not being written to you, but it pleases my sense of humour to refer to 'my wife' and also it gets me out of the way of a 'chatty' letter. Anyway I think you get more quantity if not quality!

Sweetheart, angel, honeybunch I have many more months before I call you these again. Sometimes great waves of longing come over me and leave me feeling quite sick and tired and at night I try to read or write late so that I feel tired and soon sleep. Sleep and not dwell on thoughts of what might be.

Goodnight darling, God bless. I love you Diana, your husband, Robert xxxxx

THE NEXT DAY:

Brief history of trip: after sailing for a few days zigzagging in convoy westwards, we awoke one morning to find the escort vessels gone and the convoy dispersing in all directions—an extraordinary sight to see half a dozen ships all close to each other and going in quite different courses. After that rough seas and very cold for four or five days. Three or four days ago we started to sit out on deck and now the sun is almost dangerously hot. Excitement at seeing another ship. We keep off shipping lanes and away from land.

We have many types on board, a few of whom I really dislike, one or two with whom I find little fault but the majority are companionable and amusing.

At the head is the captain. He is a bit of an enigma. Shrewd, brave—he ran the British blockade at the outbreak of war, very uncommunicative, observant, but absolutely poker-faced. A round face, typically Dutch with little, rather piggish but attractive pale blue eyes. He says little of his own accord except if spoken to or to tell sometimes one of his port and agar stories. He has a good knowledge of English and the various words which a man might use but a woman never hears. He has a wife and a daughter and hasn't heard anything of them since the invasion of Holland. He likes his food, good company and, I am sure, his women.

I like him and he has a lovely dry sense of humour which is usually directed at 'Mac'. Mac(lean) is a Canadian: over six feet, broad-shouldered, narrow-hipped, large head, huge hands and feet 'a small 11½ in shoes', very outspoken. His father hates the English and he too always runs them down. His pet aversion is what he calls the 'lower classes'—which embraces anything affected, aristocratic, huntin', shootin', fishin', and lots of money.

Today marks the first flying-fish, the erection of the swimming pool and some very hot sun. We daren't stay out too long. I'm rapidly going through red to brown and keep thinking of the last time I did it—in May nearly a year ago.

Our evening walk round the decks is a very pleasant institution. The night is warm, the moon has lately been full and the sea looks lovely. Before the moon rises, it is beautifully phosphorescent with little stabs and flashes of light, some like sparkling diamonds flowing by in the water.

We stroll round and note how the stars are moving position. After the heat of the saloon—we are blacked-out all the way—it is most refreshing.

Don't vanish, angel, before I come back will you? And not then either—I expect you would like to hear that I still love you. People say that we'll like each other better for being apart but I'm quite sure I'll not let it happen again. Five or six wasted months.

19th January, 6.30. [Bob started dating his entries again]
MS Meliskirk. Lat 9°30'N, Long 20°00'W.

My darling, sitting now in the saloon and taking advantage of the comparative solitude to play some of the classical records they have on board. Some of them are quite good.

It gets hotter and hotter each day. We perspire in nothing at all and of an evening wear khaki shirt and shorts. The officers all went into white yesterday. The pool has been filled for the last two days and is a most popular spot. Last night it was too hot to go to bed so we sat up until 1.15 doing a jigsaw puzzle!

11.10 It's no good going to bed—still too warm to sleep. When I'm really tired I'll go off and drop asleep at once. Four of us are on the jigsaw tonight. The fans as usual going full blast. In about an hour or so we are supposed to be going to bathe before going to bed.

20th January, 6pm.

My dearest—to continue last night's story.

At 11.30 there was the Canadian officer and myself alone left but Lindsey came in a few minutes later to read.

We finished the jigsaw at ten minutes to two and then had a bathe in the moonlight in our birthday suits. It was glorious. Got into bed and I soon dropped asleep.

It has been very hot all day—could only sunbathe for a couple of hours although I'm pretty brown now. A short while ago we ran into a school of dolphins which we chased along in front of us and it looked marvellous to see sometimes as many as fifteen or twenty jump at the same time out of the water.

Tomorrow we cross the Equator and I expect we shall have some special fun then, although the captain won't say what they are going to do.

This afternoon we had some rain rather to our surprise and it looked quite threatening when it came down. I had pictured the Equator as being always very hot with never a cloud in the sky ...

21st January, 10.30am.

Last night the captain had a radiogram brought to him during dinner and after reading it he said it was for us, we all had visions of about-turning for home, Libya, Greece and so-on but it was a telegram from Neptune and his wife to say they would be aboard at 2.30 this afternoon. So the fun will be on.

Well Neptune has come and gone ...

At 2.30pm we were all assembled on the forward hatch next door to the pool when the whistle blew and a large bell started clanging forward. Neptune, wife and son appeared.

Neptune had on a bathing costume, wellingtons, a skirt of string, a gaudy blouse, false moustache, crown and sundry trappings of coloured streamers etc and a painted face—he was soon spotted as the first officer. He carried a trident with half a dozen herrings tied to it. His 'wife' wasn't recognised for a long time—he was the purser. His outfit consisted of a white dress with blue ribbons, sandals, scarlet toe and finger nails, an old befeathered hat and lots of make-up. Also two balloons. He looked most impressive. The son was one of the crew— the gunner—and he looked an absolute old pirate. A very old felt hat painted, a pair of trousers cut off at the knee, wellingtons and lovely painting and tattooing of fish, swords etc over his body and face.

One by one we sat in the chair and were given a medicine glass of salt water: as we tried to spit it out a runny porridge was plastered all over our face and if your mouth was open in it went. At the same time the herring was rubbed well in and finally the sea water hose was squirted in your face. Before the hosing the large wooden razor came into play and the scraped off porridge was wiped off on your hair. Next came the hosing, then flour was plastered with an immense shaving brush. Finally you sat on the end of a plank to be catapulted into the swimming pool.

Each man was dealt with in turn and as the last man was shot into the pool, Neptune and his ménage were rushed and thrown in too. It was all highly diverting and everyone enjoyed themselves a lot and didn't regret the wet siesta.

Now sitting in the cooler afternoon sun having laboriously worked the porridge out of my hair. There is really too much wind to write—this paper gets blown about too much. If so I'll be finishing now for a bit darling and if I don't write again—goodnight. I love you, Bob.

THE DAY AFTER:

After I had stopped writing I read a few pages of my book and stopped to admire the sunset. I was alone on the afterdeck and saw the sun sink, slowly at first but with ever-increasing speed, behind a bank of cloud to reappear in one last brief burst of glory before going behind the horizon. Sunsets are always impressive at sea: romantic, vivid and fascinating. No two are alike and an endless stream of different cloud formations and colours are amassed each evening.

Last night was so warm that I sat on until it was time to go and prepare for dinner. I was in a sheltered spot (from the wind). The sea was perfectly calm and the only noise was from the silk and bubbly murmur of the sea and the subdued throb of the engines.

We scarcely seemed to be moving. It was utterly peaceful. A few stars could just be seen appearing in the sky and I counted seven and wished while I thought of leaning out of the Alexandra [Hotel] window at Hastings and wishing. A few clouds scuttled quickly out of sight and I found myself drifting for the first time on this voyage into that blissful hypnotic state of happiness which Julian Green describes so well.* Not ecstatic yet not just contentedness. An intense feeling of harmony with your surroundings, of thoughts aptly expressed.

During dinner—or, rather, before we started, the captain made a little speech thanking Neptune for letting us off lightly, and us for co-operating so well and finally giving us our 'certificates' of baptism. Rather nicely we are all named after birds and not fishes: I will enclose the certificate with the letter if I remember. During dinner we had a very nice white wine on the company. The captain also told us that our certificates also made us automatically bachelors again: wasn't that nice of him?!!

NEXT DAY:

5.15. Hello darling, I've just woken up from my afternoon sleep. I haven't yet written a single letter except this and a few pages home: so I must really get down to it as we will be in Cape Town within the week.

There is a good sunset tonight but a game of deck-tennis is in progress, watched by the captain and a few others, which rather mars the tranquillity. Sometimes I hate every single person in the RAF yet it is so petty. Pettiness seems a vice of human nature—it is of mine anyhow. I get mad with people sometimes for no reason at all and hate myself and them for making me do so.

24th January, 5.15pm.

This evening there was quite a crowd sitting by my favourite hatch so I'm sitting right aft up on the gun platform with a block of wood as a seat and

---

*   Bob had been reading Julian Green's *Personal Record*.

leaning against the gun and right underneath the barrel. I should at least get peace and quiet here. Today has been one just as another—nothing of any interest. The only difference seems to be that everyone gets browner each day. I'm now about the colour of brown shoe polish.

This place seems to be singularly ill-chosen as regards smuts—I'm quite dirty already and I have to keep blowing them off the paper, blast them. I refuse to move tonight but it's too filthy to come again.

Extraordinary to think, sitting here, that we've been plugging away for nearly a month now at about 14 miles an hour and we've got as far as this—a nice example for the moralist in 'sticking at it'. Surprising, too, that in a week one can change from rough green seas and a biting gale to smooth blue waters, a cloudless sky and warm caressing breezes. If only you were here dear everything would be perfect.

We are supposed to arrive now in a week's time and I keep making hasty calculations as to the earliest we might be back. The trouble is that the RAF is such an unknown quantity. They will probably keep us waiting at Cape Town for some days then, when we get to wherever we are going, there will probably be more delay and, yet again, when we come back, they're bound to waste time. The very earliest that we can get back is about the end of June but I imagine that the end of July is more likely. I expect we shall hear more of that when we arrive at our destination.

25th January, 6pm.

Tonight I found another more secluded spot in one of the lifeboats but it has the disadvantage of being rather windy and smelling of paraffin. But there are no smuts and I hope to be left in peace.

11.15. In bed. It's cooler of an evening now that we are away from the Equator and with the fan it's bearable to sit in bed and write. Also, as we are now only a week off Cape Town, I want to get plenty of sleep so as to arrive looking and feeling really fit. I am quite well now but, with plenty of sleep for a week, I should then have plenty of energy in reserve.

26th January, 11.15pm.

I've been writing duty letters all day today and only just finished them. I'm left with a few I like writing to—to Uncle Harvey, Tony and Ruth. Today, for a change, it rained at lunch time and we had showers all afternoon. It is now cooler and I'm going to bed early as I also missed my afternoon siesta. Otherwise there is no news at all and I'm not feeling 'chatty' tonight. So goodnight my angel. Sleep well and please don't worry—I'll be back soon. All my love sweetest xxxxx xxxx Robert

27th January, 1.10am.

Well my darling, the good resolution to be in bed early has broken down. I've finished all my letter writing except one which I'll write in Cape Town or wherever we are going to.

It struck me today how absurd the RAF is to choose nine married men out of twenty-two on this trip when they could easily get five hundred volunteers to fill their places. It's just one of those things that makes me really mad.

I am sorry there has been so little news on this trip, darling, and that I found so little to talk about but I am quite surprised that it wasn't the dreary sort of journey that I had imagined. But there you are: my brain has been absorbed in material things and has failed in all those high things I planned. I've tried sometimes to write some verse but the words and inspiration isn't there. Nothing comes. Must go to bed. Sleep well my angel. All my love, all me. Your husband Robert xxxxxxx

27th January, 10pm.

I'm tired and a bit head-achy tonight so I'm going to bed early. Must just write a few lines before I turn in though. We are now getting near the 'Cape swell'— and we should arrive in a couple of days. Must do some packing tomorrow.

Goodnight my love. I'd give the world away to have you here. Goodnight my angel, darling wife xxxx Robert

31st January.

Cape Town is now a glow in sight and we expect to land tomorrow. So I'm going to finish this off more or less in case there is barely time to post it.

Last night was a surprise one—the captain's dinner. We all had paper hats, red, white and blue ribbon on the tables and streamers. The captain made a little speech and then a 'good evening was had by all'. There was a marvellous dinner and lots of food: I've kept the menu. We also had one glass apiece of champagne, red and white wines. It was a very good party and ended with a lot of water being thrown about: eventually we got to bed about 2.30am.

Today has been full of incidents. We have seen albatrosses, whales, three other ships and tonight we sighted land—Table Mountain—in the distance. After dinner we had a wonderful thunderstorm.

Now twelve o'clock so I'm off to bed angel. If I get no more time to write tomorrow, goodbye my darling and look after yourself. I shall be back soon. All my love dearest, all me.

xxxx xxxxxxx Your Robert

◊♦◊

Bob was soon to discover that his posting was to George, a town about 250 miles east along the coast from Cape Town. The South African Air Force was part of the Joint Air Training Scheme, a major programme for training RAF, SAAF and Allied air crews during the Second World War. Based at George was No. 61 Air School for navigation and reconnaissance training.

16

The burden of grief

LETTER TO DIANA:

George Hotel
George
South Africa
4th February, 1941

12.15am. My darling,

At last we seem to have a little peace and quiet again. At last we know what we are going to do and there is an end to uncertainty and eternal rushing about. I have not written the last day or so because we were either always on the move or else seeing the sights—or being shown them. But I'll begin at the beginning.

On our last morning on board at five o'clock the captain himself came round to tell us that we were approaching Cape Town and that we ought to take a look at it. It was worth turning out of bed for. At the back in the distance was Table Mountain, a hard clear line against the dawn-lit sky behind it. At the foot of it about six miles away lay the sights of Cape Town. It was like a lot of fairy lights hung on the side of the mountain in a shining skirt.

The town is built back up the foot of the hill and the lights we saw followed their path diminishing in breadth to the top and so forming a sort of triangle. The sea was dead calm and reflected back a distorted, twinkling imitation of the lights. In front was the black shape and red and green lights of another ship. Lunch soon and I've got to sew a button on first.

11pm. We docked at nine o'clock and at about 10am an immigration officer of sorts came on board and wanted to know where we were going. We of course knew no more than he did. However he phoned up some RAF depot and a squadron leader was down in half an hour to deal with us. He was able to tell us where we were going and a few scant details of the place.

We then separated our luggage into essentials and non-essentials for the next few days as the non-essentials had to follow up to George by goods train. We had to stay in Cape Town that night as there was no train that day.

By eleven o'clock we were loose in Cape Town. We headed at once for the bank and Post Office, there getting money and sending mail and cables. We also hopefully asked if there was any mail for us. At one o'clock we went to the hotel where we were staying—The International Hotel—but the unfortunate sergeants had to go to a camp about twelve miles out from the town—at a place called Wynberg [to the south of Cape Town]. However most of them stayed in the town that evening.

After lunch I got my khaki uniform fixed by the hotel and then we went out to tea in the town. We were 'rubber-necking' around after tea when an officer in a car picked us up. He took us (Lindsey, Mac and another officer) to a place called Del Monico where we sat for a while drinking and talking. Presently a friend of the first officer came in. They were both instructors from a near-by training school (nearby that is to George not to Cape Town) and told us lots of interesting odds and ends. They went off about seven so we went out to get some food.

After dinner we fell in with a South African Air Force fellow who introduced us soon after to some girls who had been flag-selling all day. We gave them drinks and the SAAF officer suggested that we visit Cape Town's one and only nightclub. To be continued ... tired now and sleepy—just 11.45pm. So goodnight angel, all my love darling. xxx your Robert

8th February. The night club was a bit of a flop—crowded and we had to take our own drinks of which we couldn't get much as all the shops were shut. However we danced until about two when the SAAF man took us all home. After we'd dropped the girls we had quite a hectic ride back as he'd had a little too much to drink, but we got back without incident. The next day I felt lazy, and not like moving at all. Nearly forgot, Lindsey and I shared a room in the hotel but one of the sergeants who was with us came back too as he didn't want to go right out to Wynberg and I slept on the mattress on the floor and he had the bed and some blankets.

We got up about ten o'clock and had baths and packed. It was about midday before we were up and about so we sat on the veranda until lunch-time. At three o'clock transport arrived to take us to the station and at 4.20 we left Cape Town. We were four in our compartment which had beds that let down making four berths in all. They were very comfortable and we also had a basin in the compartment. Before we started we bought a dozen peaches (1/6^d) and six pounds of grapes (1/-) which stood us in good stead.

The journey was about twice as far as the direct route because we had to go round a mountain range. However it was very lovely, especially the first evening as we wound our way along the foot of the mountains until we came to a narrow defile which was our way through. We passed through just as the sun was setting so we only saw a little of the other side.

The next day we awoke to find ourselves on the veldt, a dry treeless rocky plain on which little flourished except weeds. This went on all day until about ten o'clock when we started to go downhill. Presently we saw mountains in the distance and then the sea. It was Mossel Bay about twenty miles from George. From Mossel Bay we climbed up again to the foot of the distant mountains. Here everything was green again (the mountains cause clouds and thirty-six inches of rain a year. Danbury [near Diana's home] is about twenty-four inches). At 12.30am we arrived in George.

11th February, 1941. Your wire arrived this evening, darling, and I still can't quite take it all in. I keep saying to myself 'we are going to have a baby' and try to realise all that it means. Try to imagine you and I as parents, wonder what a child of ours would look like and grow up. Oh dearest, I hope it won't [tire] you too much. I know it must a little. Are you glad?

I wonder if anyone else knows yet, it's so marvellous. I like to think of [just] you and I alone knowing anything about it. And what shall 'it' be called. I don't very much mind what names we give a boy but there are heaps of girls' names I've read of and liked—Fleur (Galsworthy), Toinette for Antoinette, Anne I like, and dozens of others. My dear I'm so happy—I hope you are too. Thank heaven I shall be back before it comes.

Just can't think to write tonight dearest: my brain is too full and wanders all the time. Will finish this now and tell you all about George and 'the Wilderness' next letter. Look after yourself, my darling, oh God I wish I could be with you now. Nobody can understand why I hate this place.

All my love, all me, darling, dearest I love you xxx Robert.

LETTER TO DIANA:

George
17th February, 1941

Dearest, I realised with a shock today that I've been here a fortnight and only posted one letter to you—so much seems to happen and has to be done yet it is all the same—one day is like another. I haven't even written a letter home yet. I really must get down to it.

George is a funny place—named after a bastard son of George IV who founded the place. A very relaxing climate—you just want to sit around and look at nothing. We work from 8.30am–12.30pm, lunch 12.30pm–2pm and work 2pm–4.30pm. Not a hard day's work but we have to get two miles home for lunch.

We are billeted in the George Hotel and luckily transport is provided for us though most people take their own cars. Four of us have bought an old thirty-six horsepower Buick for £40 and hope to sell it to the next course coming in when we leave. It is absolutely essential out here to have a car and we were lucky to get this one quite cheap as prices have gone right up.

As soon as we get back in the afternoon, we get tea and then I usually go off for a bathe (ten miles away in the Wilderness) or more often for nine holes of golf. There is a good course here and I've managed to borrow clubs.

Wednesday is a half-day and we go down to the Wilderness after lunch to lie in the sun, bathe, tennis and golf. Usually though it's sunbathing and a swim—

quite good surfing—followed by tea at four o'clock at the hotel then croquet (!) until time to change for dinner. We also spend Saturday afternoon (and morning if we have it off i.e. every other week) and Sundays there just lying in the sun until tea-time.

For lunch and food we take about four or five peaches each, pounds of grapes, bananas and perhaps a pineapple!

After dinner we either do some work or go to the flics. There is only one flic house here but they have three changes of programme.

So actually we only spend four evenings a week here and that usually means flics two evenings and work the other two.

The hotel makes us laugh a lot as it is a honeymoon paradise and at 9.30pm hardly a soul is left about. One or two of us have got friendly with two married couples from the Gold Coast (aged about thirty-five to forty) who are most interesting to talk to.

Some of the people have been round about sight-seeing but I'm quite content doing nothing.

Except for the aerodrome, the golf course and the road to the Wilderness I've never been more than a hundred yards from the hotel! The weather here is warm and relaxing although they sometimes get heavy rain. When it gets colder some of us are going to climb up the mountain behind the town. A very easy climb but quite a long one. It should give us a wonderful view. Apart from the one letter I had from you and one from Mother, that is all the mail I've had and no one else has had any at all.

It is delightful to be out here now and would be just ideal for us if I were an instructor here. There is no black out of course and you can have no idea what a joy it is to wander round the lighted streets or sit as I am now on the upper balcony and see the lighted tree-lined road in front of me. If only you were here life would be perfect. Some day after this war we must come down here, or rather to the Wilderness, together.

And how are you my darling? There are so many questions to ask, so much I want to hear about—when is the baby due—about September or October? Whom have you told and what do they all think or what will they think? Will your mother be pleased or not? I know mine will. Do take care of yourself dear won't you? I'm longing to hear of all you have been doing. So glad to hear you have been writing verse, write some more, and we'll publish a joint book one day when we've got enough.

We had an exam today—the first of many. I think I did alright. Also flew for the first time since I've been here. We do most of our work on the ground and have to learn quite a lot.

Well, my darling, it's nearly ten o'clock and as we get called at 6.30am (with tea thank heaven) I'll be turning in. Will post this now and write again soon. Really soon this time now that we have got settled in and there are no odds and ends to worry about.

Give my love to everyone will you and if they wonder why I don't write just say I'm working too hard! Wait till you see the colour of my back and you'll realise the work I've put in.

Goodnight angel, do take care of yourself, don't absent-mindedly walk in front of a car and don't stop loving me. I couldn't stop loving you if I wanted to and if you stopped loving me ... too bad to think of. Dearest, all my love and all me and lots and lots of kisses your ever-loving ever-wonderful husband

xxxxxxxxxxxx

Robert

xx

◊♦◊

On 4 January 1941, Bob's younger brother John, by then a sergeant pilot stationed in Newmarket, was on a local daytime training flight aboard a Wellington L7783 from 99 Squadron Bomber Command. The plane crashed at 1250 hours.

All of the crew were injured and were taken to the White Lodge Community Hospital in Newmarket. Both Flight Officer John Davidson and John were described as dangerously ill. Davidson died at 1315 hours and John at 1600 hours. The other crew members survived their injuries—Pilot Officer Denys Bellerby had a fractured arm and pelvis and Sergeant Gordon Trustcott facial injuries that were described as 'not serious'.

John was just nineteen years old. He had served in the RAF Volunteer Reserve for 325 days and had been recommended for a commission. His father was informed of his death the day he died. He was buried at St Margaret's church, Downham, on 9 January.

◊♦◊

LETTER FROM PILOT OFFICER BELLERBY TO BOB'S MOTHER:

RAF Hospital
Ely
22nd January, 1941

Dear Mrs Keddie

I am so glad you wrote as I could not remember your address.

Something was very wrong with the aircraft and we all felt we would probably crash yet no one was at all perturbed. I could hear John and the captain talking quietly together as to the best course to take. John had been piloting but when he found that all was not well the captain took over control and was attempting to land when we crashed. The impact was so swift that he can have suffered no pain but must have been unconscious at once.

In John's death not only have I lost a real friend but the airforce is robbed of one pilot of the finest type who would have made an ideal officer. He thoroughly enjoyed the air + died as he would have wished doing his duty.

If there is anything I can do to help you in your great loss do please let me know. I am now much better.

Yours very sincerely
Denys Bellerby

LETTER TO DIANA:

George
22nd February, 1941

6pm. My angel,

Five letters all at once from you on Thursday. Now Saturday. Including the one about John. It seems so odd and far away as if it were someone else's John and then suddenly some little detail makes me realise in a bang.

The realisation is gradually sinking in though. More than grief I feel blind mad anger overcoming me in waves. I don't really want to talk of him though but please find out for me exactly what happened—though I suspect Father will tell me. His life is not wasted 'not pointless'—although he may have only been a 'passenger' at the time of his death and the reason for it may save many a life in the future—perhaps a whole squadron from destruction during operation.

I wish I could have been home. Now there is nothing I can do—no comfort but which will re-open the hurt and the pain. Poor Mother—her eldest brother in the last war, her youngest son in this. What faith to still believe in God as good. What can I write now, what can I say. I find it hard enough to write to you.

I am going to tell Mother about 'our it' darling if you don't mind: and by the time this gets to England I think you should make it generally known but I think the knowledge would help to make Mother happier too. In death, life. Give her an interest. Another 'baby' to 'manage'. John was always supposed to be the 'baby'. I hope you don't mind, darling, and any how Mother won't tell a soul. Should we call it 'John' if it is a boy? Incidentally, my sweet, you'd be pretty clever if you managed to keep 'them' in the dark until a few days before it arrived!

23rd February, 1941. After much re-writing I've managed to write a letter to Mother and Dad. My angel I hope you don't mind me telling them about 'it'—I know you won't or else I wouldn't. I'm sure it will help Mother a lot and darling please tell everyone as soon as it is necessary—for you I mean because you really ought to have advice of some sort and as I'm not there to look after you, please see that someone else does.

Yesterday two of us started to climb a mountain but the clouds came down and it rained like hell so that we came back as quickly as we could looking like a couple of drowned rats. In the evening I started these letters then went to bed early. Today I went to church at 8am and then went down to a bathing beach in the morning with Lindsey. A remote, rocky, lovely spot. Something like Cornwall. This afternoon we slept until tea and then played tennis.

Now ten o'clock and I feel tired and stiff so going to bed. But will post this tomorrow, short as it is, because I want you to get this before Mother gets hers, so I'll hold hers up for a day or so. Darling I daren't tell you how much I miss you: I hate to think of it—it makes me so sad and wild and longing. Bathing, surfing, golf, tennis, flics is all an effort—not to forget but to divert my mind. I'd go mad if I thought of you too much.

My dearest I love and love and love you. All of you—now 'it' too: there seems to be so much love that I've plenty to spare for it. Do you want a boy or a girl dear? I'm dashed if I know. Goodnight my angel, take care of yourself. I love you always. All me

Robert

xxxxxx

PS sorry this is so short but writing to Mother and Dad takes time.

17

I'm so sorry,
sorry for you, for 'it', for us

LETTER TO DIANA:

George
9th March, 1941

9pm. My darling, I've tried so often to explain to you how sometimes I can't write: perhaps it's all to ease a guilty conscience which says I should have made more effort—made myself write. But I just couldn't. Although we are now working full steam—two exams a week—there was yet time for a visit to the flics and two games of golf and a whole Sunday lying on the beach doing nothing. Dearest I'm sorry—I hope there is not a long gap between mails for you—but I hate the thought of <u>having</u> to write you. Not any wish for independence but if I ever start to write to you from a sense of duty I shall hate myself.

I've wanted to write, sat down to it once, and nothing came, but all the last fortnight I've been restless and unsettled—almost the feeling one gets before going away. Just wandering around doing nothing. I couldn't even work properly, my mind kept drifting. No doubt the news about John had something to do with it—but not so much the personal feeling as the implication of the whole thing, the utter futility and wastefulness of war.

Two letters from you on Friday, written before the last, when you were still at Waterhall and also one from Mother dated the 18 January. Apparently there are others in between. They may be at the bottom of the sea, but I think it is the erratic mails out here. Some of the lads have had no mail at all yet.

When we finish here we'd better have a code so that you can tell what I'm doing as I shall not be allowed to tell you. You can expect a cable any time after May 10 but it might be a couple of weeks or more after that—you remember how Uxbridge hung about?! The possibilities of coming home are very good, I think, but one can never tell with the RAF. Nothing I can do will make any difference as all postings are controlled by some little clerk in London like the other one we saw. However if you get a telegram signed Wallace that'll mean that I'm sailing for England sometime in the near future and if it is signed Arthur that will mean that I'm sailing practically immediately. Convoys home take about six weeks from here I believe, but may take longer as we stop on the way to pick up others. Coming out we were all on our own after the first few days and could go as fast as we could.

On Saturday morning I set out to climb this wretched mountain again and thought I'd try a new and apparently shorter route. I got hotter and hotter pushing through scrub stuff up to my waist and eventually took my shirt off and hung it over the haversack I had with me. Also took my watch off as I was perspiring so much and fastened it round my belt. After another hour I got deeper and deeper into the wretched undergrowth and had to admit that way was impassable. When I looked at my watch there was nothing but the strap and the glass cover. The stuff must have caught on the winding handle and pulled all the inside open.

I could have sat down and wept. I retraced my steps as far as I could but no sign of it. It was a forlorn hope from the start as the grass and weeds were about two feet deep and the heather and small trees were waist high. When at last I got back to the track I realised that my shirt too was gone so I had to stop at the first house near George and ring for 'Mac' to come out with another shirt for me. The shirt, thank heaven, was a very cheap one and didn't matter. In fact the humour of it cheered me up quite a lot. That evening we went down to the Wilderness and celebrated—Mac's first infant, a 7lb 4oz one which was three weeks overdue. Darling, you won't let ours be 'overdue' will you? I should just about go crackers.

I've written [to] Father and asked him to put some of our money in investments as it should pile up quite a bit in the next few months. How much do you think we shall need for the 'Baby'? Perhaps, from a financial point of view, it is a good thing I came out here as we should never have been able to save this money otherwise! Anyhow be prepared if he asks you how much you'd like left untied!

My dear, I'm so glad you thought too that Mother would like to know of our little effort, I'm sure it would cheer her now as nothing else could and I'm sure she'll long to help us as she had an exactly similar time in the last war [when her brother died and Bob was born].

Well, there's ten o'clock just sounded. Time for bed as we were late last night. Bought two books here the other day—'Winnie-the-Pooh' and a book of modern French verse. I hadn't read the bear of very small brain for a long time and I thought it might come in useful—later! The other is quite a nice little book and well bound. If we have no furniture in our future house we will at least have some books and as a wall decoration I'd ask for nothing more.

Must go to bath and bed now. My angel I must be home soon—by the time this reaches you, you should have got half-way through it. Was the Millom job very trying?* You sounded most unhappy. If you are still at Mullion try and go and see Uncle Harvey—he'd love to see you and you'd love <u>him</u> I know.

---

*   Diana wrote in her diary about the loneliness of Millom, near the Lake District, where she
     was a governess.

I'll write again in a day or two, there's lots more I've got to say but I'm too tired now to write any more. My honeybunch I love you past all knowledge—take care of all of us now won't you? And please darling try and get some advice as soon as you think you need it. If you are in Essex go and see Dr Macdonald if you want to. Darling, only another three or four months I hope. I feel I can't possibly live and wait all that time. I shall languish and fade away with longing.

All my love and all of me, my darling my own. I love you, I love you, I love you, your own husband Robert

LETTER TO DIANA:

George
16th March, 1941

9pm. Two more letters from you darling and one from Mother. I don't know if any of yours have got lost but some from Mother and Dad apparently have so I'm not sending any more photographs—I don't want to lose them. One of yours is from Yelverton and with other letters from Patsy, Pauline and Sally. I wonder if you are still there—crocus time, while out here the heather is in full bloom; it's now 'September' but it never gets really cold. With any luck I should get back towards the end of June to enjoy my second summer.

I shall probably go some way north when I go back and if I manage to get onto flying boats; almost certain to go to a place about fifty miles west of the Connal's where I was billeted [he might have meant Stranraer, further south than Monktonhead]. That should give no information away.

Time seems to be passing faster now—another week and we'll be half-way through our course. I've never absorbed so much knowledge in so short a time before. We are going strong now with our two exams a week and by the time the weekend arrives most of us feel pretty weary.

And you, darling, have you learnt to be resigned yet? You must have had a miserable time at Millom—Peter Hall lives at Lancaster and knows how drear it is—but it all will have helped to pass the time.

Incidentally I must have missed a letter: last I had heard was that you were thinking of leaving and then comes a letter from Cornwall, now Yelverton. I addressed my last letter to Mullion: I'll address this to Yelverton, just in case you are there still.

You needn't worry about money for the baby, dearest, by the time I get back we should have about £150, I think. The trouble will be when we have to live on my pay afterwards. The RAF only gives 10/6^d a week for the baby! But we shall manage and by next November I should get promoted to flying officer which is worth twice as much as a baby—£1 a week extra! Odd financial brains they use in the RAF.

In case you don't know still where George is here in a very rough map <u>not</u> to scale. Names are odd here. Imagine a small village at home called 'the Wilderness'!

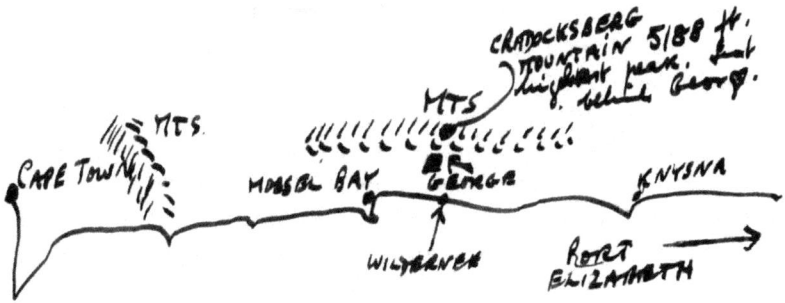

Hope you are wiser!

Must do some work now—exam tomorrow. Goodnight my darling, I love you now as always and ever. Keep well, keep happy and the days will go more quickly. Take care of yourself. Every care and don't do anything silly. Oh dearest I will be back soon, must be. All my love angel and all me.

Love love and love; all love for you

xxxx Your husband Robert

LETTER TO DIANA:

George

23rd March, 1941

The weather is now definitely cooler, but it's still warm—warm enough, just, to bathe. We had to work Saturday morning and in the afternoon I slept till tea-time and then played golf until dinner. After dinner I was lugged off for a drink at the Wilderness but we got back quite early. This morning I wrote letters, then this afternoon I again slept until tea-time. After tea I had nine-holes of golf and a swim with David Batley,* who shares a room with us, and a girl, darling (you are the darling, not the girl). She is engaged to a S. African airman so it is all quite proper dearest.

So far we had about six or seven exams but there are eight or nine more which we take in the last fortnight and they are the ones that really count. However, up

---

* Pilot Officer David Batley had shared Bob's cabin during the passage to South Africa. He was killed in a flying accident later in the year.

to now there are about five of us at the top within ten marks of each other. I made a mess of one paper—carelessness—but got 100% in four of them. So I may get those flying boats yet.

So tired now darling and so wanting you. I miss you like hell. People out here are amazed at the way we want to get back home: anyway it's a lovely country and I hate it. Enclose some heather I picked for you on the golf course. I wonder whether it will survive the journey. In case it doesn't some was white and some the ordinary colour. Darling, darling I'm going to be home very, very soon if wishing has anything to do with it. I love you more and more each day. Keep well, keep safe, and take care of yourself for me won't you angel? I love all you with all me xxxxx

Your own Robert

LETTER TO DIANA:

George
25th March, 1941

9pm. Angel, a shattering blow to-day—we are to move into the mess in about a week or a fortnight's time: that means, instead of about 16/6^d allowances, I shall only get about 4/6^d or a difference of about £18 a month. However I shall probably save about £4 or £5 on food and lodging. All the same it is a great blow: a pity we can't burn the place down or something.

To-day we've had what is known as the Berg wind, a kind of Sirocco. It's a wind from the Karoo or high hot country which comes over our hills and down to George. Coming downhill always makes the air hotter so it is very warm by the time it reaches here. So after flying this afternoon we all felt bits of headaches and shot down to the Wilderness for a bathe. We found the water very cool and refreshing—almost cold in fact as it was six o'clock before we got in—and now feel much better.

All this week I've been saying to myself 'we are over half-way through' or 'only another six weeks'—but the trouble is that, when we've finished, we are quite likely to be held up for days waiting first for our postings and, if we come home which I think is probable, then for a ship. If you get my coded telegram, please don't tell anyone who won't keep it strictly to themselves because it is quite possible or probable that we should sail in a trooper and, if Jerry got the slightest suspicion of that, he'd be all ears and eyes. 'Arthur' means 'sailing almost immediately' and Wallace means 'sailing shortly' i.e. in a few days or even weeks. I hope that is the way I said it last time, because that is how I remembered it and anyhow is how I'll send it.

I hope you are still feeling full of the 'joys of spring' my darling. I was so glad to get your letter from Yelverton to say that you had been really 'happy' again—that same happiness of Julian Green's? Wonder where he is just now? I miss my books and miss my music but above all miss you dearest—strange to say. I hate this place—this hotel and the country around: I don't want to see any of it yet it is very beautiful and grand. I'm sure that if only you were here I could enjoy it more, in fact it would be just ideal if you and I were here for the rest of the war. Lovely climate, no one seeming to realise there is a war on ... and yet ... I wonder? Wouldn't we want to get back? There is a peculiar fascination about England or one's homeland ... any homeland, I suppose, just the wish to go back from whence one came ... dust to dust ...

Must go and do some work now, darling. Look after yourself won't you like a good wife—so far I've kept out of all sickness and colds, but it is easier here in this climate.

Honeybunch, all my love and all me, you don't know how much I miss you—or perhaps you do—yet I'm 'happy' too in a way. I like the work and now it's bringing me nearer you.

All your angel dearest, all yours for ever and a day, whatever that means—in thought and mind and body, your own husband

Robert

xxxxxxxxxxxxxx

Wallace Arthur Robert Keddie

PS Just found we can send letters from the camp for nothing, but as this one has something in that might be censored I'd better pay 1½d once more. Incidentally believe you can (could have!) written me for 1½d too—

LETTER TO DIANA:

George
30th March, 1941

4.30. Just woken up from my afternoon siesta and would give anything for a cup of tea—but that I'm afraid won't come. I'm Orderly Officer, which is one of the nasty jobs in the RAF where you do little except sit about and waste time. Here it is worse: because there is no one in the mess at all and I have to be here from 9am this morning until 8am tomorrow. However I've managed to get a little work done which I shouldn't have otherwise as it is a lovely afternoon and I would certainly be down on the beach.

There is little news here—as always—but either the increased work (the tempo quickened a bit last week as the exams will be recommencing in a week or two) or the air here made us all terribly sleepy last week. Went to bed about 10pm and got up 7.30 but even so could hardly keep awake when the afternoon came round. This afternoon I slept from 2.15–4.15. Now I want my tea and won't get it.

Reading these days, when I get the chance, 'Confessions of a Young Man'—George Moore, 'Penguin' edition. An intensely interesting book. Very good unintentional Nazi propaganda in parts. 'You must have rules in poetry if only for breaking them just as we dress women for the pleasure of undressing them.' Very amusing book. Also the little book of French verse. There are some charming little pieces in it from a book called 'Le Kiosque à Musique' by Maurice Franc-Nohain. If you ever potter round a book shop darling with a few spare shillings in your pocket and find that it is cheap ...

Some of the officers have to move into the mess on the 16th April—which means three weeks here. Hope to the devil our course doesn't move in but I don't think we've much hope. The trouble is that we shall live in wooden huts, two to a room with no wardrobe or dressing table or clothes-hooks and with about 100 yards to go to wash or to the lavatory. And I hate that especially if it is raining. The only blessing is that it ought to give us time for an afternoon siesta ...

So glad you told Mother you thought you were going to have a baby—she seems quite thrilled about it and most anxious that I shan't worry. She says that you can rely on them at anytime or anywhere.

Forgot to ask you last time that if you have any relatives with binoculars that they don't use ... Coastal Command urgently require them and, if they'd lend them for the duration, they'd be of immense service to me. The trouble is that I can't guarantee giving them back, but I'd do my best. Anyhow if you've any patriotic, stand-up-for-the-God-save-the-King relatives just drop a hint.

31 March. 7.30am. Just been into the airmen's mess and asked if there were any complaints. There never are usually—and, if they do complain, nothing is done. Good old RAF. Apparently I have to stay on the camp here until the next man arrives—i.e. until 9 o'clock. As lectures start then that means that I shan't get any breakfast, shan't get a wash or a shave unless I go back to the hotel at 9 and then I shall miss lectures. What a wonderful organisation.

It's a lovely morning and the mountains and trees look glorious. We are right at the foot of them and they usually have a white cap of clouds or sometimes a 'collar' effect. If only they had snow on I could imagine I was back in Switzerland.

Oh darling this is the eighth week of our course—only five more. In another six weeks we might be sailing for home. Might be ... but probably not. I never dare look too far ahead these days, and the RAF never does the logical or the obvious. All my love and all me angel, I miss and need you terribly. Don't worry about me honeybunch I love you love you <u>love</u> you, Robert

LETTER TO DIANA:

George
6th April, 1941

9.30pm. My darling, such a large quota of mail from you this [morning] and a lot of enclosures as well—Jean, John, Pat, the Padré, Jeremy, Gerald. I suppose that means we shan't have any more mail in this week. Also one of your letters—a 'missing link' posted just after you'd left Millom. Also your rather disconcerting telegram. I wonder what can have happened to all my letters—I wrote dozens on the boat and a small novel to you: I shall be livid if they've gone and let it get sunk. All that wasted energy. Perhaps it will turn up one day.

You really must be a reformed character: when first you told me about getting up at 7.15am I just sat low and said nothing. It seems to have gone on for more than a month now so perhaps you really are reformed. Don't overwork angel though will you, after all, you know, you are not used to it!! Also very glad to hear the infant is behaving quite well to date, let's hope 'it' will continue to do so the rest of its life.

We flew to Cape Town yesterday and when we started to come back one of our engines gave out so we had to stay there the night. We had no pyjamas, toothbrushes or anything, so some of the SAAF lent us civilians [civilian clothes] so that we could walk about 'properly' dressed. We returned to-day through pouring rain and pretty cold (we'd only shirts and shorts on) and found the aerodrome just about flooded when we got here. However we got down alright and we hurried home for hot baths. I still feel a bit chillsome, so think I shall turn in in a few minutes. I do not want to start a cold. We have fires in the hotel to-night—the first time.

There is no other news my angel except that the tempo of the work here gets faster and faster. By the time we've finished I really shall need a long sea-cruise to recuperate.

Must really go to sleep now, I feel very sleepy. Goodnight angel—it is comforting to think that we keep the same time here as you do, that when I get up you do, and when I'm going to bed you are too: Funny that it should be comforting but it is.

So goodnight my darling, be good and don't worry about me—I should hate my child to be born with wrinkles!

Sleep well—do you have a rubber hot-water bottle these days? I'm sure it is not as good as the original! Sleep well—my thoughts are with [you] always and I go to sleep thinking of you and if only you were here too, now. Oh darling we must be together again soon must and will, will, will. Keep wishing and willing and believing. Honeybunch I love you to distraction—all my love, all me for you and ours

Love and love, all love

Your husband, Robert

◇◆◇

Diana sent a telegram to Bob saying that she had had a miscarriage.

◇◆◇

George
11th April, 1941. Good Friday

My dearest—Your telegram arrived yesterday. I'm so sorry, sorry for you, for 'it' and for us; but most of all for you. You mustn't ask forgiveness, angel, I've nothing to forgive; it's no more your fault than mine. My only worry is how you are—you really are 'absolutely well' aren't you? You wouldn't say you were if you weren't?

Darling, please don't reproach yourself or us and though neither of us can, or want ever to forget, please try and not dwell on what might have been. We have each other for many years more and please God we shall have other children. You must not dwell on it dearest because you are young (oh, yes you are!) and it is bound to affect you, and the life we make together, and too much thought would do neither of us any good. All very well in theory but when we come to apply it to ourselves very hard.

Try and talk to someone about it—Patsy, Pauline, Patsy—anyone you can talk to. And when I come back, me. Nearly forgot myself for once. It is very sad for both of us and much more of a shock to you than to me but it is not like the cutting short of even a day old child, far less one that has a personality.

Cheer up my honeybunch—I should be home soon after this reaches you.

Today we again tried to climb the local mountain. We got up about 2,000 feet—quite the most difficult part as we have to force our way through scrub stuff about three feet high. But when we got up to that height clouds began to form and very soon the next 1,500 feet was blotted out. So down we had to come—most ignominious, especially as it began to rain about 20 minutes before we reached the car and we got soaked. However we got back in time for a hot bath and lunch and after that a siesta until tea-time. Then some work until dinner and it's now 9pm. So there you are right up to date.

Bed early tonight and up late tomorrow. If it's fine on the beach, if not—do some work, I suppose. And there you have the future.

I'll write again tomorrow. All my love dearest: I want you very much, feel lost and lonely without you.

All my love, all me—Robert

Now it's Sunday, Sunday evening and ten minutes to eight. Where did I leave off?

Today Lindsey and I got up 6.30 and staggered off to church still half asleep. It was my second visit to the cathedral (a little bigger than Little Baddow church) and for the second time the Bishop did not perform. I was rather surprised for being Easter Sunday quite a lot of people were there.

About 10 o'clock we decided to make another assault on the mountain. It being rather late we decided to go half-way by car up one of the passes. We got there about 11 and by 1pm had climbed to within about 500 feet from the top.

But an enormous chasm divided us and we had to admit ourselves beaten for the third time. However it was well worth it for the view from up there was terrific: we could see the sea and coastline on one side and all around the rest were mountains and broad valleys stretching as far as we could see. There was not a cloud in the sky. We got down again by 2:30 and then came back and down to the Wilderness for a bathe. After that tea, 'home' for a bath and supper. And now once more we are up to date and run out of things to say.

> And like a dying lady, lean and pale,
> Who totters forth wrapp'd in a gauzy veil,
> Out of her chamber, led by the insane
> And feeble wanderings of her fading brain
> The moon arose up in the murky east
> A white and shapeless mass.

Guess who wrote that before you turn over the page?

Shelley—doesn't seem to fit does it? But it describes the moon that has just risen—a faded yellow piece of cheese was what it looked like to me as it slowly rose from behind the roof-tops. But now it's clear cut—a full silver romantic moon. Two moons from now and where shall we be? Together? Together once more ... what a lovely sound that word has. Darling I want and need you so. What a pity that individual wishfulness can have no effect on our postings from here.

Angel darling, I still adore you, darling goodbye and goodnight, your Robert

UNDATED LETTER TO DIANA:

RAF Camp
South Africa

My angel, it is nice to think that I shall probably get home before this does—lovely exciting thought. In fact it seems rather a waste writing at all, but not to write might be to tempt providence too far. And if I do go elsewhere, it will be a substitute (a poor one, but still part of me).

We have now just two weeks of our course left, and this ? I'd pay quite a lot of money to know my future movements for the next two to three months.

We moved into the camp on Wednesday. It's not as bad as we expected but I'm glad we've only got to be three weeks, at the most, here. We have to go about 50 yards in the open to get to the bathrooms and ... but I believe I let out a moan about this last time I wrote. Sorry.

We only had one exam this week—meteorology—I don't think I did very well this time. Next week we have two of the most important, the final navigation paper for which we can get 300 marks and a paper called patrol and search. That leaves another four for the last week. God I shall be glad when they're all over. I think nearly everybody is pretty fed up or 'browned off' as they say in this place. You'll have a lot of RAF slang to pick up darling! And I hope bad language doesn't worry you much because some of the everyday expressions are not quite drawing room to say the least. One of the joys of the English language I think is its expressive swear words and I can see little harm in them used as they are for expressiveness and because they are onomatopoeic (spelling right?—I should ask you!) rather than for their meaning.

How short I am for news to start a discourse on bad language, but really there is nothing of real interest to tell you.

We ought to have some money saved by the time I'm back shouldn't we? Even though I had £10 transferred yesterday. We only get 4/- allowance now—but I think we ought to sell our car for £10 each before we go. We've got a nibble for it.

Dinner 'gong' just gone. Must work afterwards. So goodnight, goodbye, see you soon my darling. Keep well won't you, be well and love me won't you? Oh angel, honeybunch I want you so much I'll mutiny if they don't send us home the day we finish.

All my love angel, all me. Be good. Love you always. Lots of kisses xxxxx
Your husband, Robert

◊♦◊

Bob set sail from South Africa on 19 May aboard the Athlone Castle and docked at Liverpool three weeks later. He was about to be given his dream posting.

18

No 'slice of love' tonight

Shortly after returning from South Africa, Bob's posting on flying boats was confirmed. The first step was to train at one of Britain's largest flying boat training bases, RAF Coastal Command's Stranraer unit in Scotland. He started there on 28 June. He and Diana were able to live together outside the base in private accommodation.

Bob did not explain exactly what attracted him to flying boats but perhaps he was drawn to them because of his experience of sailing—a flying boat pilot needed to be a seaman as well as an airman.

He took up his first operational posting when he joined 210 Squadron in Oban on the west coast of Scotland in September. Initially he flew with a more senior officer on board. Diana moved to Oban and she and Bob lived together in a boarding house along the seafront to the north of the town.

On 13 November, Bob received his promotion to flying officer and, later that month, he flew from Oban via Stranraer to RAF Mount Batten in Plymouth. From there the mission was to transport small arms to Tobruk in North Africa. Diana wrote that, out of the blue, he met Dick as he passed through Gibraltar.

Bob's first operational flight as captain took place on 19 November 1941, and from 3 February he was back in Stranraer for a five-week captain's course. He wrote to Diana from the flying base servicing unit at Wig Bay, 4 miles from Stranraer, round the edge of Loch Ryan.

◊♦◊

LETTER TO DIANA:

Officers' Mess
RAF Wig Bay
Stranraer
Wigtownshire
23rd February, 1942

My darling,

Here's a short and dirty note to tell you that we are living in comparative squalor but that I hope to be back soon. Hope like hell, because even if I didn't want to, I couldn't stand much more of this. We live in Nissen huts without light, no servants and have to light our own fires with wood which we have to climb trees to get. I've never been so filthy in my life.

Had a good trip down here. Did you see my first pilot waving as we flew down Alness main street?* We came round twice actually—the first time more or less in formation with another Cat[alina]. We gave Oban a real beat-up when we went through: dived on it in tight formation as perhaps you've heard.

I've seen Holly† and asked him to tell Daphne to let you know I was OK. He's pretty 'browned off' here I think and wishes he were back in Oban.

One thing it's pretty economical living here as we never get to Stranraer itself and have nothing to spend money on at all. We've even made chessmen by carving wood and, when we have no work, play chess or 'battleships'.

Hope you are well and all my love darling

xxxx Robert

◊♦◊

After completing his captain's course, Bob moved up to Sullom Voe on the Shetland Islands, where his squadron had relocated. The northernmost tip of Britain was an easier jumping-off point for both reconnaissance patrols to monitor German activity on the Norwegian coast, and for providing an escort for British supply ships heading for Russia.

Around this time, enemy activity had increased in Norwegian waters and several German warships had moved into anchorages along the coast. The pressure was on 210 Squadron to keep the Admiralty updated with accurate information on these activities.

The squadron's 'cross over' patrols off Norway's Trondheim Fjord were codenamed Sentry 1, 2 and 3, and Prowl. The Catalina crews had to fly within 5 miles of the coast by night and 50 miles by day for several circuits in a

---

*   Bob might have been flying from RAF Invergordon.

†   Squadron Leader Frederick Undecimus Hollins was married to Daphne and had an eleven-month-old daughter.

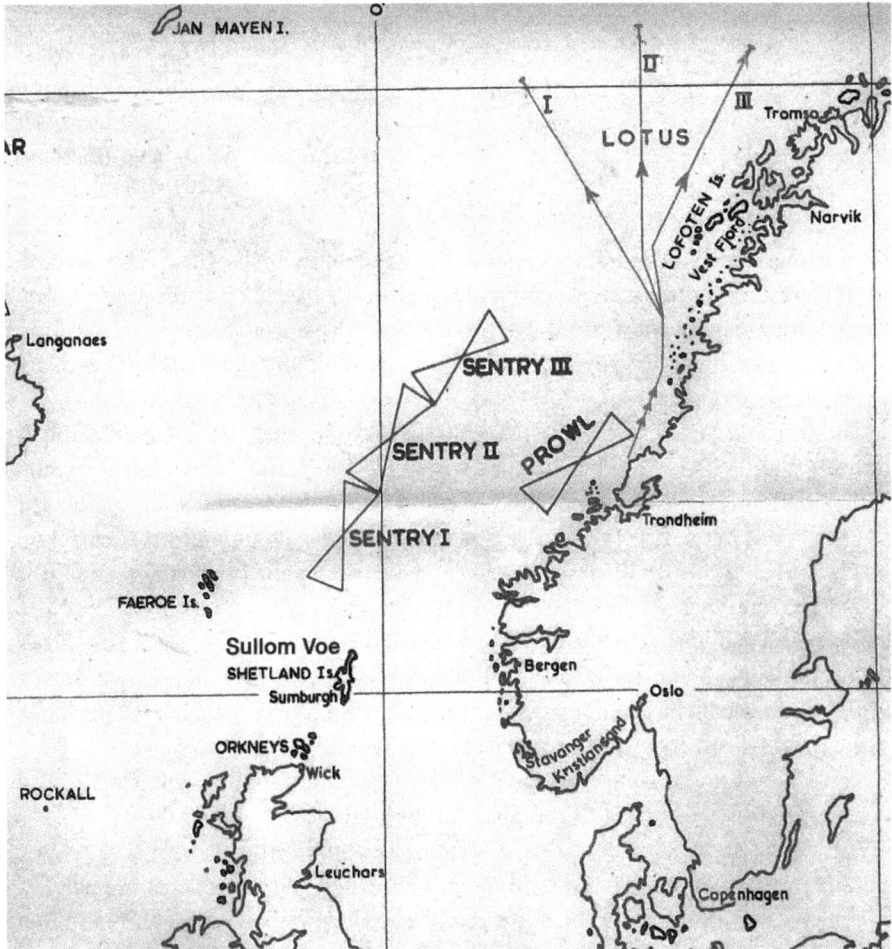

Map showing the patrol routes operated by 210 Squadron out of RAF Sullom Voe.

'straight-sided' figure-of-eight pattern. The Lotus 1, 2 and 3 patrols covered the coast off the Lofoten Islands, north of the Arctic Circle.

The patrols could be long and monotonous, often without any sightings of the enemy or land. At this stage of the war, the Catalina's anti-submarine radar was about 50 per cent accurate. Its range was up to 15 miles for medium-sized ships and about 4 miles in good weather for submarines on the surface. The Catalina could fly at altitudes beneath 50 feet, which helped it avoid enemy radar.

Flying boats needed a steady sea for take-off and landing, and the weather, which could be appalling, often made it impossible to go on patrol at all. Therefore reports to the Admiralty about German shipping could be intermittent, which did not go down well. After all, ships had to stay out in all weathers.

◇◆◇

LETTER TO DIANA:

> The Officers' Mess
> RAF Station
> Sullom Voe
> Shetland
> 12th March, 1942

My darling, hope you're not feeling too lonely—luckily I have little time to think but it's very cold and lonely sleeping alone although we have a fire in the room. The journey here went very smoothly on the whole and finally arrived 4.30 yesterday. I'm living in similar quarters as at Wig [Bay] but with adequate furnishing and our fire.

'The house' is occupied by an Army wife and the next nearest habitation is about five miles away and I think the 'Army' lives there too. Lerwick [the capital of the Shetlands] is really impossible—I never get in there and it's impossible for you to get out here. Also I think the Wing Commander would put his foot down. So it looks as if we shall have to grin and bear it again for some six months except for intervals of leave.

Played squash with Gillie tonight and as usual got soundly beaten.* Amenities are not lacking as you see but it is a hole of a place! We get a flic shown once a week—last time including a news reel of the BEF in France! Also can wear civvies in the mess—I'm very glad I brought my new jacket!

News is scarce and subject to the inevitable restriction but I think I'm allowed to say it is cold yet my health remains unimpaired.

The wireless works well and is a very great boon. Other people had to buy them from the last people and paid more for old sets than mine cost me new!

The GC [Group Captain] also is a really good man, which is a great help in a place like this. He organised a dance here a week ago and got transport to bring in about thirty girls from Lerwick—the shortage of that commodity is worse than Gib: Wrens, WAAFs and ATS not being allowed. However the mess is a jolly one and the food quite reasonable so I'll be able to last out my time I hope—anyway I'll have to!

Have decided to go on paying the £14 a month into your account: I should still save easily as there is nothing to spend money on! For once we should have some over. I'm also lazy and can't be bothered to write to the bank. Have you seen a doctor yet? Go up to London if you like and see your aunt's doctor—I think you would be wise to see one soon. [Diana was pregnant again—two months gone.]

Got to be up at 6 45 tomorrow so I will say goodnight my darling. Please do take good care of yourself my love—no weeds in the garden when I come home

---

*   Pilot Officer G. G. Potier, nicknamed after Gillie Potter. He received a DFC when flying with the squadron later in the year.

on leave! I miss you terribly and vainly try and believe I don't; not that I don't want to but it helps to lessen the shock [of being apart].

   With all my love and kisses angel—all bad things come to an end.

   xxx Robert

LETTER TO DIANA:

RAF Sullom Voe
15th March, 1942

My darling, all the news is in the letter I've written home but, in case you are not there still, I'll repeat it all.

   How are you feeling darling? Not sick I hope—getting any fatter yet? Don't swell too much before my next leave which I'm sorry to say won't be for another three months probably: I was half afraid it would be put off. However I've been very lucky so far.

   Duffield* and Frankie [Pilot Officer Frank Franklin] are with me flying—they are a good pair and easy to get on with.

   Today we had a half-day and in the afternoon borrowed bicycles and went about six or seven miles away to have some tea in what is about the nearest habitation of more than one room! They are doing a roaring trade at the moment in teas for the RAF.

   The scenery here can be quite beautiful especially in hazy weather. The water is astonishingly clear and blue and there is water everywhere—it is a maze of islands and voes as the inlets and lochs are called here. The hills are not high and generally the barren and brown grass slopes fairly gently to a rocky shore. There are some good cliffs though and the general effect is similar to Oban. More water and no trees.

   Hope to get this off from the mainland: I expect to call in for a few hours in a day or so to collect some stuff.

   I haven't sent a letter-telegram yet because they are all censored on the station and, though quite cheap (1/3^d for 35 words, I think), they are too long and 'unimportant' for telegrams and yet too impersonal and public for letters. However, when the occasion demands, I'll send one or, if you want me to, I'll send one a week.

   Take care of yourself my darling and take heed of the advice in my last letter: and try and not 'mope' angel—get around if you feel like and see some of your old friends. Incidentally re cash: I thought that for three months the £14 per month would cancel out my debt to you! And after that it can go towards 'family expenses'!

   All my love and kisses darling—I miss you terribly. Be good.

   xxxx Robert

---

*   Flying Officer W. S. (Bill or Duffy) Duffield.

RAF Sullom Voe
21st March, 1942

Darling, I was very disappointed to miss you on the telephone. We are unfortunately not allowed to telephone from here.

I'm glad to hear you saw Doctor Mac—how do you like him? The thing about Doctor Mac is he is never rash: he has a reputation, it's really a joke in our family, of being over cautious. In your case it's a good thing, I'm thinking, although, as you say, forces beyond our control separate us and you must, from boredom if nothing else, get in some rest!

As you may imagine, we are busy. Laundry is my urgent need: also one or two photos of my wife, please if you can pack them: including one of the 'glamorous' ones!

I told Mother on the phone and asked her to let you know that I shall be unable to get leave until about the middle of June I'm afraid. I've been so lucky so far and now have to pay for it while other people make up arrears. Roger Brown unfortunately has no system and now they've found out I had about twice as much as anybody else! Perhaps it's too early yet to make arrangements but I think Cornwall would waste too much travelling time don't you? Especially as I only get about twelve days in London. Suggest we spend a couple of days in town—and then retire to Essex and seclusion: what do you think? Or will London be too hot and strenuous then for you?

Played the GC squash two or three days ago and lost 3-2. Also managed to lay him out for five minutes in the middle of the game by hitting him in a vulnerable spot! Hardly diplomatic. The Wing Co beats me easily: must get some more practice.

Tonight is 'Band Night'. We have to wear uniform and the band plays until about midnight: it is actually a party night and the traditional ending is a Station versus Squadron battle if the Station can muster enough survivors! Now 9:30 so will have to join battle.

Goodnight angel: please be very careful with yourself for me. I know you will but I love you too much not to worry. I miss you an awful lot darling and hardly know how to face another three months without you.

All my love and all me darling and forever yours xxxxx to my own adorable wife from husband Robert

xxx

xxx

xxx

LETTER TO DIANA:

RAF Sullom Voe
26th March, 1942

My darling, have now had four of your letters—the last, dated the 21st, came tonight. Had very little time for writing recently and I'm afraid this will be rather short: now 9:30 and I have been at it since 3am!

Don't think I want anything just yet except my laundry (got some very welcome handkerchiefs from Mother a few days ago). I have been wearing two shirts only since I left home. I now share a room with Duffy and he's just back from leave with lots of Ovaltine etc and a saucepan. The whole thing is known almost invariably in the RAF as a tea swindle but here the new man succeeding Holly is a rhyming slang fan and tea is always known as Rosie (rhyming slang Rosie Lea—cup of tea). Hence Rosie swindles. 'Swindles' because usually guests are charged for Rosie and great profit accrues to the 'swindlers'. Did you get it all? In itself it explains one of the more enjoyable aspects of this place: namely the opportunity to retire to one's room to comfort and self-brewed refreshment.

28th, 11.15pm. As I was writing last night, Duffy came in and said we'd be called at 2 o'clock next morning so I packed up, left my clothes out and went to sleep.* Got to bed about 2:30 last night but was up in time for lunch today. Did some work and played Nigel squash this afternoon.

All your parcels arrived today—four of them with shoes, slippers and clothes, thank you very much darling. Also letter (dated 24 March)—your list of names amused me. I haven't many preferences or many dislikes either. I like Dick's third name Damyon. I don't like Adam, Bartholomew, Jonathan, Luke, Mark, Nicholas or Timothy—the last two rather a lukewarm dislike. Of girls' names I like all except Philippa, Patience, Unity, Prudence, Charlotte, Virginia and Sara. (It seems I dislike biblical connections for boys and names suggesting virtues for a girl—a bit sinister!). Of 'double names' I suggest Susan Jane (I like Susan), Jennifer Ann or Jennifer Jane, Rose Anne (Rosanne?!) or Anne Rose.

Your flower was a welcome though somewhat bitter-sweet arrival, although, as Nigel was saying tonight, it is not so much the flowers that we miss as the trees. The land here is bad enough in its sameness—all brownish, peaty, heathery, grass and rocks—completely without break or variation that cultivated fields give but it is trees or rather the lack of them and flowers that we miss most.

The trees would never live in the winds that blow here, although I believe that there are some good specimens of some wild flowers. I haven't seen any—or had the time to look for any so far.

---

*   27 March marked Bob's first action from Sullom Voe: an 'airshipping' patrol. After three and a half hours of flying, the crew sighted the Nordøyan Islands, about 100 miles north of Trondheim, and then Vega Island, just south of the Arctic Circle. They reported rain, squalls and 'icing conditions', and returned to base just after midnight, having completed a sixteen-plus-hour round trip.

Apparently your announcement at Oban that you were coming up here made no mean stir. All the other wives told their husbands that you were going and so why couldn't they. Actually I don't think you are allowed to come up and stay for short periods so I'm afraid it will be hopeless for you to come up for leave. When I do come back I hope to be able to catch flying 'lifts' so you'd better not go to Inverg [Invergordon] to meet me in case I can get a lift home. The trouble is that, if I have to go the usual way, we only get about eleven days of our fourteen because of the travel arrangements: it is most unfair.

I miss you a lot—hot water bottle time, feeding time, even breakfast time. When I finish here it's almost certain to be Inverg or Staff College. The latter if I can because it means better jobs eventually. At the moment I'm lucky to be no further away.

With all my love darling and all me—faithful husband Robert xxxxx

TELEGRAM TO DIANA:

TEL LTR MRS ROBERT KEDDIE DOWNHAM GRANGE NEAR BILLERICAY ESSEX = PARCELS AND WIRE ARRIVED LAST NIGHT THANK YOU DARLING AM QUITE WELL BUT WORK LIMITS LETTERS MISSING YOU TERRIBLY KEEP WELL AND DONT WORRY ALL MY LOVE AND KISSES = ROBERT +

LETTER TO DIANA:

RAF Sullom Voe
30th March, 1942

6.30. Hullo darling, haven't been quite so busy the last couple of days and this afternoon has been quite restful. Also yesterday afternoon when we again cycled the five miles to a place called Brae and had tea consisting of two eggs on toast, butter in large quantity, bread and marmalade: also chocolate biscuits to finish. Cost 2/4ᵈ which I think is most reasonable.

Today in the afternoon we did some PT after lunch and then we had finished for the day. I feel quite rested for a change. Gillie is on leave now and I asked him to phone you up for me—I wonder whether he has done so yet and if so whether he found you at the right house: I told him to try at Waterhall.

When I get a chance will try and get some wool here if I can but I believe it is getting rather difficult to get hold of. Also a jumper if I can find one.

Thank you for the mittens—they are a bit on the large size but it doesn't worry me at all, and they keep the wrists nice and warm. Sorry the old pants took such a lot of washing—I welcomed their return immensely—we need them. Also the rest of the washing. I don't think it's worth sending my washing back to you except perhaps the socks with holes in—they take so long to get back.

Incidentally I should much appreciate any socks your aunt might like to knit— or is she busy on other things? I read in a letter that I was censoring how an airman got a couple of scarves from the 'comforts fund' and sent them back to his girlfriend to re-knit into a pullover with sleeves. Hope you get mine finished before you get knitting smaller garments—I was relieved to hear that work has not ceased.

No 'slice of love' tonight as Tim* and I refer to our letters from our absent soul-mates. There usually is one sort of pent up after Sunday's absence of mail: but still four parcels, a letter and a wire ought to suffice for a day or so.

Saw some snowdrops are out and daffodils just growing up when we went to tea at Brae. How are the flowers and trees down south? Would you like to send me some Woolworths seeds of everything that is likely to grow here and I'll plant them and see if anything happens.

On Saturday night (band night) the Squadron took over completely. Frankie— to our great surprise—performed exceedingly well on the violin. David took the drums and George Buckle the maracas (the things with beans in them) for a rhumba while a new pilot played his guitar. A good time was had by all. Now going to make Ovaltine and so to bed. No! Just had an invitation through the wall to go visiting tonight but bring my own cup.

Goodnight angel, sleep well, be good, keep healthy and don't stop missing me. I miss you more and more each day. All my love, all me. Kisses and kisses, faithful husband (and not out of necessity—faithful I mean)

Robert

xxxxxxxxxxx

---

* Dennis Edward (Tim) Healy died in September 1942. He was awarded a DSO and Norwegian Cross for extremely tough, secret missions in the Arctic. These are detailed in *Arctic Airmen: The RAF in Spitsbergen and North Russia, 1942* by Ernest Schofield and Roy Conyers Nesbit (The History Press, 2014).

RAF Sullom Voe
31st March, 1942

Wife darling, don't expect this sudden flow of letters to last, because I'm afraid it is liable to cease at any moment, as soon as we get really busy. Have been really industrious this afternoon: two games of squash—got beaten, just, by Hutton and beat Nigel Bruce. Since when I have written Holly (enclosing the £2 I owed), Gieves (and the balance of the coupons for the shirt and a pair of pants), Ian Debenham (on the occasion of his 'fiancailles'), and the bank (just for fun).

So this is my sixth letter and all before dinner. I'm afraid it won't continue after because tonight is a party night, first we have had for about ten days, and I don't expect to be in a fit state to write after it.

Have just finished reading 'Invitation to the Waltz': it's a sweet book. My reading hours are ten minutes before I go to sleep, in the bath and a certain other time I won't mention but which you know well enough. I rather liked the name Nicola for a girl which happened to be mentioned in it. Do you?

I'm extremely healthy up here and eat my pills regularly.

We hope to be able to get into Lerwick tomorrow to get some cake, biscuits and odds and ends for our 'Rosie swindle': they are a terrific occasions when a flap [urgent mission] is on and we don't touch alcohol much. There is quite a rivalry as to who can produce the best tea.

There is little more news for you I'm afraid and nowadays we are not supposed to send xxxx at the end of letters as the censors fear that some sinister code may lurk therein so will just have to ramble on to fill the rest of the page. However no harm (or restrictions) can result from me saying that I love you, I love you, I love you, I love you—except that it sounds like a broken record. However I do love you. I miss you more than words can tell. I dream of the days we shall have together on leave and how all-too-short they will be. I hope you are taking care of yourself for me and don't do anything foolish.

All me and all my love darling wife Robert xxxxxxx

RAF Sullom Voe
2nd April, 1942

Darling, Just finished an hour's PT—all officers not on duty had to attend so there was quite a gathering—GC, Wing Co, Flt Commander, Uncle Tom Cobley and all. It was all very strenuous.

10pm. In bed—listening to Beethoven—4th Symphony. How I bless this wireless. 'Fraid I'm too sleepy to write, just going to lie and listen and drift off to sleep. We've never done that yet together have we? To lie in bed with the wireless softly playing in heaven. Next time we have a home we'll install the wireless in our bedroom.

All my love angel. Be good. All me and all my kisses. Take care and keep well. Enjoy Devon, it must be glorious just now. Your wire came tonight xxxxx Robert

TELEGRAM TO DIANA:

4th April, 1942

Hope you have a nice Easter darling. Don't forget to send me Riddles' [Diana's doctor] report. Kind regards to the aunts. Am quite well but as always missing you. Love and kisses. Robert

LETTER TO DIANA:

RAF Sullom Voe
6th April, 1942

My darling, it seems such ages since I last wrote and I seem to have such a pile of letters, photos and a jersey to acknowledge. Hope it isn't as long as it seems.

The photos and letter arrived quite safely thank you darling, and now adorn the walls of my room: did I tell you of my ingenious way of fixing them? I've got adhesive tape fixed by drawing pins with the sticky side out and on which I fix my photos. They all look very nice. The jersey arrived tonight darling and tomorrow goes into service. It is most beautiful and very warm (thank God!) I believe we get spring in another month.

Thank you too for Pauline's and Belinda's letters. I think I might have married Pauline if I hadn't met you first—poor girl she must be having a very heart-rending time. What a pity you couldn't have seen them: can't we meet them in town when on leave? I am getting this leave business worked out: when I know definitely the date I'll book some rooms in London—at Brown's Hotel, do you think?—and you could go up the night before the day I'm due to arrive and go to a hairdresser for a spit and polish so that, in case I arrive early (I might get flown part way), we'll not have wasted any time.

One of the wireless mechanics working on my boat today said he had been at Chelmsford some time ago and had a message from Papa to 'write sometime'.* It turned out he was there about the time we had gone to Inverg. But I must write sometime—feel very guilty about it, but find so little time.

I was going to write last night but we were all dragged off at 8:30 and cycled once more to Brae and had our eggs and high tea at 9:30! Cycling back in the dark. Quite fun. I'm afraid that for the next few days letters may fall off a bit but I'll try

---

* Diana's father was by now principal of Marconi College in Chelmsford.

and write as often as I can. The trouble is finding something to write about: it is much easier writing to someone you don't know well I think, because they don't know what you think before you say it! Actually I think my one sheet is worth at least one double sided of yours! Glad you got my teleg-letter OK, didn't expect you to get it so quickly. Must go to sleep now—1:00pm [*sic*]. Sitting writing this in bed.

Keep well for me darling and not too fat!

All my love all me always Robert xxx

◊♦◊

Diana sent Bob a postcard in anticipation of his planned June leave. She wrote 'June Soon ... Soon June' in the ribbon at the top, and 'God Bless Us' at the bottom. The word 'silver' lines the edge of the cloud drawn on the back.

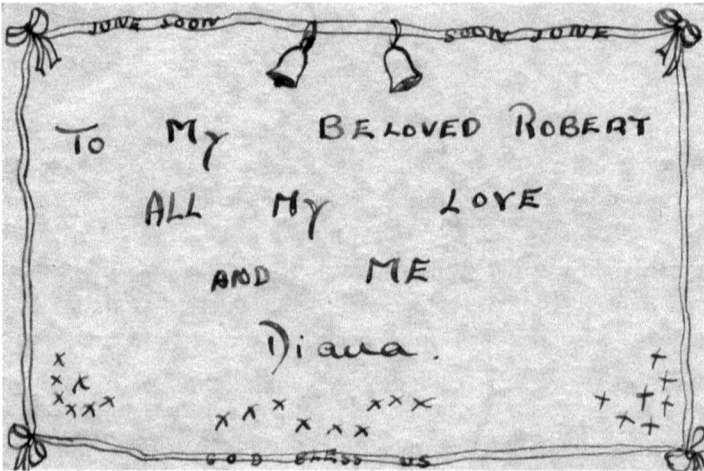

19

Flying to the edge of the earth

Sullom Voe
Friday [10th April, 1942]

Well my darling, I think this paper rather put[s] yours in the shade—doesn't it? But it has the disadvantage of taking an awful lot of filling! [It was foolscap, larger than A4, with this coat of arms.] The flowers arrived last night darling and although rather jaded then they have bucked up immensely and now flourish greatly round our room. Thank you angel, they are heavenly. Tonight if it doesn't rain I hope to start digging the ground before putting in the seeds. I hope the flowers come up alright—one thing they won't need watering here!

Very pleased to get Riddle's report: he ought to be pretty wary this time, so you ought to be OK if he says you are! Will try and write the aunts. Incidentally how does he expect you to get to Essex, without getting into a train or a car?

I'm afraid that I shan't be able to finish with this place before the winter. I'm extremely lucky, actually, not to be much further away.

Have done quite a bit of local flying recently which has been most interesting as other parts of these islands are quite exciting and great fun to explore. The west coast with its cliffs is very like Cornwall, while other parts of it look almost Tyrolean.

One little village I found by the side of a voe was absolutely lovely. About eight or nine houses clustered round a wooden pier set in transparently clear water. Two or three fishing boats lay out in the voe—varnished a golden brown. One of the houses, larger than the rest, was atop a small hill and stood out, tall, four square with large eaves, steep roof, small windows, it was quite Swiss or Norwegian and was, curiously, painted a rich mauve!

Am going to dinner now and will try and fill up the other page after my gardening—unless we have a 'Rosie' session going. Darling, I love you forever and always xxxxxxxx, but must have my food now, not that you are the less important xxxxxxxx

11.4.42. Weather cleared up last night and we cycled off for our evening eggs as supper hadn't been too hot. Didn't come back till 10:30: it's amazing how the evenings are drawing out here—still light enough to cycle at that hour, although we really ought to have lights! Still, with no cars on the road, what does it matter. After we got back the Flight Commander 'called' for a cup of Rosie, so we sat drinking Ovaltine until midnight. Thus I got no further with my letter. Now 8:30 and I've had breakfast and must close now darling—work calls!

All my love and me angel for always—I too count the days until leave. Be good and be careful!

Your adoring husband, Robert

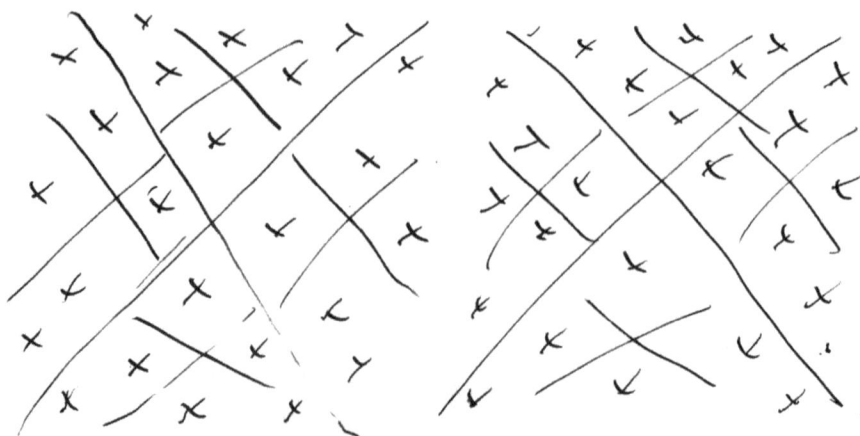

◊♦◊

On 12 April, Bob and crew went on Lotus 2 patrol duty, sighting three small merchant vessels sailing north along the Norwegian coast. They returned to base the following day to the news that Bob had been promoted to flight lieutenant.

◊♦◊

TELEGRAM TO DIANA AT HER AUNTS' NURSING HOME, KINGSBRIDGE, DEVON:*

16th April, 1942

Letters have suffered lapse don't get worried continuity resumed tonight glad to hear you are quite well angel just waiting now for my leave all my love and kisses darling Robert

---

* As the war progressed, the nursing home run by Diana's aunts was evacuated from Plymouth to Kingsbridge.

LETTER TO DIANA:

RAF Sullom Voe
16th April, 1942

My darling, hope you got the telegram OK, thought I'd send it as I haven't been able to write for a day or so. Have had quite a supply of letters from you—yours and others, and read them all with great interest. Father's list of names made me laugh—I wonder how long it took him to compose—are Penelope and Jennifer on the list?

17/4. Got called away—sorry darling! To a conference which didn't break up till late and I felt too tired to write. Today has been a lazy one. This afternoon two of the crew bathed—it felt much too cold for me. Also went for a sail in the whaler which was most enjoyable: when we got 'the other side' and went to a cottage for some tea none of us had any money so we still owe them for it!

This is a dreadful letter I'm afraid. Will close now and try and write better one tomorrow. So goodnight my angel: sleep well and pleasant dreams—I wish I were with you. All my love, all me and lots of kisses darling. Your ever-loving, devoted and faithful husband Robert

LETTER TO DIANA:

RAF Sullom Voe
19th April, 1942

Hullo wife darling, today has been a pleasant lazy day—sailing this afternoon, and a little gardening later on. Have now sown all the seeds and all I have to do I suppose is to sit back and watch and wait. Driving off the sheep is the main task from now on: actually I hope to be able to get some wire and fence my little plot in. Hope they all come up. I also have a 'compulsory voluntary' vegetable plot which I dig and plant with vegetables for the men. We all have these plots—at least there are about fifteen plots and four officers to each. As a matter of fact it is quite a pleasant way to pass these long evenings: it is still quite light now—10pm and soon won't get dark at all!

Am even considering swimming now. If it is nice tomorrow, I am going to try the little stream which runs about half an hour's walk from here and which has delightful little pools in it. In fact two of us were walking up there an evening or two ago and we discussed the possibilities of damming it! I expect we shall do that eventually. It should be quite fun and ought to make a nice little swimming pool as it is in a fairly sheltered little valley and one which ought to make the most of the sun.

Am afraid it will be later than the autumn before they 'lay me off'* unless I work very hard this summer. But later on the infant should be more transportable.

---

* The plan was for Bob to have a spell as an instructor.

If I ever get into Lerwick—which I haven't done yet—I'll have a snoop around for a pram but I doubt whether I shall be able to find one there. But you never know.

No more news tonight my sweet. I miss you more than ever and can barely wait for our ten or so precious days in June. Will let you know a week or so in advance but shall have to disguise it as 'Brown's Hotel, night of ...' or something like it. All my love angel, all me, all yours, your constant, faithful, ever loving husband!

Robert

◊♦◊

On 23 April, Bob and his crew took to the air again to provide an anti-submarine escort for Force Dimple, a battleship and three destroyers, for nearly eight hours. It meant a fifteen-hour round trip from Sullom Voe.

◊♦◊

LETTER TO DIANA:

RAF Sullom Voe
24th April, 1942

My darling—now just 12pm [*sic*] and have now crawled into bed: not drunk but tired. Today ...

And that was as far as I got. It is now the day after and 7pm. At that moment in came a runner ... report to the 'operations room immediately' [there is no record of what Bob was asked to do].

I eventually got to bed at 3:30 and did not awake until lunchtime today. I was going to say today has been a day of 'rest' and I had got up (yesterday) in time for lunch and again in the afternoon had gone up to the little river I told you about before and started to dam it up to make a swimming pool: have now a huge quantity of rocks but the next thing is to get some peat or earth cut so as to make it a bit more water-tight. It should be a nice pool when finished—long and narrow, about five feet in the deepest parts and with nice grassy banks.

After dinner we had a lecture and just when I got into bed and started writing, up I had to get again. Afraid it is a long time since I last wrote but I do find it very hard to make time: the evening is really the only good time and then by the time I have fed and had some coffee, read yesterday's paper, I'm ready for sleep. However it's no good making excuses.

Have found one or two good pieces of 'Paradise Lost' which might well apply in the various cases as follows. First of all a Catalina heavily laden—

> Then with expanded wings he steers his flight,
> Aloft, incumbent on the dusky air,
> That felt unusual weight.

or one on the evils of a pilot day-dreaming—

> ... nor aught availed him not
> To have built light towers in Heaven: nor did he scape
> By all his engines: but was headlong sent
> With his industrious crew to build in Hell.*

Just time for dinner, will finish later. xxxx

In bed now listening to, above all things, the news. Up here papers are late and I often have the news on and just listen to the summary and then any interesting items.

Another letter from you tonight angel, dated 22nd. They do come quickly, hope you've got a letter from me by now. It is funny up here how time passes: I never know how long it is since I last wrote you and sometimes get in a dreadful flap and start scribbling at once only to realise that I had written the day before.

Must log some Bo-Peep so will say goodnight my darling. Leave seems a bit nearer now, doesn't it? The thing I ought to get is compassionate leave when it [the baby] arrives! Take care of yourselves darling and be good (keep knitting!)

All my love, all me, all yours, always xxxx faithful husband Robert

PS In spite of Wrens now (said to be beautiful) stationed in Lerwick!

---

*   Slightly misquoted.

20

Searching for the towers in Heaven

On 29 April, Bob and his crew felt the heat of the intensifying enemy activity. Their mission was to carry out a Lotus 2 patrol. Two hours in, just before 2000 hours, they were flying at 600 feet when a Heinkel 115 at 100 feet flew with the sun behind it firing two bursts at a range of 600 yards. The Catalina turned towards the enemy firing thirty rounds from the port blister and forty from the starboard one. The enemy plane returned fire but then broke off the action. The Catalina could not overtake and so resumed its patrol. Soon after, the crew discovered a petrol leak and returned to base.

◊♦◊

LETTER TO DIANA:

RAF Sullom Voe
Monday 4th May, 1942

My darling, just as I was about to start your letter last night they came and told me [the official confirmation of] my F/Lt was through. Did you notice it on the back of my envelope? So off we went and had quite a party until it was time for me to lay a flare path [runway on the voe]: Finally I got to bed about 3:30. Now 12pm, just up bathed, shaved and dressed and trying to scribble a quick letter before the post goes—1.30.

Thank you for my presents darling, they were a lovely surprise. Unfortunately I have only been able to get the rhubarb cooked in the kitchen as we have no saucepan and we also get very little sugar, so I don't think it is an economical proposition sending anymore. The flowers just weathered the storm but are now sadly depleted by casualties: pansies, wallflowers suffered most and the best of the survivors was the forget-me-not. The chocolate was certainly not coals to Newcastle and much appreciated.

Had a lovely sail a day or two ago. We set out about 11:30 to get to one of the other islands but, at 1:30, we were still only about halfway because of a rather choppy sea, so decided to make for another little village higher up our own island: this place rejoiced in the name of Ollabery and there we left the whaler tied to the pier while we went for a walk. We, incidentally, were Jack Stirling, Jack Holmes ('Tom'),* my third pilot and myself.

We walked about four miles then sat down in a corner out of the wind to bask in the sun. We slept for about an hour! Then walked back to find the whaler high and dry on the rocks! We had miscalculated the tides. It took us about two hours to get her back into the water and would never have been able to do it except for a rusty old crane on the end of the pier which had apparently not been used for five years: in fact one of the 'natives' said they tried to move it three years ago but couldn't manage it! We got back here about 9:30, tired, sun and wind burnt and very hungry as we had only had some sandwiches which we took with us.

I think it is about time I told you that, since we have been here, the whole squadron has started to grow moustaches, the Wing Co included. I now sport quite a dashing specimen of the early 1900s, with little bits curled up at the corners. If you don't like it, I'll take it off, but I have to bring back a document signed by the person taking it off and stating reasons. Gillie brought back a very amusing note, signed by a girlfriend and written on Dorchester [Hotel] note-paper saying that she made him remove it on threat of catching the last train home and that it interfered with the evening's enjoyment. You mustn't tell anyone else though—I want to surprise them.

Must catch the post, so goodbye angel. All my love and kisses, all me. I miss you very much. Leave soon. Be good.

Your ever loving and faithful husband Robert

Letter to Diana:

RAF Sullom Voe

It must be about the 7th or 8th—unlike you I have too many things to keep me occupied than to have time to cross off days, and anyway time passes more quickly if you don't count every minute of it. So there's the date for you.

Glad to hear your bank account is, like yourself, rapidly growing more substantial, darling. I am afraid that I shall not have much saved for leave as my mess bills here are pretty heavy (and I don't drink as much as most people!): they are usually about £10—so I am afraid we may have to draw on your money for leave. And, talking of leave, I have still not heard when we are getting it, things like that are always most indefinite here but I believe it is still scheduled for about the middle of June.

Nobody here (except Tim) knows about your entry for the production stakes: I am keeping it fairly quiet because I ought to be able to spring it as a surprise

---

* Jack Holmes DFC (to which a bar was added in 1943). Later he was promoted to air commodore.

and get extra compassionate leave if I'm lucky! (That is when the baby is due or newly arrived.)

One thing you must not do on leave in town before I get there is to travel by bus or tube: for heaven's sake get a taxi and porters wherever you go. I must write Brown's soon to see if they will be able to put us up at short notice. With any luck, I should be able to fly down—we always try arrange it—which should save some time.

Oh angel my mind is a complete blank—not quite a blank but a dull ache and it is an effort to write commonplace dull and uninteresting news and words.

I love you so much—must close now before it all comes bubbling out again. Please forgive this short letter.

Always your loving husband Robert

xxxxxxxxxxxx

LETTER TO DIANA:

RAF Sullom Voe

Darling, just a very short note to say I'm OK. The post goes in ten minutes so I wanted to get this off in time. Will write a proper letter later.

Have just got up (12 o'clock) after going to bed at 9pm last night so feel fine. Your presents of chocolate and socks arrived OK and also the lilies of the valley which have perked up a bit but the rose looks very sad still. However both still smell very nicely. Hope you are keeping well and expect to see you soon.

All my love darling and me xxxxx Adoring husband Robert

LETTER TO DIANA:

RAF Sullom Voe
Friday [8th May, 1942]

Hello angel, I'm addressing this to Downham as I expect you'll be there by the time this reaches you or if not it will wait as a surprise for you. I'm quite busy these days darling, which is a good thing as time flies rapidly but it leaves little time for letter writing. When I scribbled that note at lunchtime I expected to be free tonight but now I'm told I shall not be. However just time to squeeze a letter in before supper.

The date you wanted to know was the 9th January—I hope this will help you put your calculations all square.*

I'm having quite a hectic time at the moment and nothing 'off' for sailing or any other lighter diversions—except for a sergeant's mess dance a few days ago where I found a reasonably presentable but spectacled army nurse to dance with.

---

* Diana must have been asking about the date that the baby had been conceived.

Did you ever hear that 'girls that are bespectacled never get their necks tickled' ... and the rest of the rhyme? I even accepted an invitation to the opening of their new hospital—house-warming, but know I shan't get away.

Now that leave approaches, I feel more and more impatient, don't you? Will try and write again day after tomorrow—all my love darling, hope you had a good journey up. Keep well, be good xxxx xxxxx Robert

◊♦◊

At the dance, one of the ground staff described one of Bob's crew as a Jonah (someone whose presence on board brings bad luck and endangers the ship).

◊♦◊

LETTER TO DIANA:

RAF Sullom Voe
Sunday [10th May, 1942]

10 minutes to 2am. My darling, as a husband correspondent I must be deadly dull and fail utterly to fulfil the promise as a husband-to-be and an attempted husband-to-be. All of which means that I am fairly nicely pickled—or drunk— and now safely in bed before I lose my mental and physical equilibrium. But as I was starting to say (and being slightly drunk and thus rather less sensitive than usual) I must write very boring letters—full of news—(when they do come)— and very barren of love. I am sorry but that is just me and you married me and not what you thought was me.

I can write good letters and beautiful letters (pat on the back, please!) but I cannot now write them to you or anyone else for that matter because ... because what? Were they dishonest, untruthful? Perhaps, a little. Posing? Pedantic? Boastful? Written with an eye to winning your sympathy and love—and you? Yes all of these.

And now at last I can write once again in the old vein, write letters which please you, I know, and why—because I am drunk.

And why? Because when drunk I miss you and need you more than ever, desire you more than always and want to kiss you and love you and hurt you so that I nearly scream; and being tight I can tell you all this and not mind. It is in my mind always, an eternal throb and desire which must be suppressed but now I am tight and can write this and seal it tonight and post it tomorrow before I realise what I have said.

My God how I miss you and long for you darling. Marriage may be a religious ceremony but you and I are wise enough to know (I hope!) that sleeping together and all that that means is a very large part of one's happiness; and that on that foundation is built the accumulated happiness and love which will eventually replace or grow stronger than the former. But how I dread the day when 'us' shall be no more. Natural, I suppose.

Oh Lord, feel so tired and not a little drunk. If I shut my eyes the whole room goes round and round. Oh my angel, honeybunch, why aren't you here to cling to and to comfort me?

It's foolish: I shall be home soon. I want only you, would be content to spend our leave anywhere, alone with you—would prefer it too. But I must go to Downham: you understand don't you my sweet? Mother and Dad are so lonely since John died and Dick gets home so seldom that they look forward so much to seeing us and they are really fond of you too. It must be hard for you, darling, but for me my cup is full: I have you and as well I have my home and my family.

I'm too tired now to see to write more my angel: what wouldn't I give to have you here now darling! I'm yours all yours, your adoring xxx Robert xxx

TELEGRAM TO DIANA AT HER AUNTS' NURSING HOME, KINGSBRIDGE, DEVON:

12th May, 1942

Hope you have received letter by now. Don't write Daphne until you get my last letter. Expect my arrival early next month. All joy love and kisses darling Robert

LETTER TO DIANA:

RAF Sullom Voe
12th May, 1942

My angel, your letter arrived last night—unfortunately I couldn't wire today—Sunday [actually Tuesday]—but will do so tomorrow (midday) unless we've gone off before then. Am very contrite and sorry that you have been so letter-starved recently. But please never worry if you do get a gap for several days or even a week because sometimes we go off for as long as that.

Have such sad news for you—perhaps you gathered from the telegram, but I didn't say so in words so as not to shock you suddenly. Holly was killed a few days ago in a crash at you know where. He was doing local flying and, so far, we have no further details. Am going to try and write to Daphne after this, but it is so difficult to find anything to say. It has made us all very sad the last few days.*

---

* Squadron Leader Frederick Hollins died in an accident near the Outer Hebrides on 4 May when his Sunderland aircraft stalled and crashed on landing. He was not the pilot at the time. It was seven days before his thirty-first birthday. His obituary described him as 'surely one of the most attractive and vivid personalities to be lost yet in this war'. He left behind his wife Daphne and their infant daughter.

I have been trying to engineer leave a bit earlier recently but doubt if it will come off. The crew is due for it before some of the others going soon, but I don't think it will come to anything. However, if you get a hasty wire from me, you'll know what it means.

Now 11.30 and David (Eadie)* has this moment come in with Duffy for a cup of 'Rosie'. Have already had mine with the Adj. (Paul), the Flt. Commander and Gillie. Duffy is off for two months on a similar to what I did recently [perhaps a flying course] and Gillie and I rather expect to share this room when Duffy goes, and if Ian Martin doesn't come back—which he may not do. It is incredible the way the chaps are moving about nowadays and I've come to the conclusion we were extremely lucky to get sent up here. Will elucidate more when on leave. All rather depressing I'm afraid, darling, but we must face facts. Also I'm sorry to say, our 'retiring' hours have been put up another two hundred I believe, although we have no official confirmation of that.

Sorry to keep dodging from sheet to sheet but have no blotting paper handy. Played rugger—a practice—on Friday and should have played a match to-day but have been standing by. If we are not off on our travels again, we hope to play soccer for the officers on Tuesday v. the sergeants. Have had very few letters from you recently, I think they must have blitzed some unless you are making the punishment fit the crime.

As usual, the news here is very small and all the same. The only progress recently is in the garden. I've not had time to sail again or visit the dam. The seeds are beginning to show and we have great fun speculating on which is which and also in driving away the sheep which sometimes get inside the fencing.

Well my angel it should only be about a month from now: it seems years and years since I last saw you and yet for me the time has gone quite quickly. If by any chance I get home between the 6th and 13th I'll go straight to Downham, shall I? and find you in bed!

Goodnight my darling, and all my love and me to bless you with sweet dreams. Be good and don't worry, or else we'll have a perpetually frowning infant or something! Don't stop loving me—ever. Love, kisses and me. Your adoring Robert xxxxx

PS Any more economy labels? xxx R

◇◆◇

On 13 May, Bob and his crew were airborne at 2338 hours on a Lotus 3 patrol. Visibility was very good, making the Catalina more vulnerable, so at 0741 hours the plane changed course to patrol further from the Norwegian coast. Between 9 and 10 a.m. the crew tried 'to hone in on enemy radio telegraphy signals' but they abandoned this when they suspected the signals 'came from an enemy

---

*   David Eadie was awarded a DFC when flying with the squadron the following year.

aircraft. An unidentified aircraft was sighted at five miles but no contact resulted.' *
They returned to base just after 4 p.m.

There were no operational sorties on 14 May, probably because of bad weather,
but tension was mounting in the squadron due to increased enemy activity.
Meanwhile, the variable weather only added to the pressure.

The next day, two Catalinas on consecutive Lotus 2 patrols sighted enemy
combat aircraft. The later of the two patrols also spotted five marine vessels.
Soon after this, the patrol had to be abandoned because of a hailstorm.

At 11.35 a.m. on 16 May, the Catalina on Lotus 1 patrol spotted an unidentified
enemy aircraft but almost immediately lost contact. The patrol was cut short by
snowstorms, bringing visibility to zero. No. 210 Squadron did not know it at the
time, but that same day the German warship Prinz Eugen sailed from the
Trondheim area towards Kiel. It was surely no coincidence that the next day about
fifty Coastal Command planes were thwarted in their attacks on the enemy. The
day after that, the 18th, the enemy warship Lutzow moved from Kiel to Trondheim.

At 0455 hours on 16 May, as we have seen, Bob and his crew set off from
Sullom Voe. Their patrol route was Sentry 3. At 1739 hours one of the crew
requested a landing forecast on the radio; nothing was seen or heard of their
Catalina after that.

At 0434 hours the next day, Flight Lieutenant Charles Owen and crew took
off in another Catalina in search of the missing aircraft. They met a submarine
also searching, but at 1240 hours they ended the search and rejoined the
submarine, which signalled nothing to report.

No. 210 Squadron recorded that a German report had been intercepted stating
that 'one of her recce aircraft had attacked and destroyed a Catalina two hundred
miles west of Trondheim'. As Bob and his crew were flying the only British
aircraft in the region at the time, the RAF assumed that it was their plane which
had been destroyed. Had the crew become disoriented by bad weather? Did they
believe they were further from enemy territory than they actually were when they
requested the landing forecast? We will never know.

On 18 May, Bob's father and Diana were notified that Bob was missing. Diana
received two of Bob's letters after she had heard the news.

Since he had been at Sullom Voe, Bob had flown with pretty much the same
crew on every patrol. The following men died with him: Pilot Officer Brian
Harmer (twenty years old), second pilot; Pilot Officers Frank Benjamin Franklin
(twenty-four) and Peter Lambert (twenty-two), observer/navigators; Flight
Sergeants David Hall (twenty-three) and William Lonsdale (twenty-two), air
gunners and flight mechanics for engines and air frames respectively; Sergeant Eric
Horton (twenty-one), fitter and flight engineer; Sergeant Bernard Short (twenty),
wireless operator mechanic and air gunner; and Sergeants Leslie Mitchell (twenty-
five) and Robert Henderson (thirty-two), wireless operators and air gunners.

---

*   210 Squadron's operations record book.

Epilogue

Letter from Wing Commander Walter Hutton, CO, 210 Squadron, to Bob's father:

RAF Sullom Voe
19th May, 1942

Dear Mr Keddie

It is with the deepest regret that I have to tell you that your son has not returned from an operational flight.

I am terribly sorry that this should have happened and that I am not able to give you any definite news of him other than that he is missing with his entire crew. Rather than that you should harbour any false hopes however I think it only fair, and I am sure you would wish it, to give you the story as we know it here.

Bob—he was known as Bob by all of us—went out on a most important task which we know he completed successfully. On his return journey to base however we have good reason to believe that he was engaged by an enemy aircraft and in the course of the combat was shot down into the sea. This belief has been more or less confirmed by an enemy claim that an engagement took place some 200 miles west of Trondheim in which a Catalina crashed.

Following Bob's failure to return, exhaustive surface and air searches were sent out which thoroughly scoured the area in which he could have come down and covering the position of the enemy claim. Weather conditions for the searches were ideal but I am sorry to say all returned without success.

Although I hate to say so, I feel that there is no chance of Bob's survival. As I have already tried to tell Bob's wife he had an excellent crew with him who were devoted to him and if they had the slightest chance I am quite sure they will have given a good account of themselves.

Bob always tackled every job given him with tremendous keenness and efficiency whether it happened to be an operational flight or some task on the ground and

I had implicit faith in him. The example he set his fellows could not be bettered and with the popularity which he enjoyed amongst us all he has been largely responsible for building up the excellent spirit of esprit-de-corps which exists in the squadron. His loss to the squadron and to the RAF which he served so well is a severe blow. It will be many times worse for you but I hope you will be able to find some slight consolation in the knowledge that Bob was lost on a duty the risks of which he knew and which he completed to the fullest satisfaction.

May I offer you on behalf of myself and all his fellow members of the squadron the most sincere and deep sympathy in your tragic loss and may I hope that if there is anything that any of us can do to help in any way you will not fail to let us know.

I have written to Bob's wife as he so wished it and in addition to telling her what I have told you I have explained about the disposal of Bob's effects.

Yours most sincerely

Walter Hutton

Poem from Diana's collection:*

Nothing of Importance, says the News
Enemy planes were overhead
The bland voice smoothly telling
Eight planes crashed and dead

Eight planes and only one of ours
Only only only one.
That's excellent! That's good news!
That's a good day's work, well done.

I wait as if expecting something
Civilization must surely fall
All life mankind come to a standstill
For their ONLY, was my all.

Bob and his crew were officially declared dead in January 1943. Their names live on, inscribed on the Air Forces Memorial on top of Coopers Hill at Runnymede in Surrey, along with 20,000 others. When the wind is in the right direction, looking out from the memorial over the River Thames, a stream of planes coming in to land at Heathrow Airport provides a fitting backdrop to the missing airmen and women of the war.

---

* Author unknown.

After Bob's death, Patsy cycled over every day after work to sleep in Diana's room. She said that Diana was terrified of losing the baby but found that chatting into the nights helped soothe her nerves.

Bob and Diana's daughter Penelope Anne was born on 12 October 1942. Her arrival was marked by drama. When walking along a beach in Devon, Diana and her mother were the target of a German aeroplane. The pilot flew over them and then came round a second time. As the bullets zipped past them, Diana suggested that they should take cover but her mother said calmly, 'Let's walk to those rocks, but not so fast that he thinks we're afraid of him ...' It was that night that Penny was born in her great aunts' nursing home, where Diana had spent much of the war and where she too had been born.

Diana was both a widow and a mother before her twenty-second birthday.

◇◆◇

Two years after Bob's death, his parents received yet another devastating blow—the death of their last surviving child, Dick. He was twenty-six years old. On 29 August the ship he captained, HMS *Cattistock*, was patrolling off the coast of Normandy with HMS *Retalick* when they intercepted German vessels evacuating Le Havre. HMS *Cattistock* was hit twenty-six times. Dick and three of his crew were killed. His short career had been a stellar one. He had been awarded the Distinguished Service Cross and mentioned in despatches.

In his letter to Dick's father, the Second Sea Lord, Vice Admiral Sir Algernon Willis KCB DSO, wrote: '[Dick] was undoubtedly a born leader with a very high moral sense of duty and loyalty and had an excellent influence on all those with whom he came into contact. His appointment in command of a Hunt Class destroyer with less than four years' seniority as a lieutenant was some measure of his ability as an officer and the Navy has indeed suffered a severe loss in his untimely death.' He went on to say that 'Dick's commanding officer had described him as being by a wide margin the most impressive and outstanding young officer he had met during the whole of his service career.'

Dick and John are buried with their parents in a joint grave at St Margaret's church, Downham. Bob's name is also recorded on the grave though his body was never found. In 1946 the Keddie family commissioned a bell for the tower at St Margaret's in memory of their three sons, whose names are on the bell. It was a tenor B flat bell, named Sursum Corda (Latin for 'Lift up your hearts', part of the Eucharistic prayer).

Diana spent the rest of the war in Essex. On VE Day, when everyone was celebrating the end of a long war, she was sad and cross that Bob was not coming home. She visited Mrs Foster who tried to cheer her up over a cup of tea. She said, 'Bill Dawkins is home. Why don't you go over to see him?' Bill's older brother John was Diana's sister's husband. Having risen to the rank of major and been mentioned in despatches, he had returned from fighting the Japanese in

Burma with the Sierra Leone Regiment. Diana cycled on to Bill's family home, a ride that would mark the beginning of the next chapter in her life.

Diana and Bill soon married, and when Bill took up a career in the Colonial Service, Diana went out with him to Sierra Leone. Her daughter Penny joined them too.

Diana never lost her faith that life must go on. When my mother died, she wrote to me saying, 'Live again as soon as possible.' Near the end of her own life she had a cruel stroke, which left her unable to walk, but it could not deprive her of her sense of humour. Just before she died, she said that she was looking forward to seeing her two husbands again—though she hoped they would not fight over her.